November

Ann Stevens took up writing in ~~later~~ years, after
working and bringing up her two children. Her writing
career took off quickly, with numerous short stories being
published and winning competitions. She lives with her
solicitor husband in a thatched cottage in a Devon village.
November Tree is her first novel, and she is currently at
work on her second.

NOVEMBER TREE

Ann Stevens

HarperCollins*Publishers*

HarperCollins*Publishers*
77–85 Fulham Palace Road,
Hammersmith, London W6 8JB

This paperback original 1996
1 3 5 7 9 8 6 4 2

All Souls' Night by Frances Cornford quoted from *Collected Poems*
by kind permission of Hutchinson Publishers

A catalogue record for this book
is available from the British Library

ISBN 0 00 649685 7

Set in Linotron Meridien by
Rowland Phototypesetting Ltd
Bury St Edmunds, Suffolk

Printed in Great Britain by
HarperCollinsManufacturing Glasgow

For Andrew

The Beginning

ONE

Watching from the window, Rowena knew with a sudden breathtaking certainty that one day she would strike Phyllida.

They had lived together for four years, in Rowena's house which had belonged to her parents. Now, everything Phyllida did was predictable, like this critical picking and poking at the soil on top of the front garden wall. Unable to bear it, Rowena stepped back from the window.

'I'm back, dear.' The front door slammed, making the announcement redundant. Rowena took a deep steadying breath.

'I'm in here.'

Phyllida came into the room. She stood squat in her red raincoat, grey-white curls clinging damply to her broad, smooth forehead. She had been a pretty woman, though inclined to plumpness. At sixty-two she could be irritatingly smug. It made Rowena want to smack her face.

Phyllida said now, 'It's coming on to rain. And that front wall needs weeding again.' She held up a dandelion whose broken root had smeared her glove with mud.

'It's no good pulling them out,' Rowena snapped. 'You have to dig up the roots or they just grow again.'

'So you say, dear.' Phyllida's voice was mild, her expression obstinate. 'But you've never really been a gardener, have you?'

Rowena sighed and moved towards the door. 'I don't fiddle about like you, if that's what you mean. But I managed the garden for a good many years on my own. However . . .' For this wouldn't do. Silly bickering, so easy to slip into, was the start of the slippery slope. Irritation could so quickly grow into animosity, animosity into unpleasantness . . . Her smile was

3

propitiatory and she reached out for the shopping bag. 'Everything all right? You got it all?'

'Oh yes. Dreadful queues in Waitrose, though. Why don't they open up all the tills?'

'I know, ridiculous isn't it.' Suddenly Rowena wanted to laugh. They were like a music-hall duo. Same old script every day. Waiting for the applause which never came. Two has-beens on the stage of life, propping each other up while they drove each other mad.

Yet what else could they do?

It was Friday so lunch was fish. In the kitchen, Phyllida unwrapped the two fillets of plaice and displayed them for inspection. 'The haddock was very expensive and it didn't look fresh. I've got baby carrots. I love them when they still have their frilly bits.'

Rowena nodded, notwithstanding that one paid through the nose for the frilly bits. It would have been better to have the haddock, and some frozen peas. Personally, she found plaice pappy and insipid, but it wouldn't do to say so. This was Phyllida's week. It was an unwritten rule that the one who did the shopping made the choices.

A lot of unwritten rules developed when two people tried to live together. Another was that the cook didn't lay the table. Phyllida always cooked when it was fish. Rowena didn't like handling it, found the smell lingered on her fingers and baulked at the sticky cling of scales and bones. She opened the sideboard drawer and took out two fish knives and forks from their green-lined section. They belonged to Phyllida. Beneath them, wrapped separately in baize, lay a silver fish slice, a relic of better days. Rowena hadn't seen it used since a dinner party, years ago . . .

'A whole salmon,' someone says admiringly. 'I've never seen a whole salmon.'

'Henry's been to Scotland.' Phyllida is prettily flushed, enjoying her role – wife, mother, hostess.

Rowena tries not to meet Henry's eyes, but she is driven to

4

look at him. She sees so little of him she is hungry to watch his hands, deftly now dissecting the fish, his silky brown hair falling over his forehead, the brown eyes behind his glasses that can dissolve her with a glance. Suddenly he looks up and she is unable to look away. There is a taut line stretching between them, remembering Scotland. She is afraid as she always is that they'll give themselves away. Part of her, with a reckless bravado, wishes that they would. She wants to wipe the smile off Phyllida's face, see the eyes round the table swivel towards her dumbstruck, accusing.

How could you? Your oldest friend . . . ?

How could she indeed? But then, how not?

The plaice was poached in milk with a knob of low-fat margarine; pale and bland, invalid food. The carrots were sweet but overdone, as Phyllida's vegetables always were. Henry had used to complain about it, mildly, so that she wouldn't take offence but so that she took no notice, either.

After lunch Rowena went purposefully to the garden shed for gloves and a trowel and set about weeding the front wall. Built with the house nearly sixty years ago, its stones were crumbling and coming apart. Small plants had taken root in the cracks which would have been impossible to remove without causing the whole structure to collapse. Most people in the road had long since replaced the soft grey stones with crisp brickwork, topped with tilted bricks or large flat stones rather than the soft random disorder of plants. It would have been sensible, but Rowena didn't see the necessity of being sensible. Besides, she liked it. It reminded her of her girlhood, when she had swung on the wooden gate across the concrete path leading to the front door. The gate had rotted away years ago, to be replaced with intricate wrought iron, impossible to swing on, even if there had been a child in the house, which there hadn't.

Now she thrust her gloved fingers between the springy cushions of aubretia and saxifrage, shoving the pointed trowel in deep and, with a deft twisting motion, hoping to lift the tapering parsnip-like roots of the dandelions without breaking them. She threw the discarded weeds into a plastic trug on the pavement beside her, noticing that a crust of litter had formed at the base of the wall. There was dog's mess along the kerb, and some of the paving stones were cracked. She sighed. It had never been like that when she was young, when her parents were alive, when the stonework of the wall had been sound and strong and never the tiniest weed had escaped her father's weekend manicure.

It is Sunday morning. The bells are ringing out from the church across the valley where the countryside begins. Their house is on the edge of the green belt, in the very last road before the suburban sprawl of south London gives way to fields.

Her father's black Riley is parked on the short drive leading to the garage. She has helped him to clean it, rubbing at the curved mud-guards until she can see her distorted reflection in the sheen. Rowena loves the car, which is a recent acquisition. She loves the smell of the ribbed, red leather seats, the glossy walnut dashboard, and the fur-trimmed footwarmer into which her mother slips her feet. There is a blind at the back window which can be elevated by pulling on a ring attached to a cord. On long journeys, she and her brother Mark squabble over this simple gadget, raising and lowering the blind until their father, in exasperation, threatens to put them out of the car and leave them. They slump back into the deep seat, pushing each other's arms off the armrest between them, sulkily asking when they will be there.

Now she is swinging on the gate while her father trims the edges of the small square lawn. There is a pyracantha below the front bay window, its berries turning red amid a framework of stiff, clipped branches. Beneath it the last blooms of the geraniums are red also, and the brickwork behind seems to glow in the rich October sunlight. The world this Sunday morning looks peaceful and contented, but it is 1938 and Rowena at nine years old can read, and listen to the wireless,

6

and she knows that people are worried and have been talking about war.

'Daddy,' she asks now, leaning on the gate towards him. 'Will you have to go away if there's a war?'

He straightens up, easing his back and letting the shears drop to his side. He sees two brown plaits framing a thin and worried face, a blue jumper knitted by his mother which brings out the colour of her eyes, and the most precious object of his joy and love. His first-born, after whom his son had always rated second-best. But to leave either of them, or for that matter Helen, his wife, would be unthinkable. With relief he is able to say, 'No. Remember I told you I'm in a reserved occupation? Well, that means I would be needed here.'

She has heard this before but asks, puzzled, 'But what would you be doing?'

'I'm a surveyor. I would be needed to assess the damage caused by any bombing, and to organise re-building programmes.' Privately, he doubts the weight of this necessity, feels that if any offensive is to be protracted then the tentacles of enlistment will reach out for him. But her face has smoothed out and she nods.

'I remember.' Satisfied, she pushes the path with her foot, and sets the gate swinging.

Phyllida came to the front door and called, 'I've made a pot of tea. Are you coming in?'

The threatened rain had passed, the autumn afternoon was closing in and there was a touch of frost in the air. Rowena had decided to lift the geraniums and was now in the garage, storing them in boxes on a high shelf among the rusty tins of paint containing colours long since vanished from the house. The flower bed beneath the window looked bare and scarred. The pyracantha had disappeared long ago, when its encroachment on the window had become a nuisance.

Phyllida, waiting for Rowena, looked sadly at the empty bed. She hated the autumn with its dying fall, its threat of the winter which, when it came, had its pleasures after all, with fires and stews and electric blankets. But now, with the last blooms of summer still in evidence, she wanted to grab at the skirts of the season and haul it back with its sun and warmth and long light evenings.

Rowena pulled down the garage door and locked it. She disappeared round the side of the house, re-appearing after a while in the kitchen where she washed her hands at the sink.

'Crumpets?' she asked, seeing that the grill was on. 'That makes it feel like winter.'

'Tea cakes. They were on offer in Waitrose.'

Rowena smiled and bit back her objection. She herself bought such things at the baker; at least then she knew they were fresh.

'I'll switch on the fire.' She felt a reluctant contentment. There was something to be said, after all, for coming in to companionable toasted tea cakes by the fire.

'I've been talking to Kathryn, she's bringing the children over on Tuesday.' Phyllida set the tray on a low table and drew the curtains.

'Oh yes?' Rowena had been flicking through a magazine; it was one of Phyllida's, which she took monthly for its patterns and instructions for embroidery and tapestry work of such immense complexity that Rowena could only marvel that she found it relaxing.

'They both have dental appointments, then she'd like to leave them here while she does some shopping. I said I was sure you wouldn't mind.' She looked at Rowena with both uncertainty and defiance stamped on her smooth face. For some reason her position in the house had begun to feel tenuous.

'Why should I? It's your home.'

'But it's your house. I don't like to be always filling it with my family.'

'Well, I'm hardly able to fill it with mine! Now surely that tea is ready? And the tea cakes are getting cold.'

She bit into one, gaining comfort from its buttery sweetness, telling herself as she so often did that she wasn't really alone.

She had Phyllida, after all. Incredibly, she still had Phyllida.

The house is plain and grey and many-roomed, standing in its own grounds overlooking the lake. The gardens are run-down but there is a gravel terrace largely free of weeds, and gracious trees hiding the view of distant Keswick with its backdrop of purple hills.

Rowena doesn't want to be here, she wants to be at home in the suburbs with her father, who has been left behind in his reserved occupation. She isn't really afraid of being bombed, but her mother is and so is Mark who at eight is a nervy child, prone to asthma attacks and eczema. He is already having nightmares although the war is only weeks old and nothing has happened yet.

Her father's firm has rented the house for the families of its employees. There will be other children, Rowena has been told. They will go to school, and everything will be as usual. Except that her father will not be there.

He has left them after all.

She scuffs at the gravel with her sandal. The sun is low, slanting across the water into her eyes. Hearing the crunch of footsteps she looks up, half blinded by the light. She sees a short, stocky figure in a tartan kilt and long brown socks. The figure stops in front of her, looking up into her face which is gilded by the sun.

'Hello,' she says. 'I'm Phyllida.'

TWO

In the four years that Rowena had shared her home with Phyllida she had been adopted by Phyllida's grandchildren, now aged six and eight, as an extra grandparent, from whom additional favours could be expected and extracted without too much difficulty. She was surprised at her complicity in the relationship. She had always rather resented the claims of small children for priority at every turn. When Phyllida's twins had been young her envy had been complicated and she had resisted the role of favourite aunt. She was still envious, but it was an envy soothed by indulgence.

It was her turn to shop that week. Wandering round Waitrose she found herself tempted by chocolate fingers and Battenburg cake, notwithstanding her usual rules about bakers, and the fact that Phyllida was at home making scones and one of her splendid fluffy sponges. Rowena never had been able to equal the lightness and height of Phyllida's sponges. But then she hadn't had the practice.

She dropped the sweet treats into her basket, reflecting rather guiltily that even now the children were at the dentist and she was hardly encouraging them in good habits. But she had spent her working life in schools encouraging good habits in other people's children, largely without any thanks. Cravenly now, she needed to see the smiles of pleasure that told her she was appreciated.

When she got home the children had already arrived, and were sitting at the kitchen table with Phyllida eating boiled eggs with bread and butter soldiers.

She felt a rush of hurt exclusion.

Phyllida showed not a trace of discomfiture. 'Sorry, dear,

they were too hungry to wait. I offered them the casserole but they preferred eggs.'

'Oh.' Rowena had made the casserole the night before. She lifted the lid regretfully saying, 'I was going to add dumplings.' Then she smiled brightly and said, 'Those eggs look good. I think I'll join you.'

Jake said, 'Daddy says that eggs used to have lions on them. I don't know why.'

'It was to show that they were fresh.' For the life of her, lowering her own egg into the saucepan, Rowena couldn't remember how the system had worked.

'I remember, during the war,' Phyllida joined in, 'when eggs were rationed and there weren't enough to have one every day, or even one each. When my mother boiled one for me, she used to eat the lid and dip one soldier in the yolk. I had all the rest.'

Jake regarded her solemnly. 'Daddy sometimes has two.'

'Yes, well that's not considered good for you now. Neither is butter for that matter, but we'll forget about that today, shall we?' Phyllida pushed her eggcup aside. 'Did you get the cream for the scones?'

'Yes. And everything else.' Rowena began to unpack her bag, coming guiltily to the cake and biscuits. 'I bought them a little treat. It's not often they come to tea.'

Phyllida looked across, taking in the packets at a glance. 'Really, Rowena. You'd better not let Kathryn see those. She's so careful about their teeth.'

'But just this once.'

Hannah had finished her egg, upturned the shell and was smashing it with her spoon. But she had seen the chocolate biscuits and now asked, 'Can I have one of those?'

'Not till teatime.'

'Couldn't they have one now?' Rowena decanted her egg into a wooden cup and sat down between the children. But Phyllida looked obstinate.

'Kathryn always gives them an apple,' she said, reaching into the bowl and handing them one each. Jake bit into his obediently but Hannah shook her head, sliding from her chair.

'Obviously not always with success,' muttered Rowena, knowing herself to be childish. After all, what did she know about the responsibilities of parenthood, of being a grandmother? But did Phyllida always have to make it so obvious?

Hannah had come to her side, leaning on her knee as she ate, and Rowena felt a warm loose feeling that reminded her of sex. The little limbs were bony; from her hair rose the smell of apple shampoo. Not for the first time, she wished the child were hers, flesh of her flesh, to pamper and spoil and mould in her own way. But she belonged to Kathryn and, to a lesser extent, to Phyllida.

As everything always had.

They are placed next to each other at the local school, squeezed into the back of a classroom already over full. The school is built of grey stone augmented by two cold wooden huts in the bleak asphalt playground. The toilets are outside, and have concrete floors which are always wet.

Rowena mourns her substantial brick-built suburban school with its parquet-floored corridors and assembly hall. Its windows were tall and bright and were opened with a long pole with a hook on the end. These windows are tall also, but narrow, with high stone ledges cluttered with bird's nests and shrivelled fungi and stiff arrangements of autumn leaves. The desks are small, and too cramped for Rowena's long legs, their lids heavily indented with laboriously carved initials to which she quickly adds her own. She likes having a desk with a lid to cover her possessions. Before, they only had tables.

As the only outsiders in a class of forty-four nine- and ten-year-olds, Rowena and Phyllida are thrown together for support and companionship. The other children close ranks, regard them wide-eyed as members of another species with their London accents, which they describe alternately as posh and funny. It is Christmas time and the class party before either of them feels accepted, and then it seems only on the strength of the superior refreshments their mothers have contributed.

After the party one of the boys, a sturdy farmer's son with muddy boots and chapped knees beneath his grey serge shorts, hands Phyllida a Christmas card, which she accepts with a gracious and insouciant smile, then opens eagerly while she and Rowena are walking home.

'Look, a robin on a pillar box. He's put kisses inside.'

'How soppy.'

'No it's not.' She flushes prettily, with annoyance and excitement. Though plump she is a pretty child in a fetching, fluffy way, whereas Rowena is tall and thin and gawky.

Rowena tries not to mind about the card, although she does. It is the start of being envious of Phyllida.

Kathryn arrived to collect the children just as they were finishing their tea. She looked pale and tense and complained of a headache.

'It's the shops. All that awful pop music.' She slumped on the sofa and Hannah climbed onto her knee. She pushed her away. 'Not now, darling.'

She leaned back and closed her eyes while Phyllida dissolved aspirin and made fresh tea. Rowena took the opportunity of removing the chocolate fingers, telling herself even as she did so that it was ridiculous, she had a perfect right. But did she? It was her house; yet they were not her grandchildren.

Phyllida offered her daughter a piece of sponge but she shook her head. 'I'm putting on weight.' She drank the aspirin with a shudder. Phyllida couldn't see much evidence of weight. At thirty-five Kathryn was as rangy as she had ever been, as Phyllida had never been herself. She had been grateful that both the twins had taken after their tall, trim father. When they had been small it had been hard to tell them apart. Even now, Kathryn had rather a hard, masculine look about her. Intimidating. Phyllida had to confess that she often found her daughter intimidating.

'How's Ben?' she asked.

Kathryn frowned. 'Far too busy. As usual.' Ben, an accountant, worked for the local council, in the treasurer's

13

department. Staff cutbacks, the new rating system and short-age of funds all seemed to land with increasing pressure on Ben's shoulders.

Jake said, 'Mummy says that's why Daddy shouts so much.'

Kathryn looked at him warningly, narrowing her eyes which were darkly ringed with pain.

'Yes, well everyone shouts sometimes.' Phyllida fidgeted nervously with the plates, gathering them into a pile on the table.

'I'll wash those up,' said Rowena, wishing suddenly to be gone.

'And you two – run and wash your sticky fingers,' urged Phyllida. She looked anxiously at her daughter. 'There's nothing really wrong, is there?'

Kathryn looked fierce, withdrawing herself as she always did. 'Of course not.' She sipped her tea.

'You would tell me?'

'Not necessarily.'

Phyllida made a small nervous smile. It was easy for Kathryn to put her down. She did so want to feel she was of use to her, but ever since Kathryn was a little girl she had preferred her father. Henry. Phyllida had never found a way to take his place, to offer the comfort that was required.

She should have been able to help. After all, she knew what it was all about, losing a father.

In the Lake District, Phyllida and Rowena talk a lot about their fathers. They miss them.

'I had a letter today,' says Phyllida. 'Some plaster fell off the kitchen ceiling into Daddy's breakfast. It's called bomb damage.'

'I know. That's what Daddy sees to. He told me.'

They are seated side by side on the swing in the garden, facing one another. As they soar and descend Rowena can see the lake, glittering under a wintry sun. The hills swoop down to the water, cornflake coloured with bracken and leaves. Phyllida can see the grey house and her mother shaking a yellow duster from her bedroom window.

14

Rowena leans back, legs outstretched. She says, 'He's coming at the weekend. It's been ages.'

Phyllida looks at her jealously. It's been ages for her too.

'It means I'll have to sleep with Mark. I hate that, he scratches his eczema.'

'Ugh!' Phyllida is deliciously disgusted.

'But it's worth it because next morning, Daddy will be here!'

Phyllida's mother never tells her daughter that her father is expected. She tells herself that it is to avoid over-excitement on Phyllida's part. But really it is so that she can have him to herself for a few hours. He always arrives late at night and she wants Phyllida to be safely in bed, not clinging possessively to Charles when that's all she wants to do herself. She knows it is selfish. He belongs to both of them. But she is so lonely, she cannot find it in her to be unselfish, even for her only child.

But one day, he doesn't arrive as expected. He is knocked down, in the blackout, on his way to the station just before Christmas 1940. The parcels he was bringing them scatter in the road and no one finds them till the morning. They don't find him for a while, either, because the driver, intent on getting home before the raid, doesn't stop. And by then, it is too late.

It is so ridiculous, so unnecessary, when people are dying by bomb and bullet, to be killed by a car. Now Phyllida's mother turns to her daughter, latching onto her as she had once latched onto her husband, cleaving to her in desperation so that Phyllida squirms, and longs for someone strong, someone grown-up, to lean on, to help her.

She turns to Rowena's mother, Helen, so practical and sensible, so comforting in a business-like way, which dries up the tears and points the way ahead.

But when Rowena's father comes to visit, Phyllida stays away. it is too painful to watch how Rowena glows and expands when he calls her 'princess', and pulls her plaits affectionately as she sits on his knee. Though Phyllida is always told she is welcome, the family seem to close in on themselves.

Phyllida has only her mother, who has collapsed like a post that is riddled with woodworm.

It is the beginning of being envious of Rowena.

The October air was crisp and nostalgic, the sun offering the last of its warmth to the turning leaves. Phyllida walked as briskly as she could, along Queen Anne Drive and into Tudor Gardens.

There was no shopping to do today but she had offered to return Rowena's library book. She liked to take a daily walk, thinking, incorrectly as it happened, that it kept her weight under control.

She often made the outward journey along Tudor Gardens, although it was a much longer route. She would pause and glance nostalgically into Tudor Close, a select development of four detached houses that occupied what had once been her back garden. Here, where pink and cream Marley blocks now met a geometric rockery of muted heathers, her father had pushed her on a swing beneath an apple tree that seemed to Phyllida now to have been in constant blushing bloom. There, beneath a double garage with turquoise up and over doors, her father had planted runner beans and carrots which her mother picked, singing, in the days before the war. Beyond the houses, screened in those days by trees and shrubs, Tudor House had stood, substantial, ugly, unremittingly Victorian in its solid respectability.

But bomb damage had dislodged its apparent invincibility, loosening everything ever so slightly so that sashes, their panes shattered by the blast, had begun to stick in their runners. Inside doors had either jammed or rattled; old tiles, blown loose and smashed, had been replaced by new so that the roof had a speckled, pockmarked, appearance.

In 1953, in the post-war building boom, Phyllida's mother had been glad to accept a local builder's offer for her house and land and retreat with her daughter to a modern flat in a purpose-built block where there was no garden to attend to, and someone else was responsible for the roof and outside paintwork. Phyllida had never forgiven her. She felt that they had betrayed her father, who had loved the house, and left him behind in the untended garden. She was ashamed of the poky flat near the station, opposite a Shell garage. In the event she didn't live there for long, because less than a year later she married Henry.

It had been to Tudor House that she and her mother returned two months after her father's death when his employers, along with a conciliatory cheque, had indicated on their headed notepaper that it was no longer appropriate for them to shelter in Cumberland. The following autumn, when the worst of the air-raids were over, Rowena and her family had returned also to their house on the edge of the fields.

'You ought to get in touch with Phyllida now you're back,' says Helen. 'She'll be hurt if you don't and you're bound to run into her eventually.'

'Oh, Phyllida.' Rowena looks mutinous. In the weeks before Phyllida left, Rowena had grown tired of the pale and puffy face always hanging round her mother, of the fuss everyone made of her at school, of her feeble and ineffectual parent who seemed only to compound Phyllida's soggy misery.

Helen frowns, not liking her selfish daughter. 'You've had it too easy,' she rebukes her. 'There's no harm in being friendly.'

Rowena sighs but she knows when she's beaten. She knows too that her mother is right. She agrees to cycle round to Tudor Gardens feeling, as she does so, both resentful, and guilty that she didn't answer any of Phyllida's letters.

Phyllida herself opens the door. She is overjoyed to see Rowena – and Rowena is overjoyed to see that pretty Phyllida has put on weight; at thirteen she is not now attractively comely, but actually fat. Sweets may still be rationed, but bread and potatoes aren't. Her mother, comfort eating herself, allows Phyllida to do the same. Rowena, still flat-chested, is reassured. There can be too much of a good thing. She eyes Phyllida's pink-wrapped breasts with triumph as she says, 'Hello, Phyl – I thought I'd let you know we're back.'

'Come in.' Phyllida is shy. It has been nine months. But then she hugs Rowena so that Rowena feels her soft, surprisingly fragrant flesh and the brush of a velvet cheek. Phyllida's skin is smooth, clear, peaches and cream, whereas Rowena is sallow and has blackheads beneath her lower lip. She feels suddenly sour again.

She looks round the square, panelled hall with envy. It is very different from the suburban villa which she had always regarded as the archetypal home. For the first time she realises that not everyone's lives are the same. There may be something else, something better – some other way to live.

'How are you, Phyl?' she asks, more warmly now. 'I'm sorry I didn't write, but there didn't seem to be anything to say.'

Walking the length of the high street on her way to the library, Phyllida reflected that it hadn't improved since her girlhood. Where there had been small independent traders, there was now a huge Boots with automatic doors, and far too many fast food takeaways, estate agents and record shops catering for the young. Waitrose occupied a big corner site which had once housed a half-timbered inn, a teashop and a greengrocer. Phyllida thought now, as she had done many times before, of the times before the war when her parents had taken her to the teashop to have toasted tea cakes dripping with golden butter. Life had been safe and secure in a way it had not been again until she married Henry, and she gave a sad little smile. The war had a lot to answer for, and sometimes she felt she was still paying the price.

Beside the supermarket there was a huge car park and, beyond this, stood the library, a single storey redbrick building dating from the sixties. The lobby was displaying children's paintings, the winners of a competition, and the lurid colours and bold shapes lifted her spirits. She remembered her own children's similar offerings, brought home proudly from school. She still had them somewhere in a folder. Sentimental nonsense, she had told herself when she packed them up to move to Rowena's. She had had to get rid of so many things, why keep them? But she had been unable to throw away this part of the precious past. Looking at the paintings on the library wall, she was glad she had kept them, and resolved to find them and look at them again as soon as she got home.

Joining the queue at the desk Phyllida glanced at the book she was returning. It was a literary tome, a Booker prize-winner by a Commonwealth writer whose white-toothed smile graced the glossy dustjacket. Phyllida looked inside. The large, close-printed pages looked tedious, almost unreadable. Mystified as she often was by Rowena she snapped the book shut. A customary feeling of inadequacy invaded her and she fought it back. After all, as her father used to tell her, it wouldn't do if we were all the same. It would make for a very dull world indeed.

Phyllida didn't read many books herself. She liked women's magazines – the weekly sort to read, the monthlies to leave about, and in particular her sewing and embroidery magazines. Last Christmas, Rowena had bought her a large hardback book on the history of embroidery but to her shame she had hardly looked at it, apart from skimming appreciatively through the illustrations in Rowena's presence so that she wouldn't feel hurt. Or censorious for, increasingly, she feared Rowena's censure. She genuinely didn't want to annoy Rowena but it sometimes seemed that she did, and then Phyllida was frightened that Rowena would ask her to leave, which was such an unthinkable prospect it made her feel physically sick.

As she was leaving the library, her eye was caught by a display of leaflets spread on a low table by the door. Information on home insulation, burglar-proofing, remedial reading classes and residential courses for writers and artists had been fanned out by a careful hand. In a plastic dispenser were a few yellow leaflets on adult evening classes at the local secondary school – previously the grammar school she and Rowena had attended – which was now known as a community college and was co-educational, with carpets and condom dispensers in the sixth form block.

Without really thinking she took a leaflet. It was already November and the courses had been running for a month. Rowena was well into her second year of bridge and German conversation, which she called keeping her brain alive now that she had retired. Phyllida never felt she herself had much of a brain, but she had hands. Maybe there was something she too could learn?

Rowena's German class was on a Tuesday. If she could attend on Tuesdays too it would save getting the bus. Phyllida had never learned to drive. Henry hadn't encouraged it. Later on, she had neither the heart nor the confidence.

She turned to Tuesday: yoga, French for beginners, Grade II guitar. And pottery. With a start of recognition, Phyllida knew that it had to be pottery. She marvelled that she hadn't thought of it before. She pocketed the leaflet with a satisfied smile. She would ring the organiser at the school as soon as she got home.

Rowena didn't seem terribly pleased when Phyllida told her. The truth was that she had enjoyed her evening classes on many levels, one of which had been that they were something she did without Phyllida. Retirement at fifty-eight had deprived her of much of the like-minded company she had enjoyed. Phyllida, cosy and comforting at first, was not intellectually stretching. Latterly, when she had begun to annoy and frustrate as well, some evenings apart had become an essential to survival for them both.

And now Phyllida was coming with her. Tuesdays would be robbed of their almost clandestine sense of escape as they climbed together into the Renault, Phyllida armed with overall and rubber gloves and wreathed in anticipation. Rowena could picture it already. Then, driving home through the quiet streets, the constant chatter, the reports on progress, the descriptions of the other students, as Phyllida was already excitedly calling herself.

20

But there was nothing to be done. As she had so often resolved over the years where Phyllida was concerned, she must make the best of it.

It is Rowena's first day at the girls' grammar school she should have attended since she was eleven. She is looking forward to renewing the acquaintance of friends she remembers from before the war. But she will also find Phyllida, already installed, having scraped through the entrance exam in Keswick and now unreservedly lording it over her friend.

For she thinks of Rowena as a friend, even if Rowena fails to return the compliment.

Phyllida had been privately educated before the war, and destined to continue so until her father's death had changed her prospects at a stroke. She is struggling at the grammar school, apart from the art and craft classes where she holds her own. She has a few friends, but none among the high flyers. Rowena she already recognises as a high flyer, intimacy with whom will add to her personal standing.

She waits in the playground, agog with self-important anticipation.

When Rowena walks in alone on that January morning, her badge bright with newness on her old blazer, her beret straight on her lank brown hair, loose now, the plaits gone, brushing the white collar of her stiff new poplin blouse which has taken so many precious coupons, she looks for a familiar face — and sees only Phyllida, beaming with pleasure and welcome. Rowena is both repelled, and grateful. She looks hopefully around, sees no better option, and moves, fatefully, into Phyllida's ambit.

And thus, in ways as yet undreamed of, she will remain.

There were only four of them at the German class on a foggy late November evening, when Rowena herself would have stayed at home if it hadn't been for Phyllida.

'Please, Ro, I'm so looking forward to it.' After three weeks of hand-modelling, it was to be her first turn on the wheel.

21

'Well you could get the bus if you must turn out. If they're running, that is.'

Phyllida pulled back the curtain. 'It's not that bad.' She looked obstinate, implacable, and Rowena gave in. She didn't really want to miss German, and an unexpected evening at home was a poor alternative.

Now she was glad she had come, for Derek Stadden had braved the fog as well. She had begun to notice that his presence gave an added frisson to the class, and this evening the four of them clustered together in the front row so that she sat next to him instead of behind in her usual place. She was able to note the firm regularity of his handwriting and the clean square nails on his short fingers, surprisingly short for so tall a man, for Derek comfortably topped her own five foot nine when he joined her in the queue at the vending machine. He had grey hair, neatly cut, and when he smiled, as he did now, his rather studious face seemed to split in two. Rowena found herself beaming back.

'Do you think you'll use your German?' he asked conversationally as she watched the thin brown liquid jet into the plastic mug.

'I hope so. I plan to go walking in the Black Forest next spring. The trouble is, of course, everyone there seems to want to speak English! It makes it all a bit pointless.'

'If we took that attitude we'd none of us learn any languages.' He flicked the knob to tea. 'Why did you choose German?'

'Because I already had a smattering, and I'm not too bad at French. This coffee really is disgusting. I think I'll start bringing a flask.'

'If you want a challenge you should try Finnish. I spent a year in Helsinki. It's a beautiful language, but completely mysterious.'

She laughed. 'I'm not sure I need to be quite so stretched.'

'This tea is dreadful, but at least it's hot. Why don't we go somewhere afterwards and have a drink?'

Pleased and startled, she remembered Phyllida with fury.

22

'Oh – I give someone a lift. Besides, maybe in view of the weather . . .'

'Of course. Another time.'

She was disappointed that he was not more specific, but had already relegated Phyllida to making her own way home next week.

It was still foggy the following afternoon when Rowena was due to visit her mother. She decided to take the bus.

'I'll come with you,' offered Phyllida. 'It will be company.'

But company was the last thing Rowena wanted. She hadn't forgiven Phyllida for spoiling the previous evening, forgetting that if it hadn't been for her, she wouldn't have seen Derek Stadden at all.

She spoke brusquely. 'There's no need. It's a filthy day. You'll just get chesty.'

Phyllida looked pained but patient. 'You shouldn't feel guilty. She really is in the best place, you know.'

'What are you talking about?'

'You always get tetchy when you visit Helen. It's because you feel you let her down, letting her go into a home. But she's happy enough – and how would you have managed while you were working?'

'It's nothing to do with feeling guilty.' Rowena had heard it all before. Phyllida's homespun philosophy may have been true once, but not any more. Besides, what right had she? Ever since their childhood, when Helen had taken Phyllida under her wing, Rowena had been jealous. She had known herself to be unreasonable – after all, she had so much, Phyllida so little. But over the years, when Phyllida's affectionate gratitude had changed to a certain possessiveness, Rowena's resentment had grown. Now, stabbing her arms angrily into her coat, she snapped, 'Why do you go over and over the same ground?'

'I'm sorry, dear.' Phyllida now looked anxious. 'I've always been so fond of your mother. I like to visit her sometimes.'

'It makes no difference. She doesn't know you.' It would

23

have been a cruel thing to say if, increasingly, Helen didn't fail to recognise Rowena herself. She picked up her bag and turned to Phyllida, taking in her unhappy but defiant face. It wouldn't do to leave on that note.

'I'll bring in some shopping. You can stay in the warm.' She tried a smile. 'Perhaps light a fire? We could eat on our laps this evening.'

Phyllida brightened. She watched Rowena disappear with startling suddenness into the fog, then closed the door with satisfaction. She would light the fire and settle down with her tapestry. There was a play just starting on the radio. She would cook whatever Rowena chose to bring in for supper and they would have a cosy evening together.

Everything was still all right.

Adelaide House was double-fronted Edwardian, extended in the sixties by ugly concrete wings which had worn badly. Each room in the three-storey blocks had a balcony fronted by a laminated panel, but no one ever sat there. Rowena's mother's room was at the back, securing a view over the well-tended garden, but no sun. It was a characterless box which she shared with another woman, who was prematurely senile in her early seventies. Helen had been allowed to take her own wing-backed armchair, a small bookcase which was largely covered in knick-knacks she no longer recognised, and a bedside cabinet. The bed was high with a plastic mattress which made her sweat. There was a tiny windowless bathroom which always smelled musty, with a shower she could no longer cope with on her own.

Rowena passed through the front door with the customary feeling of anguish and related panic at the prospect of her own old age. Adelaide House was not cheap and eight years had seen alarming inroads into her mother's capital.

When it had become obvious that Helen, at eighty-two, could no longer live by herself, and that Rowena, then head-mistress of an independent girls' school in an adjoining suburb, was in no position to look after her, Adelaide House presented the obvious – indeed the only – solution. In the event, Rowena had seemed to suffer more than Helen, who allowed herself to be prised from her home of fifty-seven years with very little protest other than that it be sold to 'somebody friendly'.

But for some reason the house failed to sell at all. At the time Rowena herself was living in a small new house not far from her school, and it eventually proved easier to sell this, increase her mortgage for the final years of her working life, and buy the house from her mother. She moved in, not without reservations, and found that she liked it.

Far from feeling that it was a retrograde step, she had taken comfort from the familiar rooms and steadily begun to change them to suit herself. Meanwhile the money produced by the sale was invested carefully by her mother's solicitor, who reported to Rowena every six months. In bald terms, her mother's life expectancy was measured against pounds and pence. Should they run out first, Rowena had not the slightest idea what would happen. Helen was now far beyond being cared for at home. Council homes were being closed down and social security payments were known to be inadequate for private care. She herself would be hard put to subsidise the fees from her own pension – and at the end of it all there was her own old age to worry about.

Rowena took a nervous breath of the disinfected air, and trembled.

Her mother was in the sitting room to the right of the front door. Its bay windows trapped any sun there was but today looked onto a swirl of grey, the glass running with condensation. The air was oppressively hot and Rowena opened her coat.

Plastic-covered chairs were ranged round the walls facing a television on whose gigantic screen rotated the bronzed protagonists of an Australian soap-opera. The vertical hold had gone but nobody seemed to notice. There was an empty chair beside Helen's and Rowena sat down, taking her mother's hand.

'Hello, Mother.' She spoke gently. She had never been a gentle person but she found it easy, in the face of such childlike docility, to treat her like a child. Her mother turned to look at her. Her eyes were hooded and sunk in khaki, so that she looked both bruised and hawklike. Someone had curled her hair and left it uncombed, a white astrakhan helmet. She had been dressed in a blue pinafore dress, a green jumper, a red cardigan and her favourite amber beads. Her stockings sagged and Rowena wanted to cry.

'It's Rowena, darling,' for her mother looked totally blank. 'I've come to see you.'

'Is it time for lunch?'

'No, you've had your lunch. But I expect there'll be a cup of tea soon. I hope so. It's foggy outside, I had to wait ages for a bus.'

'How's Phyllida?'

Rowena was startled. Nowadays, her mother's lucidity was more shocking than her senility, for it had ceased to be normal.

'She's well. She sends her love.'

'Why doesn't she come and see me?'

'She does, darling. But you don't remember.' She felt guilty. Phyllida would have come.

If her mother had felt any resentment at Phyllida moving in with Rowena instead of herself, she had never shown it. Even then, she was beginning to withdraw from life; indeed Rowena had never expected her to last so long. But, warm, fed and removed from all concern, she was ticking over physically like a run-in motorcar. It was only the driver who was out of control.

'Poor Phyllida.'

To Rowena's dismay tears began to run down the desiccated cheeks, gathering under her chin where a few bristles protruded, shining in the moisture. Rowena wiped them carefully with a tissue, though her mother seemed not to notice.

'Why poor Phyllida?' she found herself asking touchily, but her mother had closed her eyes on Rowena's resentment which even now could surface uninvited. Her mother had always been there for Phyllida, and when Rowena objected she had been rebuked, and told how lucky she was.

Still holding her mother's hand in a token, unacknowledged gesture of love, Rowena sat helplessly, waiting for the tea trolley.

Rowena and Phyllida are sitting on Rowena's bed, sewing petticoats. It is school work and the fabric is peach rayon, stiff and unsympathetic. They cannot imagine when they will ever wear them and they are giggling, in the way of fourteen-year-olds.

'Perhaps Mummy would like it.' Rowena stares hopelessly at a cockled seam.

Phyllida's needle is flying through the cheap fabric. It doesn't matter to her what she is making, she simply enjoys sewing. She also enjoys doing something better than Rowena. She smiles, smugly now it seems to Rowena, who flings hers aside impatiently onto the satin eiderdown.

Helen comes into the room. She doesn't knock and is carrying two cups of tea on a tray.

'That's excellent, Phyllida,' she says when Phyllida holds up her seam. 'How about yours, Rowena?'

Rowena makes a face. 'It's rubbish, an utter waste of time.'

Helen holds up the shapeless garment – and laughs. 'Oh dear. Well perhaps it can go for salvage.' And Rowena smarts, although she doesn't care about sewing and never will.

'Don't sit on the eiderdown, dears. I've told you before. And come down and join us soon. Dad and Mark are back and supper's nearly ready.'

Rowena jumps up. 'What did the doctor say?' She is half-way to the door.

'Oh, the usual. It's asthma and he'll grow out of it.'

'Poor Mark.' Rowena is overly protective of her younger brother, who is a weedy twelve-year-old unable to play games, though passionately interested in football. She is half-way down the stairs when Helen calls, 'What about this tea?'

Phyllida follows more slowly, carrying her cup, hanging back as she always does when Rowena's father is about. Her round face is a study of wistful envy; her heart knows the ache of exclusion, the degradation of being pathetic. More than anything she dreads being thought pathetic, yet cannot help feeling it. Rowena's family, closing round her like a clamp, underlines her own lonely partnership with her mother. Although Helen turns to her in the hall and says, 'Come on, Phyllida, into the warm,' she cannot help seeing the hug that Rowena gives Mark, nor the way her father looks at her when he greets her: 'Hello, princess, how has your day been?'

For Phyllida is no one's princess, and thinks she never will be.

'Why so sulky?' asks Helen, when Phyllida has departed after supper, carrying her admirable sewing.

'I'm not,' says Rowena sulkily.

'You mustn't begrudge her successes,' Helen tells her knowingly. 'She doesn't grudge you yours. Phyllida really loves you and you don't often find that in a friend.'

'But it's you she loves,' bursts out Rowena.

Helen smiles sadly. 'That will pass. But she'll be your friend for the rest of your life, if you'll let her.'

The rest of my life, thinks Rowena, unable to grasp the concept.

Returning from Adelaide House Rowena purchased steak for supper, anxious to make amends. She would cook it herself – well done for Phyllida, rare for herself. But she found it forcibly taken from her hands, herself ushered towards the bright fire where a bottle of wine stood open on the coffee table.

'How lucky I chose red,' beamed Phyllida, who liked to do things properly. 'How did you find your mother?'

'She asked after you,' Rowena told her generously and was rewarded by Phyllida's pleased look. It wasn't so much to give, after all. She drank a glass of warm wine quickly, steeped in a sudden good will.

Eating her steak, which was rather too well done after all, she inconsequentially remembered Derek Stadden. 'I was telling someone at my class last night about my holiday plans. As soon as Christmas is over we must get it booked. I think May is the time to go.'

Phyllida said nothing.

'You don't mind do you, Phyl? I mean, you wouldn't care for all the walking.'

Phyllida, who hadn't been consulted on this point, chewed on her steak thoughtfully. It didn't seem to be best quality – probably a special offer. Rowena liked to feel she was getting a bargain, but then she'd always had to be careful. After a measured interval she answered, 'I've told you I don't mind. You go off with your bridge friends. Kathryn and I will take the children down to the caravan.'

'You'll like that.' Certainly better than she had liked France, thought Rowena. Last year's holiday in Provence had been a disaster, with Phyllida dubious about the food, without a word of French and unable to share the driving. She had also been bitten by mosquitoes and burned by the sun and they had both returned exhausted. A caravan near Padstow with her grandchildren was far more Phyllida's sort of thing.

That it would have been Rowena's too, had she been given the chance, Rowena always strenuously tried to ignore.

'Lovely wine,' she said now, refilling her glass. 'Is there any pudding?'

THREE

At the last but one German class Derek handed Rowena an early Christmas card and asked her to come to the George Hotel for a Christmas drink the following week, giving her plenty of time to make arrangements with Phyllida.

She said to her in the car that night, 'Next week perhaps you'd get the bus home, dear. I'm going out for a drink after my class.'

'Oh. Well, all right. That's nice. I didn't realise you were that friendly.'

'It's just one man. Derek Stadden. The others keep themselves pretty much to themselves.' She negotiated a corner carefully. It was a frosty night and the car windows were smeared with the defroster that Phyllida had insisted on applying, thinking that she was helping. Rowena preferred to scrape the ice off. 'He's a widower,' she heard herself explaining, and wondered why she had bothered. Was she implying that the assignation was innocent, or that it had possibilities? And why did it matter, anyway?

'That's nice,' Phyllida said again.

The hotel looked festive, its old beams hung with greenery and a tall tree in the foyer, brightly lit against brick-red walls. Wide red-carpeted stairs led invitingly to unseen bedrooms, suggesting to Rowena deep quilts and hot radiators and large accommodating bathrooms. From the restaurant came lingering smells of roast meat, redolent of pleasures others had enjoyed.

The bar was crowded and they had to perch on stools. Rowena didn't mind. It reminded her of the days when she had first gone into pubs, sitting up at the bar, smoking experi-

30

mentally and drinking beer. To sit on a stool, one's feet crossed on the foot rest, one's reflection gazing back from the mirror behind the bottles, was to be young and free and hopeful. She asked for a glass of Madeira, feeling it to be Christmassy — more interesting than sherry, less exotic than a gin and tonic. Derek ordered a pint of Guinness.

'So – what are you doing for Christmas?' he asked, turning on his stool and opening his sheepskin coat to reveal a bottle-green, hand-knitted sweater. Several threads were pulled around the neck; perhaps he had a cat? Irrationally, Rowena hoped he had a cat, though she had never had one herself. But a cat-lover spoke of kindliness, comfort, and a certain peace.

'Do you have a cat?' she found herself asking.

He looked surprised and answered, 'No,' with a querying tone.

He laid his gloves on the bar and once more she admired his fingernails.

'Christmas,' he prompted, as she stared down at his hands.

Flustered, she looked away. 'Oh, I shall be joining Phyllida and her family. It's very good of them. Children really make a Christmas, don't they?'

He agreed. 'I shall be going to my daughter's. She lives in Wales.'

'And you have grandchildren?'

'Three. All marvellous of course!'

'Of course. That goes without saying.' She sipped her drink, drawing in its comfort.

After a while he asked, 'You never married?'

'No.'

'I hope you don't mind my asking.'

'Why should I? It's the luck of the draw, I suppose.'

He smiled, saying generously, 'I'm sure you had plenty of chances.'

She sipped again, not answering, wishing neither to agree nor to deny.

'I was a headmistress before I retired,' she explained. 'I've had a very rewarding life.'

31

'And now?'

'Oh, I fill my time. As you do, I suppose.'

Now he didn't answer, drinking deeply and swivelling on his stool to look out over the crowded room. 'Everyone getting into the Christmas spirit,' he remarked. 'And there's still two weeks to go.'

'I shall miss our classes, five weeks off is a long time.'

'You will be carrying on next year I hope?' he asked.

'Oh yes. Weather permitting of course. February can be difficult.'

'The fireside is a draw, I agree.' Now he looked at her, smiling full into her eyes. 'And you're lucky, you have somebody to share it with.'

'It has its compensations, certainly.' She was momentarily confused by his gaze, which seemed both intimate and meaningful. She looked down, fiddling with her bag like a young girl at her first dance. She wanted to tell him all the disadvantages, too, but it would be petty, disloyal, and too soon. She hardly knew him, so now was not the time for confidences, for involvement. And yet, surely . . .

He was still looking at her, still smiling. 'I shall look forward to seeing you in January.' There seemed to be a promise in his words and, like the young girl that she had suddenly become, she accepted it.

Phyllida was in the kitchen in her dressing gown, drinking hot chocolate.

'Good time?' she asked.

'Very pleasant.' Rowena would say no more, not just yet. She smiled, secretively, hinting at more. 'You got back all right?'

'Oh yes.' There was a pregnant silence as Rowena poured milk into the saucepan and turned on the ring. 'I had a lift, actually.'

Rowena turned. Phyllida's eyes were dancing, she had noticed it at once, yet chosen not to see.

'Another potter. I had a lot to carry, your Christmas

present . . .' she indicated a large box on the worktop. 'And you're not to look.'

Rowena waited, her eyes on the rising milk. There was going to be more.

'He's very nice,' said Phyllida, inexorably. 'His name's Bob, Bob Duffy, and he's asked me out to supper. Isn't that a surprise?'

Rowena made herself turn, lifting the saucepan as she did so. She had a fleeting fantasy of herself throwing the scalding milk, its arcing across the kitchen and spreading itself across the smug, plump, still pretty face.

Her own small triumph dissipated in the milky steam.

And wasn't that how it had always been?

They are waiting at the bus-stop after school, waiting for the boys. The boys' grammar school is further up the road and strictly out of bounds, but school is over now and the journey home is a free for all.

Rowena hates it. She would rather get an earlier bus but usually Phyllida persuades her.

'Go on, Ro, be a sport. I can't go on my own.' Which isn't true at all.

'I don't like them, Phyl. They're silly and noisy.' What she means is that they don't like her. They never grab her beret or jostle to sit beside her.

With Phyllida it's different. Phyllida is different, when the boys arrive. She pouts her mouth and slides her eyes sideways. She has a way of slinging her raincoat over her bunchy body that is both challenging and sexy. And Helen has taken her in hand recently, encouraging her to be careful about what she eats. She will never be thin, but at nearly fifteen the puppy fat is falling away. Rowena watches the transformation resentfully, angry at her mother who should have left well alone. Her own body is reluctant to round into womanhood, her periods have only just begun, she is impatient with herself and malcontent. Phyllida on the other hand seems to be bursting open like a baking loaf, warm, succulent, full of promise.

'Hi, Phyl!' It's Alan, sixteen years old, a hockey player, acne behind him and a smudge of beard on his chin. Sourly, Rowena admits in secret that Alan is attractive. Phyllida pretends not to notice this, but she has a very special smile reserved for Alan which she gives him now so that he asks, not realising that he has been hooked, 'What are you doing on Saturday?'

She looks at Rowena. 'Ro and I are going to the pictures.'

Rowena waits, mutinously. She is not going to help them.

'Well how about me joining you?' He looks at Rowena cockily, waiting for her to back out. She says nothing.

'Would you mind, Ro?' Phyllida is looking both triumphant and doubtful. She doesn't like doing this to her friend, but other currents are pulling her and she has to go with them.

Rowena shakes her head. 'No, let him come.'

But her heart is heavy because she knows how it will be.

Bob called for Phyllida in his Jaguar the following Saturday. Hours before, Phyllida was fussing around, applying make-up and fiddling with her hair. Rowena was startled to see her with blue eyeshadow and eyeliner, which she hadn't worn for years. Far from foolish, it made her look almost indecently young, with her smooth cheeks and bright eyes. Coils of feeling Rowena had hoped to have forgotten tightened round her chest: envy, dislike and — now — a sense of foreboding. To loosen them she said, 'You look wonderful, dear. What are you going to wear?'

'Oh, my blue I think. I was saving it for Christmas, but I think it's called for, don't you? We're going to the George Hotel, and it's quite smart.'

Rowena pictured the sparkling tree, the dining room with its pink napery and unctuous waiters. She thought, inexplicably, of the bedrooms, private and warm, and wanted to scratch the bright blue eyes with their painted lids. She smiled painfully and said, 'I'm sure you're right.'

She let Bob in herself, anxious to grasp the nettle. He was

short and tubby, balding and affable, with a small hot hand that gripped her own and a lazy, south London accent.

'Pleased to meet you, Rowena. I may call you Rowena, I hope? Phyllida's told me all about you. I must say this is a very pleasant house. I've only a flat, in Croydon.'

'You come a long way for your pottery classes.'

'Only one I could get into actually. Local one is very over-subscribed. Ah, here she is. Doesn't she look a treat?'

He rubbed his hands, as if anticipating a feast. Rowena looked away. Gross little man, what on earth did Phyllida see in him? But Phyllida was exuding a pleased charm which had been buttoned up for years.

'Bob, how nice.' She extended her hand graciously, like the Queen Mother it seemed to Rowena, who swallowed hard on her own ungraciousness.

Phyllida turned to her. 'You'll be all right, dear?' she asked, as if it made any difference.

Feeling patronised, Rowena said sharply, 'I'm playing bridge, you know that.'

'Of course. Well at least I shan't feel I'm in the way.'

Touché, thought Rowena.

At the hotel Bob unbuttoned his short camel coat and handed it to the waiter, who hung it with Phyllida's fur on a curly hatstand. She had thought long and hard about the fur coat. These days it was hardly the done thing to be seen wearing real fur. But for reasons far removed from discretion and good taste she hadn't worn it for fifteen years. It had hung under its cloth cover in her wardrobe for all that time, and some bravado had caused her to remove it that afternoon, give it a good shake, and try it on.

It felt good. It looked good. There was nothing like fur next to the face, her mother had always said. She had leaned her cheek into the collar, closing her eyes languorously and savour-ing both the sensation and the coming evening with all its possibilities. It was a long time since she had dressed up for a man. She would wear the fur, and take the consequences.

35

'I'll have a sweet sherry, please,' she responded to his offer of a drink. 'Let's have it at the table, the bar looks crowded.' She had no intention of perching on a stool as if she was waiting to be picked up. Besides, the tight skirt of her blue silk dress would not be shown to advantage.

The waiter showed them to a table beside the window where heavy aubergine drapes shut out the winter street with its Christmas lights and the litter of a Saturday's shopping.

'This is very nice,' she murmured, looking round at the pink tables and shaded lights.

'So it is, so it is.' He rubbed his hands happily then picked up his campari and soda. 'Well, here's to you, my dear. It's very good of you to accompany me.'

'It's good of you to ask,' she fluttered. 'It's a long time since I've eaten out like this. And I don't suppose I've been here since before I was married.'

'Have you always lived in these parts?'

'My married life I spent in Guildford. Well, just outside, it was countryside really.'

'Ah, the country. I'm not a country boy, I'm afraid. Give me the city streets any time.'

The waiter handed them the menu. 'The boeuf en croûte is very good today,' he told them, handing the wine list to Bob. He unfolded Phyllida's napkin with a flourish, spreading it on her taut blue lap. She found herself flushing with pleasure and stared at her menu with growing anticipation. Tonight she intended to indulge herself.

While they were eating Bob told her that he had been the manager of one of a chain of betting shops in Croydon. 'But I never touch the gee-gees now. And I've got a nice pension, and only myself to please.'

'Your wife has died?' she asked experimentally.

'Alas, no. Well, I mean, alas we divorced, many years ago. No children, which is a sadness but perhaps just as well.'

'I have two children. Twins. And grandchildren now, of course. But I don't often see Stuart. That's my son. He lives

36

up north. He hasn't a wife. I think it's the women who like to keep in touch don't you?'

'I wouldn't know, my dear. But perhaps you're right. I seemed to lose touch with a great many people when Marjorie left.'

'People take sides, that's the trouble.'

'And quite unnecessarily. No one can know the truth of it, after all.'

She said no more, concentrating on her food. The vegetables were a little crisp for her liking: *al dente*, she thought it was called. But the veal, swathed in a Marsala sauce and nestling on a bed of spinach as the menu so fancifully described it, was tender and the sauce savoury. She sipped her wine, smiling at Bob with pleasure.

'Do you like to dance?' he asked her suddenly. 'That's something I really miss.'

'Oh yes. I haven't danced since . . . since . . .'

'When did you lose your husband?' He spoke with a kindly concern, reaching out a plump hand which she touched lightly, then withdrew her own.

'He died six years ago.' She found herself screwing the napkin in her lap, its crisp folds crumbling into dampness.

'I'm sorry. But then, you had him to the end. In a way that's better than divorce.'

She stared at him in silence, her blue eyes bright with what he took to be tears.

'Tell you what, why don't we start to enjoy ourselves? New Year's Eve, we'll go to a dinner dance.' He rubbed his hands with a sort of glee. 'You'd like that, wouldn't you?'

She and Rowena had already booked dinner at a country pub where there was to be live music and entertainment to see them through until midnight. 'Oh . . . dear. I'm afraid Rowena and I had already made arrangements.' But she was looking at him longingly.

'Well, she could come along too.'

'Hardly. Not to a dance. And I don't think Rowena does . . .'

'What a shame, what a shame.' He sat back while the waiter

took their plates. He folded his hands comfortably across his distended stomach and looked at her appreciatively. Her cheeks were pink, her hair fluffy, her lips, though pulled down in disappointment, were nonetheless soft and glossy. He leaned forward. 'Another time then, eh? We'll not let it slide.'

'I hope not.' She smiled at him gratefully. They chose their pudding and she let her eyes wander round the dining room, which was almost full. At a table near their own sat a woman in her thirties in a black velvet suit with a multi-coloured silk scarf thrown about her neck in a casual way that Phyllida envied. Opposite her sat a girl of about fifteen, dressed in a baggy sweat-shirt printed with 'Peace and Love', rattling with bangles, her hair languidly draped across her forehead and necessitating frequent sweeps of her beringed hand as she talked.

They seemed to be enjoying themselves. The woman laughed frequently at something her daughter – for Phyllida presumed it to be her daughter – was recounting. But Phyllida, comfortably conscious of Bob sitting opposite, looked at them with pity, for there was no man at their table.

The dining room at the south coast guest house is already full, though the sounds of the gong in the hall have only just died away. There are tables for four in the two bay windows, filled with happy families. Other tables for two have couples, mainly middle-aged though two are honeymooners, who are always late for breakfast.

There is another table for two near the kitchen door, and here sit Phyllida and her mother. They are always the first to smell the food, and the last it seems to be served.

This is the second year that her mother has brought her away on holiday, thinking that a week by the sea will do them both good. Last year, they had befriended another family. The barbed wire had been cleared from the beaches and Phyllida had been happy to play childish games, digging and damming and throwing a ball about with the younger ones. This year, at fifteen, she is too old for that, and too young to do anything else. She is self-consciously aware of their isolation, that everyone else has a father, a husband, a man. Everyone must be feeling sorry for them. She wishes they had not come, yet feels guilty because of this. Her mother must be lonely too. She is old enough now to realise this, but too crushed by her own deprivation to offer companionship.

At one of the other tables a mother and son had been alone, too, for three days. Sensing a kindred spirit she had asked the boy to play table tennis after dinner one evening. He had been much better than her, and played in a concentrated silence, throwing down his bat at the end with nothing more than a thank-you. Then on the fourth day, his father had arrived from London, and everything had seemed worse than ever.

She toys with her shepherd's pie and carrots, wondering whether to send a postcard to Alan and if so, what to say.

'Bob's invited me to a dance on New Year's Eve,' she told Rowena next day as they cleared away the breakfast.

It was unfair. She should never have mentioned it, never put Rowena in the position of feeling guilty. But the miracle she hoped for had occurred. Rowena's face, far from falling apart, actually brightened.

'You'll go of course. You always liked dancing.'

'But how about our plans?' Phyllida held her breath.

'Well, in fact . . .' and Rowena actually looked uncomfortable, 'Robert and Joyce have organised a bridge party and asked me if I'd like to go. I said not, of course, after all we have booked up, but if you'd rather go with Bob . . .'

'Well if you don't mind, dear. As long as you're not alone.'

'I won't be alone.'

'Fine. I'll give him a ring.' She started scraping round the base of the taps with a knife, causing Rowena to give a tut of irritation. If there was one thing she couldn't stand . . . She clenched her hands tightly, trying not to speak.

Then Phyllida dried her hands and bustled to the door where, turning, she said, 'And we'll be together for Christmas.'

'Yes, dear. We'll be together for Christmas.'

* * *

Uproar greeted them on arrival at Kathryn and Ben's on Christmas morning.

'We've all been up since five,' Ben explained, opening the door and letting out gusts of heat and turkey fat and childish wailing. 'Hannah's ready for bed again already and Jake's being impossible.'

'Well, we're here now. We can take them off your hands.' Phyllida looked pleased. 'I don't expect Kathryn will want me in the kitchen.'

'I don't know what Kathryn wants,' he said sourly, taking their coats. 'She muttered something earlier about a nunnery.'

Rowena laughed, then realised he wasn't being amusing. He looked drawn and exhausted, and was still unshaven. She had to stop herself suggesting that he go and do just that, and maybe have a nap as well.

Kathryn came out of the kitchen looking dishevelled and unfestive. 'Happy Christmas,' she said mechanically, kissing her mother and offering her cheek to Rowena. 'Oh – you've brought more presents! They've had so many already.'

Rowena saw Phyllida flinch. 'We'll put them round the tree,' she intervened. 'They can have them later.'

'You try telling them that!'

The sitting room was spread with torn paper, boxes of Lego, cars, books, dolls and electronic games. Hannah was tearing at the intricate clothing of a Barbie doll, while Jake lay on his back amidst the paper jeering at her.

'She's stupid, she's got boobs with no nipples.'

Hannah's face was flushed and angry. 'I don't care. I didn't want nipples.' The tawdry pink net dress came off suddenly in her hands, revealing skimpy underwear. She lifted the brassiere and stared doubtfully at the smooth pink plastic breasts.

Phyllida seated herself on the William Morris covered sofa, pushing aside a somnolent cat who jumped to the floor philosophically and began to claw the hearthrug.

'Come to Grandma,' she crooned, holding out her arms to Hannah. 'How about a Christmas kiss?'

Hannah sidled up to her, red tights wrinkled over her thin

legs, her Stuart tartan kilt twisted askew. 'Are those for us?' she asked, watching Rowena arrange their parcels in the fallen needles beneath the tree.

'Yes, darling, but later.' Phyllida hugged her and received a wet kiss in return.

Jake laughed loudly and rolled across the floor to the tree. 'I bet it's a book,' he said to Rowena. 'You always give us books.'

'Yes, well we'll see,' she answered tartly. 'You seem to have plenty of everything else. How about clearing up some of this mess for Mummy?'

'Mess mess mess!' he shouted in delight, clutching his knees to his chest and rolling.

'You're being silly.' Phyllida looked nervously at the door. It would be as well to regain some sort of control before Kathryn came back. She looked at the end of her tether.

She slid to her knees, pulling armfuls of paper towards her. What a waste. Some of it looked hardly used, but it was crumpled now and useless. In her day it had been carefully smoothed and folded and put away for the following year. But young people these days knew nothing about rationing and making do, darning socks or sides-to-middling sheets. She crammed the paper into the log basket beside the fire and began to gather the toys into a pile, while Hannah watched droopy-eyed from the sofa with her thumb in her mouth and Jake lay on his back, humming and watching a paper bell turning in the warm air from the fire.

Rowena leaned down to pick up the Barbie doll and her abandoned dress. As she did so she felt an annoying twinge of stiffness to remind her once again that she was not as young as she was. She straightened carefully and looked at the dress. The flimsy fabric was already torn. She sat down and began carefully to ease it back over the doll's stiff arms.

'No, no!' Hannah shrieked, rushing at her from the sofa. 'She's got to go to bed.'

Rowena caught her close, feeling the fragile bones beneath the too-warm clothing. The child needed fattening up. A few more sweets and a little less muesli wouldn't hurt. 'Why don't you take her up to bed with you?', she suggested in a calm and reasonable voice. 'I'm sure she'd sleep much better if you were there.'

To her surprise, Hannah nodded. 'But she hasn't got a nightie.'

'Well I'm sure we can find something. Come along.' She stood up, taking Hannah's hand.

They passed Kathryn in the hall, carrying a tray of bottles and glasses. Her eyes looked stark but she had run a comb through her thick hair and removed her apron.

'Sorry to be so long. Where are you two off to?'

'To put Barbie to bed.' Rowena gave her a conspiratorial wink and together she and Hannah climbed the stairs.

She could hear Ben in the bathroom, and the buzz of an electric razor. He was humming 'We wish you a merry Christmas', which sounded hopeful.

After lunch Rowena and Ben took the children for a walk while Phyllida, for once resolutely ignoring Kathryn's protests, helped with the washing up.

The children ran ahead. They scuffled through damp leaves which had gathered in the ditch along the lane and Jake stooped and gathered up a sodden pile and threw them over his sister. She shrieked and looked back at her father, who took no notice.

'How are things at the Council?' asked Rowena.

'Gruesome, but I don't want to think about that now. I'm on holiday until the New Year.'

She felt rebuked. 'I'm sorry.' They walked in silence. She found her thoughts wandering to Wales, to Derek Stadden and his grandchildren. Pulling them back she said, with a glance at Ben, 'Actually, you look as if you could do with a holiday. I mean a proper one, not just the caravan with the children.'

'Chance would be a fine thing.'

'Perhaps we could have the children? You and Kathryn get away on your own for a while?'

What temerity, she thought. Such suggestions were Phyllida's prerogative.

He shrugged. 'It's a nice idea. But there may be problems. It all depends . . .'

She waited. He said nothing so she prompted, 'On what?'

He looked at her sideways, then away, up into the leafless trees behind which a late sun was flaring between the clouds.

'On the results of Kathryn's tests. She has a lump in her breast.'

Rowena looked at him, shocked, already embracing all the implications, not the least of them Phyllida's reaction. She would be beside herself with worry. Rowena felt a rush of pity for them all.

'Oh. Oh Ben.' She wanted to touch his arm, instead called to the children, 'Jake, Hannah, don't get too far ahead.'

They ran on, ignoring her.

'Does Phyllida know? No, of course not. She'd have told me. Perhaps Kathryn is telling her now?'

'I doubt it. The last thing we want is her fussing. You won't say anything will you? Time enough to worry if there is anything to worry about.'

'I see. If that's the way you want it.' She wished he hadn't told her. It put her in an awkward position. 'I'm glad you told me,' she said reassuringly, drawing his arm through her own. 'A trouble shared and all that. And maybe it will all come to nothing.'

He stopped walking, standing stock still in the road looking into the sunset. 'Let's go back now, it's getting cold.'

She called the children again, shrilly, and this time they turned and seeing their still figures, began to run back up the lane, wellington boots flying, faces bright under their woollen hats. Hannah grabbed her hand and said, 'Can we have our presents now?' and Rowena nodded indulgently, pushing down the anxiety that had prematurely darkened the afternoon.

That night she dreamed of the air-raid shelter.

*   *   *

43

It is June 1944. The Normandy invasion has taken place, the tide has turned, they are beginning, just beginning, to relax. But out of a clear blue sky have come the flying bombs, raining down on southern England with a menacing roar. and an even more menacing silence.

They hadn't thought to use the shelter again. It is a purpose-built brick and reinforced concrete structure just outside the french windows, and her father had used it while they lived in Cumberland. They themselves had slept there on occasion since their return, and she remembers vividly standing at the doorway while her father took his air-raid warden's helmet from the hook by the door and went out into the roaring night. She had wanted to drag him back into the musty safety of the shelter, where Mark was sleeping on the bunk bed and where she would join him and listen to him coughing in the damp air.

Now, her father insists they sleep there again, every night, although the bombs fall night and day and, as Helen says, they can't live like moles, life must go on.

In her dream Rowena knows again the nameless dread born of the drone of aeroplanes overhead, the distant crump of death in London, the sense of someone evil up there seeking her out. She huddles under the grey blanket, shutting her mind lest she summon that evil with the very force of her imagining.

But the flying bombs are mindless, indiscriminate. No amount of deception or evasion can divert their random destruction.

Despite her fear, she sleeps, pressed against her brother while her parents murmur in the other narrow bed. And in the morning they are all still there.

Rowena had met Robert and Joyce through her newly acquired interest in bridge. They had a large detached house on the edge of the woods, reached by a private road which Rowena, Mark and their parents had often walked up when she was a child, peering up the long drives and marvelling at

44

the wide brick and stucco façades. It had never occurred then to Rowena that people actually lived there. Not until she visited Phyllida at Tudor House did she realise that houses could be large, excessive to requirements, profligate of space both inside and out. Now she got a peculiar pleasure from driving up to Birchwood and parking her car on the raked gravel outside the pretentious colonnaded porch.

Robert and Joyce were not pretentious. He had made his money in a merchant bank and now wore cardigans, walked the dogs and dug manure into the garden. Joyce did Meals on Wheels and washed hair in the geriatric ward. They had invited Rowena to join the bridge club in the New Year, and now she had come to their New Year's Eve bridge party.

She hoped she would deport herself well.

Four card tables were set up in the long drawing room where a bright fire sparkled and leapt in a mock-Adam fireplace.

She drew near, holding out her hands. 'What a lovely fire.'

'It's not real. Gas,' explained Robert, handing her a glass of sherry. 'All the effect for no trouble at all.'

'Oh.' Rowena was disappointed. She had imagined him chopping logs, probably taken from trees in his own garden. Now, looking closely, she saw that the logs were artificial and there was no tell-tale drift of ash beneath them, no smell of wood-smoke. It was a pity, but she had to admit that the effect was cheering.

'Perhaps I should do the same,' she suggested, thinking of Phyllida fussing over the dust, the humping of the smokeless fuel which became increasingly onerous.

'Hello, Rowena. Happy New Year.'

She turned and saw Betty Simpson, her partner, dressed elaborately in a swathed silk dress with a large amethyst brooch at the cleavage. She was a big woman with lumpy features and heavy hair coiled into a bun. Rowena, whose own still-dark hair was cropped short and simply brushed back, always felt drab in comparison to Betty and she regretted her choice of a simple wool dress. But she hadn't thought of it so much as a party as a game of bridge.

She said nervously, 'I hope I'll be in form for you tonight. I'm still a beginner.'

'Nonsense. You're better than me any day. You know how to concentrate. We must get together soon, about the holiday.'

'Yes.' They sipped their drinks and helped themselves to little savouries that Joyce had set out on the coffee table. More people arrived and greeted each other jovially. Rowena knew no one else and engrossed herself in studying the Christmas cards on the mantelpiece. She was irrationally pleased to see her own there, beside the clock, as if endowed with some importance, though common-sense told her this wasn't so.

Then Robert bustled up and led her round, introducing her to everyone. 'I shall never remember so many names,' she laughed. She hoped that they couldn't see that she was nervous. She hadn't felt so nervous for years and years. Maybe it was just growing old, this uncertainty of her worth, of her abilities.

Then they took their places, and the cards were dealt.

Phyllida was whirling and whirling in Bob's arms, small feet flying, laughing breathlessly at the sheer joy of it all.

Though short, he was an excellent dancer, and held her firmly against his round body so that her feet followed his unerringly, remembering . . .

Though she and Henry had never danced so exuberantly. Taller, he had been graceful, almost stately, and she had felt graceful and stately too, and grateful. They had made a good pair and she used to hold his arm possessively as they left the floor, claiming him as her own.

The Viennese waltz over, Bob kept her hand in his and led her back to their table. She sank onto her chair, realising that her feet in their gold sandals were beginning to swell and ache. She reached for the bottle of mineral water and poured herself a generous glass.

'Nearly midnight,' he told her. 'I'll pour the bubbly.'

The sparkling liquid filled the glasses to the brim, catching the disco lights which revolved overhead. There had been something for everyone – disco music, the Valeta and the Gay Gordons, spot prizes, excuse-mes and ballroom. It had been a wonderful evening and now Phyllida told him so, leaning across the table so that her breasts pressed up above her dress, traversed by lights, red, blue and yellow. Bob gazed down at them as if transfixed. Suddenly the music, a rock and roll number, stopped abruptly and the Master of Ceremonies seized the microphone.

'Here she comes folks, a brand New Year! Let's raise our glasses and wait for Big Ben.'

Someone had switched on a radio and there was a pregnant silence as people reached for their glasses. Bob's other hand picked up Phyllida's where it lay damply on the table. He squeezed it. Then the clock began to chime. She held her breath in a crazy anticipation. On the first stroke, she raised her glass to her lips and drank, smiling into Bob's eyes.

He drank, deeply, then lowered his glass, and said, 'I have a feeling this is going to be a good year. Don't you?'

And he leaned forward and kissed her, wetly, on the lips.

His mouth tasted of champagne.

At Robert and Joyce's, things were more restrained. Joyce switched on the large television in the corner and they arranged themselves on chairs and sofas, holding their glasses and chatting as the merry-making ranged across the screen. At the stroke of midnight, they all took a formal sip and smiled at each other. Robert cried, 'Happy New Year everyone!', hugged Joyce, then gave her a warm, prolonged kiss. One of the other couples followed suit.

Rowena looked down into her glass. This had always been a bad moment, with no one of her own to kiss. She was relieved when someone suggested 'Auld Lang Syne' and she could jump up, dispose of her glass and clasp hands with strangers and sing of friendship.

Friendship. There had always been Phyllida. But there had been others.

* * *

47

The war is over. There have been bonfires in the streets, and the shelters behind the school hall have been converted into changing rooms.

Rowena is sixteen, and doing well. She has moved ahead of Phyllida into a more academic stream, and is being steadily pulled away, leaving Phyllida on the shore, gazing after her bereft and wan. But Rowena doesn't glance back; she sits in the library with Julia and Pam, heads down over their books, delving, exploring, stretching their minds. Together they discover Molière, Mephistopheles, *The Miller's Tale* and Karl Marx. They circle the playground, heads together, talking, changing the world, changing themselves.

And Rowena decides to be a teacher.

At seventeen, Phyllida leaves school and enrols in a beautician's course. With her perfect, perfumed skin and soft plump hands she is ideal material to practise on. She sees herself in the mirror, accentuated and adorned, and for the first time thinks she might be beautiful.

FOUR

In the New Year, Rowena had a letter from Mark, from New York where, he said, snow lay thick in Central Park and the breath from the horses drawing the buggies condensed in the bright blue air.

He also said he was coming over to see her.

She wasn't often so honoured. When he was twenty-two, fresh from the London School of Economics, he had taken himself off to America to 'bum around' as he described it. Rowena had been worried, protective as always. Mark was still asthmatic – suppose he had a bad attack? When she voiced her fears to her parents they seemed uncaring almost in their dismissal, leading her to wonder if they were pleased he was going. Her father pointed out that Mark had been living his own life for three years already, but she was still uneasy, unable to accept that he could do without her. Throughout their teens, until she had gone away to university, Rowena had fussed and cosseted and pandered to her baby brother. He had given her little thanks and gone off to digs in London without a backward glance. She had been hurt. She had always looked out for Mark. Who would do so now?

Her father told her, gently, that Mark would.

He had eventually settled down in the States, and he didn't come home. An English firm of management consultants, something new in 1955, had put him into their New York office and he got himself an apartment in an old brownstone building in Greenwich Village. He seldom wrote and this too her parents seemed able to accept. Indefinably, Rowena sensed that they had washed their hands of him. She wondered if she, too, could prove so easily dispensable.

This year he hadn't sent a Christmas card, but his letter

explained all that: *I've been in hospital with a touch of bronchitis, so Christmas rather escaped me. But I'm coming over in March. Can you put me up?*

There was a spare room, a third bedroom where they kept suitcases and brought on the bowls of bulbs. There was no problem that Rowena could foresee, although Mark had never stayed with her before. Nonetheless she knew a feeling of sick anxiety. Was this at last what she had been dreading?

She told Phyllida that Mark would be coming but Phyllida, dizzy and preoccupied at receiving a bunch of roses from Bob Duffy, hardly heard her.

'I haven't had roses for years,' she gloated, arranging them stiffly in a cut glass vase that had belonged to Helen. Pettily Rowena had wanted to snatch it away, whining, 'Use your own vase,' like a child.

'They never last,' she said instead, caustically. She knew she was being ungenerous, but couldn't think how to make amends.

Trying hard to be pleased for Phyllida, she wandered up to the spare bedroom. The heating was turned off and it felt damp. She would have to have a clear out, give the bed a good airing, maybe replace the curtains. Would it be worth replacing the curtains? How long would Mark be staying? She didn't know. She didn't know anything.

It is her first Christmas home from college, and she has walked into a family crisis. Her mother has clearly cried herself to sleep; her father, having met her at the station with an abstracted air and a disappointingly cool reception, has disappeared into the garage and is hammering, wildly and incongruously, for he has told her he is making bookshelves for her college room and he never nails, he always uses screws. But the irregular battering goes permanently into her head, along with the smell of austerity corned-beef pie and the blasted look on her mother's face across the kitchen table.

'What's happened? Have you and Daddy had a fight?'

'No. We never fight, you know that.'

'Well, what is it? And where's Mark?'

'He'll be back. He's – we've – there's been a bit of an upset. I suppose you'll have to know.'

'Know what? Is he ill? Honestly, I go away for a few weeks . . .'

'He isn't ill. Well, I suppose some people would say he was.'

'What?'

'Your father will tell you.'

But he doesn't. He comes into the kitchen, washes his hands and they sit down to a silent lunch. Rowena is too frightened to ask, his eyes, usually full of love and admiration, have gone in on themselves, like the eyes of someone very old. Sometime during the bread pudding, she hears the front door open, and Mark going upstairs to his room. His tread is heavy, weighted down, the slam of his bedroom door final and defiant.

Later, she knocks on the door and when he doesn't reply, she goes in and finds him lying on the bed staring at the darkening ceiling. His football posters gaze down from the walls; there are books on his desk, covered in equations. There is a square of patterned carpet set on brown linoleum and undrawn blue curtains at the window. She can still see the holes in the frame where the blackout was fixed. His shoes are resting on the satin eiderdown, careless of their mother's prohibition.

She trembles at such recklessness, such oblivion. Mark usually obeys the rules.

'What's up? Nobody will tell me.'

And to her horror he rolls onto his front and begins to cry like a baby.

Rowena found herself sitting on the spare bed, smoothing the cover. The same bed, the same room. Not the same eiderdown. A pastel duvet now, with matching valance. But she heard again his strangled voice telling her of things she barely under-stood, of a teacher called Robin, whom he loved, and who loved him, and who had been found with him in the changing room after school and had lost his job and now their parents knew, they knew everything about him, the things he had been trying to tell them but had been too frightened and now he was proved right for he had never seen them so angry, so disgusted. It was as if they hated him.

And Rowena had reached out a hand, experimentally, to see if he still felt the same, and he did, and she had leaned down and hugged his thin shoulders and sworn to stand by him, saying she understood. Though of course she didn't.

Now she stood up and went to the window. The street outside was quiet, and Phyllida was going down the path with her shopping trolley. Rowena waited. As she knew she would, Phyllida peered at the dormant winter wall and flicked at a recalcitrant weed. She sighed. Mark's visit would at least provide some diversion.

And whatever he was coming to tell her, she would try and understand.

Phyllida was humming as she walked down the street. 'Little Brown Jug' – they had watched *The Glen Miller Story* last night on television. She enjoyed watching films about the war, liking to identify with them though she had only been a young girl, a child almost, when it ended. But she felt proud to have lived through the last great cataclysm, to have suffered loss and hardship. It had amused her over the years to regale her children with her memories.

Jake and Hannah however were too far removed. It meant nothing to them to talk of egg allocations and coupons and sweet rationing. And they suffered rationing of their own, Kathryn's stingy allowance of a few jelly babies or dolly mixture after lunch on Sunday. Kathryn had forgotten how she used to spend her pocket money in one go on Crunchie bars and sherbet dabs. Phyllida had permitted it, remembering the intoxication when sweet rationing ended and the shops were cleared in one fell swoop, only to have rationing imposed again. She had eaten herself sick, although no longer a child, and only stopped when she found she was putting on weight. She had never wanted her children to suffer such deprivation.

Phyllida was happy. Bob Duffy had sent her flowers and she had had a telephone call from Stuart in Newcastle. The New Year had started well, and tonight was the first pottery class of the term. She had plans for a set of cereal bowls for Kathryn, something rough and artistic from which to eat their muesli. Bob would be there of course, and they would hug their secret to themselves. Nobody would ever guess, and when they did find out they would be amazed, delighted.

She hugged herself through her thick coat, and trundled her trolley into Waitrose where, she noted, only two of the tills were working.

When she got home Rowena told her, 'Kathryn rang.'

She looked tight-lipped, with disapproval, Phyllida thought. Rowena had never entirely seemed to accept her children, though Jake and Hannah she adored almost as if they were her own.

If Kathryn wanted to speak to her, it was tantamount to an order. And Kathryn led such a busy life. It was a question of finding a window of availability if you wanted to catch her. Phyllida suspected that the window was already closed; Wednesdays were Kathryn's afternoons at the Citizen's Advice Bureau, where she headed a team of volunteers. It was worthy work which Kathryn performed with a fierce dedication that privately Phyllida considered must have been more off-putting than it was reassuring.

She wanted to call back at once but Rowena obviously had different ideas. 'I'm sure it will keep. Here, I've just made coffee. I'll unpack the shopping.'

She seemed tense, Phyllida felt, and unduly considerate. Nevertheless she was glad of the coffee. Her hands and feet were cold. She warmed her fingers on the cup, watching as Rowena unloaded fats and sugar, flour and lamb chops from the trolley. She opened the fridge, her arms full of butter and lard, and gave an irritated tut.

'What's all this?' She turned, a clump of butter wrappers in her hand. 'You're hoarding them again.'

'But they're useful, dear. When I'm baking.'

Rowena sighed. 'They make such a mess of the plastic door.'

Phyllida said mildly, 'Well you don't do any baking so you don't realise how useful they are. For greasing the tins.'

'I know what they're *for*, but there must be an easier way.'

She depressed the pedal of the rubbish bin and dropped the papers inside, scattered the packs of fat on the worktop and pointedly ran the dishcloth under the hot tap. Removing the greasy smears from the shelf and door she was conscious of Phyllida sitting in silence behind her. Her face would be either mutinous or ashamed. Either was insupportable, particularly under the circumstances. Kathryn's call was undoubtedly going to be upsetting.

'After all,' she suggested, 'perhaps you'd better ring Kathryn. You may just catch her before she leaves.'

Thankfully, like a child released from detention, Phyllida got up, carrying her coffee into the hall. She closed the kitchen door firmly behind her.

There was no reply. She let the phone ring and ring, but obviously Kathryn had left.

'I wonder what she wanted?' She had returned to the kitchen, setting her cup on the draining board. 'Did she say?'

Rowena didn't look at her. 'No. But I'm sure it can wait till this evening.'

'Would you like me to cook the lunch?'

'No, dear, I'll do it. I've had an idle morning.' Rowena could be equally obliging. 'I've lit the fire, why don't you go and read the paper?'

'Yes – I might do that, if you're sure. There was such a queue in Waitrose, only two tills were open as usual.'

Rowena watched her go in silence. She thought, 'Oh dear . . .' irritated and anxious in equal measure.

At six o'clock, as Phyllida was toasting crumpets and Rowena was struggling through the back door with another box of smokeless fuel, the telephone rang.

'That will be Kathryn. Can you watch the grill?'

54

She snatched up the receiver. 'Kathryn? I did ring you back but you'd left. I was waiting till later, when you'd had your meal.'

'Okay, Mum. I only wanted to ask if I could pop round tomorrow. Something I want to talk to you about.'

'Oh. What's that?'

'I wouldn't be coming if I wanted to tell you on the phone. I'll come for coffee, okay?'

'Yes, well I suppose so.' She didn't want to leave it at that. 'Is anything wrong, dear?'

'Why does all news have to be bad news?'

'Oh, I don't know. I suppose it's just being a mother.'

There was a short silence. 'Right, well about eleven then. I'm glad I caught you.'

'I would have rung, dear.'

'Yes. Well – bye for now.'

'Goodbye.' Phyllida heard the phone click down, but continued to stare worriedly into the receiver as if it could give her an answer.

Rowena passed through the hall carrying the tea tray. Phyllida followed her into the sitting room. 'Kathryn wants to come for coffee tomorrow. To talk to me about something. What do you think it could be?'

Rowena was busy with the fire, stooping stiffly to add fuel. 'Now how should I know?' she asked, and turned with glowing cheeks to pour the tea.

They arrived early for their classes. Phyllida could scarcely contain her excitement.

'I've got such plans for this term,' she enthused. 'I can't think why I didn't take this up years ago.'

'That's good.' Rowena felt indulgent. 'And it's got a little to do with Mr Duffy, I suspect.'

'Oh Ro! He's just a friend. But it's nice to be appreciated.'

'Yes.'

But Phyllida had always been appreciated. By Helen, the twins, Jake and Hannah.

By Henry.

Rowena wondered if Derek Stadden would be there. She wanted to tell him about her holiday plans. She took her usual place in the second row, nodding greetings as others arrived, opening her notebook at her last homework, checking her work. It seemed a long time ago, she felt quite rusty. The tutor arrived, an earnest young woman almost fresh from college, augmenting her teacher's salary with evening classes. She enjoyed it more, dealing with sensible, well-behaved and motivated grown-ups who didn't whisper and giggle or gaze pointedly out of the window, removing themselves from the class. She laid her books and notes neatly on the desk, plugged in the tape recorder and looked at her watch.

It was seven thirty-five. And Derek Stadden didn't come.

'Mrs Sullivan's not so good today. She wanted to stay in bed.'

The care assistant was fat, middle-aged and careworn. She looked tired and Rowena felt guilty. This weary woman, probably with a family of her own, was paid to look after her mother while she . . . But it was no use thinking like that. The woman probably needed the job.

She hurried down the hot, carpeted corridor, carrying a potted chrysanthemum. It was fortuitous that she had chosen to bring it today for she could place it at her mother's bedside, a suitable gift for the sick. She wondered what was wrong, whether this was the beginning of the end, and knew a guilty spurt of hope.

Helen was asleep, head thrown back on the piled pillows, toothless mouth agape, eyes deeply sunk. Her hair was wispy, uncurled and uncombed. Her breath was so slight that for a moment Rowena wondered whether she was actually dead. She looked dead; pale and shrunken and helpless. A wrench of terrible pity twisted Rowena's insides. Life shouldn't hang on so long, outstaying its welcome, piling up time against a fragile mind and body so that they bent and shrank and cracked under the sheer weight of living. It was time for her mother to go.

She put the plant on the bedside table amid the tissues, drinks and the glass containing her mother's teeth.

The other bed was empty, the pink coverlet drawn up tight and smooth over a mountain of pillows. There was a photograph on the cabinet that she had never noticed before, a kindly man in a dinner jacket with a smiling woman in a cocktail dress, her hair back-combed in the smooth wide style of the sixties. So life moved on, from dinner dances through bereavement to senility. She pulled up a chair and sat down, staring out of the window at the winter garden.

Her mother was suddenly awake. Rowena heard her dry cough and turned to see the eyes bright, fixed on her with a curious intensity.

'Is it time to go?' Helen asked.

'Go where?' She leaned over and took her hand. It was cold, brittle under the silky skin. She picked it up and tucked it under the covers.

'It's Rowena, darling. Not so well today?'

Her mother looked at her blankly.

'Would you like a nice hot drink?'

'No thank you.'

'Well I would. I'll organise some coffee.'

She waylaid an assistant in the corridor and said that her mother was awake. She arranged for the coffee and returned, expecting that someone would come and attend to her mother but no one came until a waif-like teenager arrived with two mugs on a tray. There were no biscuits and Rowena felt unreasonably angry. They were paying enough, were a few biscuits and a bit of attention too much to ask?

She was left to heave her mother up onto the pillows herself, feeling the tug on her back. She would have to be careful, she wasn't used to this. No way could she ever cope with full-time caring. With a relieved sense of justification she sat on the bed and sipped her coffee, watching her mother's thin fingers circling the mug, the unsteady ascent to her lips. She had put in her teeth in Rowena's absence, her mouth had regained its normal shape. Rowena remembered that she had once had rather a beautiful mouth, with a pronounced cupid's bow and a natural pinkness. Now it was puckered, the lips so soft to kiss as to be almost absent. She held herself in readiness to steady the mug, but Helen held it firmly, and scarcely dribbled.

'Mark's coming to see us soon,' Rowena told her. 'I've had a letter from him. Sometime in March.'

'March?'

'Yes. It's the second week in January now, then it will be February, then March. About eight weeks. Isn't that good?'

'Mark?'

'Your son, Mark. He lives in America.'

'I had a letter from his wife. She's not well.'

Rowena spoke gently. 'Mark hasn't got a wife, dear.'

'She has the same as me, but she had an operation.'

'Yes, Mother.' What was the point, after all?

Helen held out her mug. 'I've had enough. I want to get up.'

'Are you sure?'

Her mother was trying to release her legs. 'And don't sit on the eiderdown, I'm always telling you.'

Rowena got up, helping her mother lower her legs to the floor. Her body smelled sour and bedridden; she needed changing. Rowena rang the bell above the bed. Really, this wasn't her job. Why didn't somebody come?

Phyllida and her daughter were sitting opposite each other beside the fire. The fire wasn't usually lit until after lunch but Phyllida had deemed today to be special. She was sure Rowena would understand; nevertheless it wasn't until Rowena had left to visit Helen that she had swept the grate and set the kindling.

The coffee tray was on the table between them but the cups were empty, the coffee unpoured, for Kathryn had said, 'Leave that, Mum. Sit down, I've something to tell you.'

'Is it you and Ben?' asked Phyllida, who had been awake since five, wondering.

'Me and Ben? Why on earth?'

'Oh I don't know. I suppose because things seem so tense between you.'

Kathryn looked cross. 'You do fuss about nothing. Didn't you and Dad ever argue?'

She knew she had said the wrong thing for Phyllida's face collapsed. 'Anyway, let's not get onto that. I haven't got all day. The thing is, I have to go into hospital.'

Phyllida's hand went to her mouth. 'Why?'

'I have a lump in my breast. I've had what they call a fine needle aspiration. They drew off some tissue with a needle. Now they want me to go in. I wouldn't have told you, but I need a little help with the children. When they come home from school, until Ben gets home. Do you think you could come and stay? I'm not sure how long for.'

'When will it be?'

'Next Monday. Ben would come and collect you on Sunday evening.'

'All right.' Phyllida's face was taut with worry. 'What do they . . . do they think . . . are you worried?'

Kathryn snapped. 'Of course I'm worried.'

'You should have told me before.'

'What for? And have you worrying too?'

'But I'm your mother. I like to think . . .'

'Well maybe that's why. You're too involved. The last thing I want is you fussing. Please, Mum, it will only make it worse.' For a moment, Phyllida could see the little girl staring through the crossness, the little girl who had looked so like her twin until she changed into this fierce and independent woman while Stuart softened, transmuting into a replica of his father.

'I had a call from Stuart the other day, to wish me a Happy New Year,' Phyllida said, spinning off at a tangent.

Kathryn was reaching for the coffee pot. 'About time. How is he?'

'He didn't say a lot. The job seems to be going well. Thank goodness.'

'You miss him, don't you?'

'Not as much as I did.'

'How's Jill?'

'I'm afraid I didn't ask.'

Kathryn passed her a cup and a plate of homemade shortbread. 'Have this. You've never approved of Jill, have you?'

'I just wish they'd get married. And I still miss Fiona. She was like a daughter.'

'Well it was just as well there were no children.' Kathryn bit into a piece of shortbread. 'Mmm. Your usual recipe. You always made good cakes.'

'I enjoyed it. I still do. And I didn't have a job. Not like you.' She hesitated. This was ridiculous, making small talk about cakes, when Kathryn could be ill, dying even. She struggled to control her panic. 'Perhaps you do too much? You do look tired. Do you feel quite well?'

Kathryn knew what she meant. Firmly she said, 'I feel quite well. This is just a little hiccup.'

But fear was potent in the space between them.

'Kathryn gone?'

Rowena glanced at the fire, the coffee tray, and at Phyllida who was gazing into the fire, her embroidery untouched on her lap. As Rowena had expected, she looked distraught.

'She had shopping to do,' Phyllida told her matter-of-factly, but her frantic eyes said otherwise.

Rowena sat on the arm of a chair and asked anxiously, 'So, what did she have to say?'

Phyllida told her, making no attempt to hide her alarm, adding, 'It's cancer, Ro – she'll lose her breast, maybe more.' Her voice was rising hysterically.

'Not necessarily. You must ease up, this will do you no good,' Rowena told her. 'The last thing they'll want is you to worry about it.'

'You seem to have taken it very calmly. But then I suppose she's not your daughter.'

'Phyllida! I feel very involved. But Ben warned me, at Christmas. I suppose I've been prepared.'

Phyllida's expression changed to suspicion. 'Warned you? Why not me?'

'Well, not deliberately perhaps, but it came up in conversation. He asked me to say nothing, in case it came to nothing. And looking at you now, I can see why.'

'Oh, Rowena!' Her voice, her look, were accusing. 'I had a right to know.'

'It wasn't my news to give. I had no right to tell you.'

Phyllida subsided, looking hurt.

It had always been the same. Rowena, the sensible one, entrusted with secrets, turned to in a crisis.

Phyllida the protected, too silly and helpless to cope. Tears stung her eyes. She was terrified, already fearing the worst. And, worse, it seemed that nobody thought she could be otherwise.

The telephone rings shrilly for Rowena's mother, but she isn't there. Rowena is. She is on vacation, at the end of her second year. It is summer and she is sunbathing in the garden. She tans well, her olive skin taking on a deeper golden tone which makes her look if not beautiful then handsome enough, with her thick, long dark hair and direct blue eyes, protected now by sunglasses. She removes the sunglasses with an impatient sigh. Who is interrupting her idyll?

It is Phyllida. They haven't spoken for months, not since Phyllida had arrived with a Christmas present for Helen and a shy card for Rowena. Rowena had then been struck afresh by the beautiful texture of her skin, enhanced now by the skilful application of make-up which made her eyes enormous. Pools of innocence and promise, Rowena found them faintly disturbing. But now as Phyllida talks she can imagine their look of confusion, of panic, as she says that her mother has fallen downstairs and cannot move, she thinks she has broken her leg, what should she do? Her mother, gritting her teeth with pain and frustration, has told her to get an ambulance, but she doesn't know how to get an ambulance.

'I thought maybe Helen . . .'

'Just ask the operator for emergency,' Rowena tells her, incredulously. 'And cover her up, she'll be in shock, she must be kept warm.'

'Sweet tea.' Phyllida's own teeth are chattering now, she is shaking all over, wants to cry. Her mother's insubstantial support has finally fallen away, leaving her in charge. She vaguely remembers something about hot sweet tea.

'Yes, make some tea. But try not to move her.'

'How will she drink it?'

'Oh Phyllida!'

The voice bleats, 'Will you come round, Ro? I'm sorry to ask you . . .'

'I'm in my swimsuit.'

'I'm sorry . . .'

'Oh, all right. But call the ambulance. And don't get in such a tizz. It won't help your mother.'

'No. I'm sorry.'

Rowena dresses, replacing her swimming costume with the loose slacks she has begun to favour, winding a long scarf around her neck.

She gets her old bicycle from the garage, and pedals off.

She has not expected to visit Tudor House again.

'Well, I have my uses,' Phyllida now declared defiantly. 'At least I can look after the children.'

Rowena, she knew, would be envious of that.

Bob Duffy telephoned on Friday night.

'Hello, my dear. And how are we today?'

'I'm very well, Bob. All the better for hearing you.'

Rowena saw her smirking into the phone, and turned away.

'How about a day out in the country on Sunday? This fine frosty weather looks set to last.'

'Sunday. Oh, I'd love to. But I'd need to be back before six. I'm going over to my daughter's.' She would tell him later, in the car perhaps. He would be sympathetic, protective, concerned.

'Six o'clock it is. I'll pick you up at ten. We'll find somewhere nice for a spot of lunch.'

She looked doubtfully at Rowena whom she could see in the dining room. She was poring over travel brochures spread out on the table.

'I'll just check with Rowena.'

She put down the phone and went to the door, though Rowena could hear her quite well in the hall.

'Do you mind if I go out for Sunday lunch, dear?'

They always made a little ceremony of Sunday lunch, getting out vegetable dishes and wine glasses and laying the table in the dining room. Phyllida thought it made up to Rowena for all the years of solitary dining off a tray. Rowena thought it did Phyllida good to appear to be keeping up standards, not letting things slide.

She said, 'Not at all, you go if you want to,' thinking, I'll eat in the kitchen, it's warmer, and knowing an extraordinary sense of release.

The weather after all didn't last, and Rowena waved them off into a damp and murky morning, wet underfoot with mist lingering in the trees. Despite this, Phyllida was in high spirits, hugging her fur coat round her as she waited at the front window in her high heeled shoes.

'Don't you think you should wear something suitable for walking?' asked Rowena mildly.

'We won't be walking. In this weather?'

'Well, you know him better than I do. Is he an outdoor person?'

Phyllida looked at her in astonishment. 'He doesn't even have a garden, dear.'

'That's all the more reason, I should have thought.'

But Phyllida would not be persuaded. When Bob bounced up the path in his camel coat and suede lace-ups she said with satisfaction, 'He's hardly dressed to go mountaineering,' and hurried to open the door.

Rowena shut it behind them with a satisfactory click.

The house closed round her, silent, empty. Her own, to do as she liked in. She would take a long, hot bath, using all the water. And then she would telephone Betty and talk about their holiday.

And after that she would lightly grill a piece of steak and cook some oven chips and make herself a green salad. With plenty of garlic in the dressing.

Life had its compensations.

Phyllida was wakened early by the rackety noise of children in the house and for a moment she couldn't remember. Then uneasiness arrived, reminding her that Sunday was over and this was Monday, she was at Kathryn's, and Kathryn was going into hospital. She pulled the covers higher, blocking out the day, wishing it could still be Sunday and Hever Castle and walking through the woods with Bob, even though it had ruined her shoes, and sirloin of beef in the Carvery in a red-brick Kentish village.

There was a knock at her door and Jake came in, carefully carrying a cup of tea, followed by Hannah who sat uninvited upon her bed.

'Shall I rub your feet?' she asked.

'No, darling. Why?'

'Mummy always rubs our feet when we're ill.'

'But I'm not ill.'

'Mummy is,' said Jake. 'She's going to hospital.'

Phyllida pulled herself up on the pillows. 'It's nothing to worry about, they'll soon put her right.' She sipped her tea.

'I made it, we have to do it at Cubs.'

'It's very nice.'

'Are you taking us to school?'

'No, Daddy will.'

'Who will meet us?' Hannah looked pathetic, twisting her long hair in her fingers.

'That's all arranged. And I'll be here when you get back.'

She finished the tea. 'Now suppose you two run along and let me get dressed. I want to be down to see you off.'

They ran off, carrying the empty cup. From the landing, Phyllida heard Kathryn snapping at them in the kitchen. Tension seemed to be coming out of the walls and Ben, when she greeted him, hardly looked up from his paper.

He said, to nobody in particular, 'The economy's apparently still "bumping along the bottom". Well I think we already realise that at the council offices. Two more old people's homes scheduled to close this summer. "Care in the community," they call it. Tell some of the old people that when they're forced to sit alone at home and wait for some community nurse to call.'

Kathryn sat down with a cup of black coffee.

'Is that all you're having, dear?'

'It's all I want.'

'Don't you think . . .'

'Mum!'

Ben threw down the paper. 'You kids ready? I'm off in five minutes. Say goodbye to Mummy.'

Hannah flung herself across Kathryn's lap. 'I don't want you to go.'

'Hush. I'll soon be back.' She bent over the child. Phyllida couldn't see her face but her voice was unusually soft. Jake stood in the doorway, shouldering his bag.

'Can we come and see you?'

'Of course, if you want to.'

'Well – cheerio.' He gave her an uncertain smile and turned away. Kathryn pushed Hannah after him and they heard the front door slam and the car start up.

Kathryn gave her mother a tremulous smile.

'An hour before it's my turn. Maybe I should think of a last request?'

To fill in time they stripped the beds and filled the washing machine.

'Ironing that lot will give me something to do this afternoon,' said Phyllida with satisfaction. She liked ironing, often offering to do Rowena's as well as her own. Rowena thought it was nonsense the way she ironed towels and polyester sheets, but she liked to, just as she ironed underwear and even socks. Then you put them away carefully in drawers and cupboards, instead of just stuffing them in anyhow. One look at Kathryn's airing cupboard had shown her that Kathryn was still a buncher and stuffer. Sorting out the airing cupboard would pass another hour or so.

She wondered if Kathryn would mind and regretfully acknowledged that she would.

Ben came back and made fresh coffee while Kathryn collected her bag and scribbled a final shopping list.

'You should get all of this from the village shop. Anything else Ben can bring in. And there's masses in the freezer. The milkman will call for his money tomorrow, it's on the dresser.' She nodded towards the stacked shelves, blue and white china, hand painted mugs and earthenware pots fighting for space with children's paintings and holiday postcards. 'The Aga will look after itself, you may prefer to use the microwave for speed.'

'You know I can't use the microwave.'

'It's self-explanatory. Just don't put in anything metal.'

'Why not? It's all these peculiar rules that bother me.'

Ben put a hand on her arm. 'Just use the Aga. Or wait for me to get back.'

'Heavens, Jake can show you!' Kathryn got up and put on her coat. 'Let's go.'

Her lips were held tight and thin as she watched Ben feeling for the car keys. She let him take her case and turned to Phyllida.

'Thanks, Mum. I hope there won't be any problems.'

Phyllida felt sick with foreboding. Would things ever be the same again? She wanted to hug her daughter but she felt fended off, as if by barbed wire through which her daughter peered, distant and imprisoned.

'Good luck, darling. I'm sure there's no need to worry,' she murmured encouragingly, holding the door of the car.

She slammed it shut and turned away to face her fear and the empty house.

*   *   *

By Tuesday evening Rowena was more glad than usual to be going out.

For to her chagrin, she found that she missed Phyllida. It was extraordinary how one got used to people. Coming down to an empty kitchen — Phyllida always rose first and made the tea — was curiously bleak, although she had done it for years, for all of her life in fact since she left home to work in Hampshire.

The first morning, she had rejoiced in the silence after the incessant babble of the radio which accompanied Phyllida everywhere, and took a perverse pleasure in seeing her Horlicks mug still dirty where she had left it on the draining board. She had the newspaper to herself and left her dishes where they lay. She took another bath, and set out late to the shops and the library. Then she spent the afternoon trying unsuccessfully to read a German novel for which she thought she might be ready. It was salutary to discover she was not.

By Tuesday she was already strangely reluctant to leave her bed. The house felt dead and cold, although the heating had come on at seven as usual. From her window she could see that it was frosty again, the twigs were thick with it and the grass was crystallised. The sky was leaden and the forecast mentioned snow.

On impulse she rang Betty to ask her to lunch, but she was going to a meeting, one of her committees. Aimlessly, Rowena frittered the day away then, too late, for a premature evening was already coming down, she decided to go for a walk.

She walked briskly, taking comfort from being out of the house, seeing other people about their business, nodding and chatting to one or two acquaintances. Eventually she found herself in Tudor Close and stood for a moment staring beyond the modern villas into the past and what had been Tudor House.

She has come to say goodbye. She doesn't know why; maybe it's finally to close the chapter, to make the break with Phyllida. Their paths won't cross again.

They are sitting in Phyllida's room. It is a large room, furnished now like a bedsitter with two armchairs and a kettle and coffee mugs on a low table. Rowena has always envied Phyllida her bedroom with its tall sash windows which rattle in the wind, overlooking the unruly garden; the marble fireplace filled with fir cones with a shining grate of dark green tiles. The carpet is flowery, fitted to the deep skirting boards, and there is a sheepskin rug beside the double bed. Why a double bed? To Rowena it seems the height of sensuous luxury, deep and warm and all embracing, like Phyllida herself.

Phyllida is telling her about her boyfriend, Michael, who is a clerk in Barclays Bank. She says, 'I know he wants to go all the way, but I don't know, do you think I should?'

'Don't ask me. Do you want to?'

'Sometimes. But it's not right. Anyway, I don't want to get pregnant.'

'Well there are ways round that one.'

'Rowena!' Phyllida's eyes are bright with excitement. 'You haven't. Have you?'

Rowena hasn't, though she wants to very much. But there is no one, yet. She has been living in hall, the rules are strict; in her case at least the boys are none too interested in breaking them. But soon she will be living alone, in a bedsitter in Andover, earning her living, independent.

She intends to find a man, and sooner rather than later. And to lose her virginity before Phyllida, if she's lucky.

She told herself it didn't matter if Derek was at the class or not. All the same her heart gave an adolescent lurch when she found he was already there.

He turned in his seat to greet her.

'Did you have a good Christmas?'

'Yes. Quite nice. Were your family well?'

'No. They all had flu, then I went down with it and had to stay on.'

She made a sympathetic face. 'Well, Happy New Year anyway.'

The tutor silenced her with a look.

'Let's all try and speak in German, shall we?'

Rowena shrank into her chair, ten years old again, and seventeen.

She wondered if Derek would invite her for a drink and, if he did not, resolved to suggest it herself.

FIVE

Phyllida was sitting beside Helen, holding her hand. Outside a late February snowfall had loaded the trees, bringing branches to the ground, smothering the shrubs in anonymity. Someone had cleared and gritted the paths and an old man in a walking frame was making his cautious way past the front window, wrapped in a coat which swamped his chest and shoulders. His cheeks were sucked in with concentration. He looked like a refugee, Phyllida thought, or one of those relics who had staggered out of Belsen after the war, and she shivered and thanked God, not for the first time, that her own mother had been spared such indignity.

Helen, however, was in fine form.

Her face had lit up when she saw Phyllida, whom today she remembered quite clearly, also the names of her children and grandchildren after whom she asked with some of her old interest. And before long, Phyllida had found herself telling her about Kathryn.

'She had cancer, I'm afraid. In her left breast. But they didn't remove the breast.' She was an expert now. 'It's not thought necessary to do a mastectomy these days, just a lumpectomy, followed by chemotherapy.'

Helen nodded, though she had forgotten what they were talking about. Phyllida saw her eyes glaze over and wander to the television where a Tom and Jerry cartoon was romping its way to a predictable conclusion. Despite herself, Phyllida's eyes were drawn. She saw Tom stretched like elastic, spun round and round, then disappearing through a door, leaving a cat-shaped hole. He was squashed flat by a roller and moments later popped up again, whole and three-dimensional.

70

Why wasn't life like that? she asked herself. In life, when you were down you were down.

When you were sick, you were sick.

Kathryn was sick, every time she had the chemotherapy. She retched and heaved and strained and groaned while Ben, or Phyllida, sometimes even Jake, stroked her back helplessly. Sweat would pour from her grey face and her eyes would sink back, rather like Helen's now, in a ghastly premonition of death.

But they were assured she would make a complete recovery. It was just a question of time and patience. They had caught the cancer early, it may not have spread and if it had, well the treatment would see to that.

'She's also doing relaxation therapy,' Phyllida told Helen, though well aware she wasn't listening. But it was an audience nonetheless. She had this compulsion to talk it out, to air the reassuring theories as if she believed in them herself so that one day, perhaps, she would. 'It's called visualisation. You visualise something nice, something happy, it offsets all the evil forces. Or you can imagine laser beams, or a knife, cutting out the disease from your body. I don't really understand it but the whole thing is to believe in it and Kathryn does.'

Suddenly Helen began to laugh. Startled, Phyllida turned to the television but the cartoon was over. The news had started, troops were huddled under a bullet-scarred wall, wrecked cars blazing in the background. Africa? The Lebanon? Eastern Europe? It was all the same these days, everywhere in conflict, tearing itself to bits.

So why was Helen laughing?

'What's so funny, dear?' She had to lean forward to intercept her gaze. The laughter stopped.

'Funny? Is it time for tea? I haven't had any tea.'

'Yes you have. We had cake as well.'

'Ask someone to bring it.'

'All right.' She pulled on her coat and gloves. 'I'll ask somebody on my way out. Goodbye, Helen.'

She bent and dropped a kiss on her soft hair. It smelled sweet, of apple shampoo. Like Hannah's.

Somebody was taking care of her.

Helen didn't watch her go, and Phyllida saw no one before letting herself out into the snow.

Bob said, 'You need a break. Why don't we find a nice little hotel somewhere for the weekend?'

Phyllida went pink. She knew precisely what he was suggesting. But old habits died hard. At sixty-three she still thought of herself as a nice girl. Nice girls didn't go away with men for the weekend.

'Separate rooms,' he persuaded, reading her mind. 'No strings.'

'And I'd pay for myself of course.'

'If you like. Come on, how about it? You choose — country or seaside?'

'Well . . . how about London? I've never stayed in a London hotel.'

He looked pleased, rubbing his hands. 'Couldn't be better. We can see the sights, be tourists, take in a show.' His plump face positively oozed with anticipation. 'Let me arrange it all. Second weekend in March suit you?'

Sodom and Gomorrah, she thought. The slippery slope to sin. But let it be. 'It would suit me very well,' she said, giving him the benefit of her smile.

He dropped her off early for the roads were freezing hard and he had to get back to Croydon. She allowed him to escort her up the slippery front path. Rowena had cleared the snow but a trickle of melt water from the day had now frozen into a sheet of ice. On the step he said, 'I won't come in, my dear.'

He slid his hands inside her fur coat and fondled her breasts in the warmth. She knew a tweak of pleasure, of remembered passion. She let him kiss her, his mouth wide and moist, his tongue probing possessively.

'Goodnight, Bob.' Her voice was faint, slightly breathless,

but her feet were cold, she was anxious to be indoors. She watched him cautiously tackling the path before putting her key into the lock.

Rowena's bridge evening was still in progress. She could hear the low voices from the dining room, saw the residue of their dainty supper in the kitchen, a trolley loaded with bone china and left-over smoked salmon sandwiches. She smiled. Rowena was learning to push the boat out. There was a shop-bought chocolate sponge and Scottish shortbread. Not a patch on hers.

While she was drinking Horlicks and warming her feet by the boiler, she heard Joyce and Robert come out into the hall.

'We won't hang about,' Robert was saying. 'The roads look nasty.'

'A good game, my dear. Thank you for a lovely evening.'

The front door opened, leaking in a blast of cold air, then closed again.

Rowena came into the kitchen. 'I thought I heard you come in. Come by the fire.'

'I'm all right.'

'It's only Betty. She's stayed to chat about the holiday.'

'I'll go on up. Say hello to her for me.'

'All right, dear.'

Rowena watched her go. There was something pink and secretive about Phyllida's face that was not necessarily to do with the cold.

She returned to the dining room. Betty had left the table and was sitting in a wing-backed armchair over the dying fire.

'I won't stay long,' she said.

'Have a hot drink?'

'No. I like that in my bed with a book. One of the advantages of widowhood. You can read all night and eat biscuits in bed if you want to!'

Rowena knew all about that.

'I've managed to change the bookings,' she told her, picking up a file from the sideboard. 'It's a pity Robert and Joyce decided not to come.'

'Well their daughter needs them, with the new baby due.'

'They could have said so before.' Rowena couldn't help feeling hurt, displaced. She had been flattered to be asked to join Robert and Joyce in the Black Forest. Now it was to be just her and Betty.

'We'll have a good time. Better perhaps. Not so many people to please. But I'll be relying on your German.'

'Let's hope I come up to scratch.' Rowena was augmenting her classes with a BBC course on television. She could book a room with a bath or a shower, with single beds, order coffee with or without cream, ask directions.

It had been arranged that Betty would drive. Her car was the newer, the least likely to require attention. If it did, Rowena could find them that as well.

Derek had said to her the previous Tuesday, 'You're really getting very good. Quite the star pupil.'

She had found herself blushing, demurring, 'I don't believe that.'

'Well, you're the only one of us who consistently gets the genders right. And your accent is commendable.'

She laughed. 'It sounds fine over here but probably no one will understand me when I get to Germany!'

'Nonsense.' His wide smile split his face. 'Another drink?'

She had said no, she had better get back as it was snowing. He had taken her, courteously, to her car, his hand on her arm. But that was all.

She decided to ask him to tea. After all, there could be nothing suspect about that. He lived alone, would be glad of the company. She was wondering when it should be when Phyllida announced that she was going to London with Bob.

Perfect. She would make it that Saturday afternoon. Not that she exactly minded him meeting Phyllida. It was just that she preferred to have him to herself. There was a record she wanted to play him, they had discovered a mutual taste for opera. She refused Phyllida's offer to make a cake.

He arrived early, throwing her into a little confusion. The

snow had gone leaving the garden sodden and strangely green, with bulbs thrusting through the mud. She had put on her boots and gone out to gather some sprigs of forsythia, and been diverted by the gold and purple of crocuses beneath the apple tree. The birds were singing like mad things, presaging spring, and her heart was uplifted. She stared up into the branches at the fattening buds. When she looked down again it was to see Derek coming round the back of the house carrying a bunch of daffodils.

'You didn't hear the bell,' he explained. 'Now I see why.'

'It's so lovely out here.' She felt fussed. She hadn't changed her dress, her boots were clumsy and mud-caked. She had wanted to have some music on, the fire at its brightest best. She clomped down the lawn carrying her bunch of twigs like a peace offering.

She arranged the daffodils in one vase, the forsythia in another, and took them into the sitting room. Not quite the same as roses, she thought, setting the daffodils in the window. But they would do. She offered him a chair, stooped to poke the fire, sending up a shower of sparks which settled again into a glow.

'I do dislike this smokeless fuel,' she complained. 'I've been thinking of changing to gas.'

'But that would be a shame. There's something about a real fire.'

'Do you have one?' She realised she knew absolutely nothing about his home.

'I'm all electric. Storage heaters, fires. Horrendously expensive, but clean I suppose. But there's something sterile about cleanliness, I always think.'

He looked momentarily sad. She said, 'Oh I quite agree. Phyllida is pathological about it. This house doesn't know what's hit it. I just let her get on with it. It keeps her happy.'

'Where is she by the way?'

'Oh, she's gone away.'

'How's her daughter?'

'Fighting back. She's a great fighter, Kathryn.'

'I lost my wife to cancer.'

'Oh.' It didn't seem quite adequate. 'I'm sorry. It's such a scourge, it seems to get all of us in the end.'

'Yes.' They looked at each other, thinking of their own uncertain futures.

'I've got out the Wagner. Would you like to hear it?'

'Yes please.' He settled himself back in the armchair while she lifted the perspex lid of the record player and operated the arm. 'I'm afraid I haven't invested in CDs. It seems too late now to change all my collection.'

'I quite agree. Though the quality is so much better. My daughter has it.'

She lowered the needle, hearing the slight scratch and hiss as it found the groove and feeling embarrassed.

They were finishing their tea when there was a knock at the door.

It was Mark, standing on the step with a large holdall covered in airline tags, looking pale and thin and strange; a stranger who was not, at this precise moment, welcome.

'Mark! I wasn't expecting you until Monday.'

'Sorry. I was asked to change my flight. I should have let you know.'

'Yes. Well I mean, no, it's fine, you're here now.' But it wasn't fine at all, though Rowena felt ashamed to be so put out. She stood back to let him in. 'I have a visitor, come and say hello.'

She introduced them and noted the spark of interest in Mark's eyes. Derek greeted him with a disappointing affability as if he didn't in the least mind the interruption. He insisted on leaving at once.

'I know how much you've been looking forward to your brother coming.'

'I'm sorry,' she said to him at the front door. 'It's been very pleasant.'

'Perhaps another time. You could come to me?'

She beamed her pleasure. She wondered if she should kiss him, just a friendly peck on the cheek. After all, they were friends. But he had turned on the step and there was nothing left to do but close the door behind him.

She took Mark up to his room. His old room, but warmer now, close carpeted, with thick lined curtains to tone with the bed covers. No rules about eiderdowns. The football posters were replaced by prints of churches in gold frames. Only the bed was the same with its mahogany headboard on which he had tapped out morse code messages to her in the adjacent room long ago, when he had joined the scouts.

She felt shy with him. It was six years since they had met, and then he had stayed in London with Lawrence, who was attending an auction, buying exhibits for the Guggenheim. Their lives couldn't have been more different and now he was to be staying under her roof. What did he like to eat, did he expect a big American breakfast with pancakes and maple syrup and a bottomless coffee pot? And what about his health – did he still have asthma? Why had he come? And did he have anything to tell her?

She eyed him anxiously, taking in the gaunt and haunted look about his face, trying to see her little brother. His accent was mid-Atlantic, his style of dress subtly foreign and expensive. Gucci shoes, Brooks Brothers shirt. He had done well for himself. He was sixty-one years old. She couldn't quite believe it.

'Are you hungry?' It was all she could think of to say; such momentous moments were always reduced to basics. Creature comforts. Concern expressed over the minutiae of life, offered in love, to cover up the irritation that someone had arrived too soon . . .

She sat him at the kitchen table while she washed the tea things, scrambled eggs with smoked salmon she had been saving for bridge, made fresh tea. He ate hungrily.

'Airline meals never seem to go far,' he mumbled, swallowing brown bread and butter.

'You need something more substantial. But I wasn't expecting you. We could go out?'

'Not out. Too tired.'

He looked tired. She felt uneasy. But then he was probably jet lagged. She remembered jet lag. She had visited him, once. He had sent her the fare.

He whisks her up with a hug at the airport and her hands are torn from the trolley, her heart full. She thinks, people will think we're lovers, but she doesn't mind. It's just so good to see him again.

He piles her into a yellow cab and they weave across the bridge and into Manhattan in the dusk. It is August, hot and dusty. Negro faces under woollen hats loll against peeling paint. Rowena has seldom seen a coloured face. She feels both thrilled and threatened.

'This is Broadway. And Times Square. And the park.'

He is proud, proprietorial. They are travelling along West Side, the Hudson River. For Mark has moved up in the world since he met Lawrence.

'Lawrence,' he tells her seriously before they arrive, 'is like a wife.' He hopes she understands, and will be comfortable with it.

She is not. She lies awake at night, wondering what they are doing. She knows about sex now. Bruce, a writer of scientific books and journals who lives in Winchester, has obliged. She likes it; sex is wonderful, even without love.

But not like that.

She found herself thinking about Bruce, after Mark had excused himself and gone to bed. It was true that one never forgot the first time, the first one. She remembered clearly how she had eyed him in the library in Winchester where she was researching a lesson on Milton. She took her work seriously, preparing lessons weeks ahead, reassured by a stock of material on which she could draw rather as, later, she kept food in the freezer for a rainy day.

He had been sitting opposite her in the reference library, scribbling with frantic haste on a large pad, his writing moving behind his pen like unravelling yarn. She had watched, fascinated. Scholarship always fascinated her. It was sexy, provocative, intriguing, admirable. Summoned by her stare he looked up finally and met her eyes and she smiled, thinking, that's the one, and said, 'Hello. Excuse me for staring but you look so busy. So absorbed. What are you doing?'

'I'm researching a book.'

'You're a writer?' She was excited. He was older than her, probably in his thirties. 'What's the subject?'

'Very boring I'm afraid. I'm translating chemistry into terms a fourth former can understand.'

'Oh.' She was obscurely disappointed. But he said, 'I feel like a break. Would you like to join me for coffee?'

She accepted. And a month later she took him to bed.

Bruce and Rowena travel together to the South Bank, to the Festival of Britain. She has seen pictures of the Dome of Discovery but is unprepared for its size, its huge smooth greyness under the grey London sky. It begins to rain, glazing the emptied plastic seats in their bright new-era colours, splashing into the turgid, dirty river beneath the Embankment.

They gaze up inside the shot tower, the tiny opening at the top making her feel dizzy, oppressed, cringing backwards away from the upward-rushing walls. They stand beneath the Skylon looking up, the rain falling in their faces, seeing its skyward thrust reduced to a tiny circle against the clouds.

'It's positively phallic,' says Bruce as they turn away. 'So proud and thrusting, so easily reduced to nothing.'

He squeezes her arm and she shudders with desire.

'I'd like to go to church,' Mark told her the next day. He had been up since six, his internal clock shot to pieces, as he put it. She had come down to the smell of coffee percolating and Mark rummaging in the fridge for orange juice.

'I would have bought some, had I known,' she said in mild rebuke.

'Never mind.' He took an orange from the bowl and began to peel it.

'You never used to be a church goer.' She was surprised, and apprehensive. Was he making peace with his maker, seeking comfort, looking for answers?

'It's been my salvation, since Lawrence died.'

'He died?'

'Two years ago.'

'You never said.'

'I knew you didn't approve.'

'Oh Mark. After all these years. I never disapproved. He made you happy.'

She is struck by a thought too fearful to voice.

'How did he die?' Her voice is timid, reluctant. But she must know.

'Pneumonia,' he told her, which told her nothing.

'Well, you remember where the church is. It's still across the fields. Thank heavens for the green belt. Though there's a car park, now, where the pond used to be. Where we fished for minnows, remember?'

'Of course I remember.' He looked at her fondly. 'We were good pals, you and I.'

'I used to worry about you.'

'I never have asthma now. Haven't for years. New York must agree with me.'

'I'm glad.' She reached out a hand and took his. It was the first time she had touched him since their first perfunctory kiss. 'Perhaps I'll come to church with you. Then we'll go and see Mother.'

Walking up the hill towards the church, Mark suddenly took her arm and linked it in his own.

'It's good to see you again. You look well.'

She smiled at him, a little breathless from the hill.

He went on, 'I'm so sorry I burst in on you yesterday. I should have rung.'

'It would have been better, I might have been out.'

'Well, that would have been my problem. But I'm sorry your friend had to leave. Who is he – anyone special?'

Pride urged her to lie. But she had never lied to Mark, so she said instead, 'He's just a friend, from my evening class.'

Mark looked at her sideways. 'I've never understood why you didn't marry. It's been a source of grief to me you know.'

Rowena was immensely touched and squeezed his arm. 'Let's just say the timing was never right.'

'But what about this Derek? He seems nice. Could he be more than a friend?'

They had reached the churchyard and Rowena stopped amongst the graves. Now the urge was to confide. 'I'd like to think so,' she said carefully. 'But maybe I'm just tired of being on my own.' She didn't say that she was envious of Phyllida, even now dallying in London with Bob. It was too shameful to admit, even to herself.

His reply was heartfelt. 'I know exactly what you mean. Poor Rowena. I want you to be happy. You always stood up for me.'

'I always worried about you. I still do.'

Mark grinned and the years seemed to fall away. It was her little brother standing there again. 'What a pair we are,' he laughed. 'Thank goodness we've got each other!'

'Thank goodness,' she agreed. Then, suddenly embarrassed, 'Just look at the daffodils. It must be spring.'

In London it felt like spring as Bob and Phyllida walked down Bayswater Road to the entrance to Hyde Park. The daffodils were already past their best under the trees. Phyllida remembered reading that it was always several degrees warmer in town, something to do with all the concrete, and no doubt also the central heating leaking out of all the offices, flats and hotels. Her room at the Post House was unbearably hot; she couldn't seem to turn off the radiator and if she opened the window she was deafened by the noise. Lying awake she had almost come to regret her solitary state. But Bob had kept his word and when she finally discarded her nightdress it was purely to keep herself cool.

Bob was chattering away, as he always did, leaving no time

for reflection. He liked to talk about his racing days, about great winners like Red Rum and Shergar, speculating on what had happened to him.

'He'd be dead by now, even if he didn't end up as dog meat.'

'Oh surely not dog meat. What would be the point?'

He shrugged. 'Well what else could they do with him?'

She shook her head. 'People's motives are always a mystery to me.'

They stopped by the Serpentine, where children were feeding the ducks. 'I wish we had some bread,' she said. 'I used to do this with the twins, in a park in Guildford. Stuart was always a bit frightened if they came out of the water but Kathryn was quite fearless. She would run towards them shouting, "Come here, ducks," and of course they'd all just run away! She still hasn't quite learned not to force her ideas on people, I'm afraid.'

'Still, she's showing spirit now.'

'Oh yes. But let's not think of that, I've come away to enjoy myself.'

'What would you like to do?'

She thought for a moment, then exclaimed, 'Madame Tussaud's! I haven't been there since we took the twins. It would be fun to see who's in there now.'

He gripped her arm. 'Everything's fun with you, my dear,' he told her, and his voice was gruff.

Phyllida was surprised to find that Mark had already arrived when they got home.

Rowena introduced Bob. 'This is Phyllida's friend, they've been to London for the weekend.'

To Phyllida she said, 'We went to see Mother today and she didn't know who Mark was. It was very upsetting.'

'Never mind, dear. Another day she could be completely different.'

'Are you a racing man?' Bob asked Mark incongruously.

'No. But I'll have a flutter on the Grand National if I'm still here.'

Phyllida had made Horlicks and they sat round the fire talking inconsequentially. Just as Bob was leaving the telephone rang.

It was Ben. 'I tried to get you earlier. I've got to go away for three days,' he told Phyllida.

'Oh dear.'

'I don't think Kathryn can be left, she has another treatment due.'

Tension plucked at her shoulders. 'You want me to come over?'

'If you could. Tomorrow week. I'll come and fetch you.'

'No. I'll ask Bob to bring me.'

'I hope you don't mind.'

'Why should I? I'm here to help.'

Returning to the fire she wondered how long the nightmare would go on.

'How do you bear it? I really can't take this on board.' Mark had made another visit to Helen, this time alone. 'She kept asking me about my wife? Said she'd had a letter from her.'

'Yes. I've heard that one before.'

'Wishful thinking perhaps?'

'Not any more. At least this time she knew you.'

'I wanted to try and explain, but I see it's too late. I wish you'd told me.'

'It's been so gradual. And I wasn't sure if you cared.'

His face was as grey as his hair, and pinched. His voice was fierce. 'Of course I care, even if she doesn't.'

'She always cared about you,' protested Rowena, though sometimes she had wondered.

'It's ridiculous, but I needed to have her take my hand, to say, "There there, all is forgiven."'

'But there's nothing to forgive.'

'In her eyes there was. And Father's.' He looked at her bleakly. 'Well, at least they had you. You never let them down.'

She smiled grimly. 'Not so that they knew. But they'd have liked grandchildren. We both deprived them of that.'

'We deprived ourselves. I'd have loved a family. Wouldn't you?'

She shrugged, refusing to admit it.

'Families can bring a lot of grief. You've seen that for yourself. And look at Phyllida now, worried to distraction about Kathryn.'

'But at least she's needed. If I remember Phyllida, she always liked to be needed.'

'Included would be a better word. Phyllida always wanted to belong. That's why she loves Mother so much. Mother always included her. It drove me mad sometimes. I didn't want her around, our lives had diverged, we had nothing at all in common. If it hadn't been for Mother . . .'

The television set is installed in the lounge, nine inches of bulbous green-tinged glass in a walnut cabinet. It has been purchased in honour of the Coronation.

Rowena has come home for the occasion. Neighbours have been invited in, salad has been prepared with precious tins of luncheon meat, and ham saved from the ration. At the last minute Helen says, 'What about Phyllida and her mother? I don't suppose they have a television.'

'I've no idea. They're not that hard up.'

'Even so, they don't want to watch it on their own.'

'They have friends, neighbours.'

But Helen is adamant, and telephones, and her invitation is accepted. They arrive with fruit and cake as a contribution to the royal feast and install themselves in the crammed ranks of chairs, in front of the set that is so shortly to become an altar in the room.

Together, they watch the tiny coach driving through the rain, the waving hands along the route like the tentacles of an insect, hear the roars of the crowd, the bells, the solemn music. Rowena is moved and impressed, both by the images, and the fact of their transmission into their home. A whole new world seems to open up, full of possibilities as yet untapped.

She helps her mother bring in the lunch and they eat, eyes on the screen, in the early stages of a love affair which is to consume them all. But as the afternoon wears on Rowena's head begins to ache. She excuses herself, saying she would like to take a walk. Phyllida jumps up too, and invites herself along.

They go into the fields below the church, then climb to the churchyard where once Rowena and her brother used to circle the gravestones morbidly reading the names.

Phyllida says, 'Mother's sold the house. We're moving to a flat.' She sounds depressed.

'Oh dear! But I suppose Tudor House is rather large.'

Already Rowena regrets the panelled hall, Phyllida's bedroom with the green tiled hearth, though she never goes there now.

'Still,' says Phyllida, giving her a slanting glance. 'I won't be there for long, probably. I'm getting married.'

'Phyl!' Rowena is impressed, jealous, excited, cross. 'Who to?'

'His name's Henry. He's a librarian.'

Rowena is astonished. A librarian? Phyllida?

'Mum didn't tell me. Does she know?'

'She knows about Henry. But I've only just decided.'

'Does Henry know?'

Phyllida laughs, hugging herself through her thin dress. 'Not yet. But he's been asking me for weeks. He's going to be thrilled!'

Of course. Who wouldn't be? Phyllida was ripe for the plucking. Now she looks serious again.

She stops beside the pond, where the water boatmen are describing fraught patterns on the brown surface and newts are crawling through the mud. The church tower rears behind her against cloudy skies as she asks, 'Will you be my bridesmaid, Ro? Now that we've met again I realise that no one else will do. You are my oldest friend.'

Rowena bites her lip. She doesn't see herself in pink satin, least of all following Phyllida down the aisle. But she doesn't know how to refuse without giving offence. She forces a smile.

'All right. I'll be there when you marry your Henry.'

She little realises what she is saying.

Mark didn't say how long he would be staying and Rowena didn't like to ask. Once or twice he took the train up to London, saying he had business to attend to, something about investments inherited from Lawrence. He was well off now. He had the flat in New York, some capital, his own pension and savings.

But no one to share it with.

'Why don't you come back to England now?' Rowena asked him tentatively. 'Is there anything to keep you in New York?'

What she really meant was, has there been anyone else since Lawrence? Are you being careful? But she said only, 'It would be good to have you home again. And Mother would like it.'

'It would make not a scrap of difference to Mother. And I don't think I could live in England now. I like the choice America offers. I can winter in Florida if I want, or ski in Colorado.'

She was astonished. 'Do you ski?'

He laughed shortly. 'No. I always meant to. Now it's too late.'

'Why?' She was bristling with alarm.

'Oh, time's wingèd chariot, all that. But you must come and stay, we could make a trip together.'

She was still dubious. 'You are all right, aren't you? I mean, quite well? You look so . . . insubstantial.'

'I'm growing old. Though you haven't changed at all. Your hair is hardly grey. You were always stronger than me.'

'I still worry about you. Life in New York is such a risky business.'

'You mean the mugging on the streets? Well I've never seen any of it.'

'Maybe you've been lucky. But I didn't really mean that.'

He gave her a long look, some sort of comprehension dawning in his pale eyes. Eventually he said, 'You think I might have Aids, don't you?'

She looked away, feeling ashamed.

'It had occurred to me. You've been in hospital. You've come home, unexpectedly.'

'If you must know that was partly to say goodbye to Mother. But not for any sinister reason.'

She knew a huge thankfulness. 'Mark, I'm sorry.'

He took her hand. 'Don't be. You always were the one to look out for me. But I don't need it, I'm a big boy now.'

She smiled suddenly, remembering him saying just that on his seventh birthday when their grandmother had given him a teddy bear. 'I'm a big boy now. I play with guns.' But he had loved the bear nonetheless and it had outlasted the gun which had gone to a jumble sale.

She said, surprising herself, 'Let's go to church together again this Sunday. I enjoyed it.'

She had never caught religion, though once, escorting a class of girls to hear Billy Graham on his first evangelising mission, she had nearly succumbed to the hysteria. They had been seated high up in the huge arena, and the girls had been given strict instructions not to leave their seats.

When emotions had been roused to fever-pitch the call came to give themselves to Christ. 'I want you to get up out of your seat. The coaches will wait . . .' A slow dribble of people made their way down the crowded rows and wavered across the arena, heads bowed, drawn by the irresistible power of his magnetism. The dribbles merged into a stream until a mass of silent, submissive souls awaited absolution.

Next to her a girl was weeping. 'I want to go down,' she sobbed. 'I want to go down.'

Rowena knew what she meant. She wanted to go as well. She wanted to be washed clean and folded up into redemption. She felt as if she would burst with angry frustration, but she did not permit herself to cry.

'Why did they let us come, if we can't go down?' implored the girl, who was only fourteen and called Janice.

Rowena put her arm round her shoulders. 'I know it seems unfair. But how would I ever find you again in all this crowd? I have to get you safely home.'

Janice looked at her with crazed, accusing eyes.

The crowd were singing, 'Just as I am without one plea, But that Thy blood was shed for me,' and they rose, and sang together in an ecstasy of short-lived piety, 'And that Thou bidd'st me come to Thee, O lamb of God, I come.'

Walking again to church that second Sunday Rowena asked suddenly, 'Do you believe in God, Mark?'

She didn't like to look at him, the question seemed too personal. She was pleased when he answered easily, 'Yes. I suppose I do. The thing is, when I was young, and realised I was different, I tried to find a reason for it. Mum and Dad seemed to turn against me. I had to belong somewhere so I guessed – I hoped, I suppose – that there had to be some sort of a master plan and I was part of it. It helped me accept the way things were. When I met Lawrence I went further. He had great faith. I've found it a comfort over the years just to believe implicitly. Does that seem rather feeble?'

'No. I think I envy you. I must say I've never seen much of a plan in my life. I wish I'd known what God had in store for me.'

He glanced at her curiously. 'That sounds sad. Do you want to tell me?'

She looked at him longingly. She could tell him. What harm would it do now? But the long habit of secrecy was hard to break. She wasn't protecting herself, but Phyllida, when she shrugged and said, 'Not really. It's all a long long time ago.'

She and Phyllida are in the church porch, waiting for Henry. It is the week before the wedding, and they have come to a rehearsal.

Rowena is curious. She has never met Henry. When he finally arrives, apologising to them all for being dilatory, she sees a self-effacing tall and earnest man, his athleticism submerged by spectacles and diffidence. He has a precise speaking voice which she finds pleasing. If she notices anything more about him, it is that he looks kind.

He is clearly besotted with Phyllida, who looks fetching and sexy in a pink angora jumper. Following her up the aisle Rowena dreads the ceremony, her pastel dress and circlet of flowers, Phyllida's obvious triumph, Helen's indulgent pride in the bride who is not her daughter.

Mostly she dreads her own irrational sense of failure.

In self-defence, she asks herself what on earth they will find to talk about, once they get out of bed.

SIX

When Phyllida leaves her mother's flat for the last time it is with a complex mixture of relief, triumph and excitement. A chapter has ended, a new page is being turned, upon which she has begun to write her own story, in her own setting, filled with the characters of her choosing. The star role goes to Henry, who loves her to distraction and whom she supposes she loves too because he is the first man she really wants to go to bed with, though she hasn't yet. She has saved herself, as she always intended, for her wedding night.

She has never ceased to marvel that Henry loves her. When she first learned that he was a librarian, she thought naively that he stamped the books and sorted tickets in the local library. She was astonished to discover that he had a degree, that librarianship was a profession, and that he worked in a library at London University. His position is, in fact, fairly lowly. He is only twenty-eight. But it is a world she has never expected to become acquainted with, as mysterious and tantalising as Mars.

Henry is not well paid, but he has inherited his parents' house near Guildford where he lives alone. He has asked Phyllida if she would like him to sell it. They could choose something else together. But Phyllida has fallen in love with the house almost before falling in love with Henry. It has something of the substance of Tudor House, without the problems, built in the 1920s in the style of Lutyens; tiled gables, mock-timbering, a raised brick terrace above the small landscaped garden.

She sees herself there, complete at last. She is leaving her job at a beautician's in Croydon and will devote herself to cooking, to sewing, to making Henry happy.

For she has what she has most wanted in all the world.

A man in her life.

She glides down the aisle in a rhapsody of lace and net, her hair a blonde froth beneath her veil, her eyes subtly enlarged, her cheeks blooming like peaches, like rose petals, fragrant, innocent and pure. Rowena follows behind in palest pink, her long hair wound into a bun, her dark height a perfect foil. Phyllida glances from right to left, savouring the moment. She gives her mother a special, pitying smile, for her mother has cried all morning and is now red and puffy beneath her picture hat, bursting with pride and grief, her emotions oozing from her eyes into a succession of lace handkerchiefs. Helen gives Phyllida an encouraging smile, and Jim beside her winks conspiratorially. But Phyllida doesn't need him now.

Her uncle is giving her away. He hands her firmly over to Henry, his duty done, and slides into the pew beside her mother. Phyllida gazes up at Henry, who is looking at her through his horn-rimmed glasses as if he has seen a vision. She smiles, her heart beating fast. She hopes she will remember her lines. Everything must be perfect. When they finally leave the church she is holding his arm as if they are locked together. She wants to cry, but doesn't want to spoil her make-up as the photographer is waiting outside to arrange them, tastefully, under the yews.

It is satisfactory to have Rowena at her side. After all, she is her oldest friend. She thinks, belatedly, that perhaps pink is not Rowena's colour. it does not enhance her sallow skin. But she is playing her part well, greeting the guests, holding the bouquet, arranging Phyllida's train for the photographer. Later, she helps her into her navy suit, her pale pink hat and gloves. Phyllida kisses her and says, generously, 'Your turn next, Ro. Make sure you catch the bouquet.'

Henry's car is waiting outside, an open tourer decorated with ribbon, trailing a line of boots. They fill it with confetti and it drives away, scattering paper petals like autumn leaves. At the last moment, she throws her bouquet into the crowd but Rowena isn't looking. She has turned away.

That night Henry is gentle with her at first. She is bestowing on him an enormous, precious gift and he has already waited so long. But at the end he forgets himself with a violence that surprises and delights her and, later, while he sleeps, she smiles into the darkness.

Jake and Hannah were squabbling and Phyllida was at the end of her tether.

'Really you two, can't you be more considerate when your mother is feeling ill?'

'She's always feeling ill,' Jake complained.

'Well just be a bit more sympathetic. You don't like being sick.' For Jake got car-sick and knew all about nausea.

Hannah said in a whiny voice, 'I want Mummy to give us our tea.'

'Well she can't, she's lying down.'

Hannah gave a tremulous sigh, all the cares in the world brimming out of her big brown eyes. 'I want to lie down with her.'

'Oh darling, she wouldn't want that. Let's just leave her in peace shall we? Eat your tea quietly and then you can go and watch *Neighbours*.'

'Wheee!!' Jake stuffed a fish finger whole into his mouth, pressing in the ends with his fingers.

'But not if you eat like that. I can't think what your father would say.'

She hated herself for saying it. Over the years she heard her mother's voice when Phyllida herself had caused displeasure. 'I can't think what your father would have said. Thank goodness your father can't see you now.' It had hurt her deeply, the implication that she had let him down, that her father would have sat in judgement, was still doing so, when in life he had been indulgent, and loved her. 'I've made you a jelly,' she said now to Jake, by way of propitiation.

She felt incredibly weary as she was washing up, too tired to prepare herself a meal. She picked at the left-overs, spooning down the last of the jelly like a child then thinking, belatedly, that perhaps Kathryn would have fancied it. As she was drying the last of the dishes – it hadn't seemed worth loading the dishwasher – Kathryn herself appeared at the kitchen door like a ghost, hunched in a towelling dressing gown, her dark hair lank and stringy, her eyes haunted.

Her voice was hoarse from vomiting. 'I think I could drink some tea. I'm dreadfully dry.'

'Oh darling.' Given her helplessness, Phyllida found it easier to show her love. She put an arm round her shoulders, feeling her thin and damp, and led her to the rocker beside the Aga. She threw off the cat and lowered her gently down. 'I should have brought you some, but the children . . .'

'I know. Don't worry. Are they watching television?'

'Yes. I know you don't approve of *Neighbours* but . . .'

Kathryn's eyes were dull. 'Don't worry,' she said again. 'We must get by as best we can.'

Phyllida took the kettle from the Aga and made tea. She cut a slice of lemon, for Kathryn couldn't take milk. 'Waitrose was packed today, and only two tills open as usual,' she said conversationally. 'It was nice of Mrs Armstrong to give me a lift.'

'She's a good neighbour. We have to stick together, in the country.'

'I remember,' said Phyllida, for hadn't she lived in the country, once?

She put the mug into Kathryn's hands and pulled a rug from the back of the chair around her shoulders, though the kitchen was warm. She stroked her daughter's hair absently. It needed a wash but she knew Kathryn didn't like to do it too often as so much fell out when she did. It was all due to the treatment. Sometimes it seemed to Phyllida that the treatment was worse than the disease, but that was absurd, the cancer could kill you, baldness couldn't. She withdrew her hand, looking anxiously at her fingers for clinging hairs.

She had thought never to feel such pain again and she felt she couldn't bear any more. Her daughter's stoical suffering was intolerable, when there was so little Phyllida could do to help. Suddenly it flashed into her mind that Henry would have been more use than she was. Kathryn had always adored her father. It was unfair. She allowed herself a little of her own grief and loss, re-emerging over the years. It seemed, momentarily, to cancel out the other pain.

'It's a pity Ben had to go away just at this time.' She cut a piece of bread. Perhaps Kathryn could manage a piece of dry toast. In fact she thought she could manage something herself after all. She pressed the toaster down, hearing it click into life.

'It can't be helped.' Kathryn laughed drily. 'It comes to something when they have to provide stress clinics on the rates for the very people who are collecting the rates!'

Phyllida had her own views on that but thought it better not to voice them. 'Well I've no doubt it will do him good. After all he's had a lot of stress lately, and not just with work.'

'The trouble is, it doesn't take the problems away. They'll all be waiting for him when he gets back.' She looked hopeless and set the empty mug down on the Aga.

The toast popped up. 'Would you fancy a piece to nibble? It would make you feel stronger.'

She shook her head. 'No, Mum.' She looked across at the toaster, at the jar of Marmite into which Phyllida was digging her knife. Her stomach bunched and twisted and she stood up, throwing back the rug.

'Oh God, here we go again.' Her voice was strangled and she was swallowing hard, sweat drenching her body.

Phyllida grabbed a bowl and ran to her but it was too late, Kathryn was doubled up, hurling her tea across the floor.

Mark wanted to take Rowena shopping. 'I'd like to treat you to something before I leave. Let's go up to town.'

Rowena didn't often shop in London. She found it too stressful. London had changed. There were bomb scares. There were dark faces and saris; Oxford Street sometimes looked more like the heart of a foreign city than a street in the capital of England. And the beggars, some of them so young, upset her, making her feel guilty if she didn't give, exploited if she did.

She remembered the beggars after the war, men in rags with one arm missing or an eye patch. 'War veteran', the scribbled card would say. 'Please give generously.' She had always hung back, wanting to give, but her mother had hurried her past.

'They've probably got more money than we have,' she would say, which Rowena thought unlikely. Why would anyone with money choose to sit on a dirty pavement dressed in rags?

But with Mark beside her it would be different. They would take taxis, visit Knightsbridge, Piccadilly and Bond Street. The dark underside of the city, the cardboard boxes and picked-over litter bins, would be conveniently invisible. As they stepped out of the new, post-modernist Charing Cross station into the sunshine she felt a lift of the spirits.

'Let's go and feed the pigeons first. Do you remember Grandma bringing us to do that?'

'Your stockings were wrinkled. I still have the photograph,' he said, surprising her.

'There's the Sainsbury Wing,' she told him, nodding towards the National Gallery. 'I must make the effort and come up sometime. I've read such a lot about it.'

'I've been in already,' he said, surprising her again. 'I did it for Lawrence really. He would have made a special trip, of course.'

'Yes.'

They bought seeds and held out their hands to the pigeons, feeling the spiky claws descend, the blunt sharpness of the pecking beaks. It made her shiver. She didn't really like it and dropped the remaining seeds onto the white-splashed ground. 'It's good to see the fountains playing, they don't always,' she told him.

'And Nelson has been cleaned, he looks very fine. They must have known I was coming!'

They took a taxi to Harrods where he bought her a cashmere jumper and cardigan in sage green.

'I never wear green,' she protested when he picked it up.

'Well you should,' he told her, when she tried it on.

They had lunch in Fortnum's and he purchased special tea and peaches in brandy and pickled walnuts. 'For when you need cheering up,' he said, smiling down and pulling her hand through his arm. She felt proud to be with this tall, well-dressed man and thought, as she had done once before, that they could be taken for lovers.

She wondered, had he ever taken Lawrence's arm in public?

They walked up Bond Street where he bought himself a silk scarf and for her a patterned pure wool wrap the colours of jewels. They reached Soho and Rowena said, 'Let's find a coffee bar? Do you suppose they still exist?'

'Well, cappuccino is supposed to have made a come-back. Let's see if we can find espresso.'

What they found was a small dark room with deafening music which almost drowned the evocative remembered hiss of the coffee machine.

There are four of them, Rowena, Caroline, Terry and Brian. They have been to Ken Colyer's jazz club. The girls have pony-tails – though Rowena thinks it makes her look too young. They are wearing loose men's sweaters from Marks and Spencer and tapered trousers with straps beneath their insteps and long, cheap beads. For Terry and Rowena it is a blind date. He says to her, 'You don't look anything like a teacher.'

'Oh.' She laughs. 'What does a teacher look like?'

'Well, you know, serious.'

'I'm deadly serious,' she says, looking intently into his eyes. He is good-looking in a way. He is an electrician, a friend of Brian who is engaged to Caroline who lives in the flat beneath her own and thinks it's about time Rowena had a boyfriend. Rowena has never really known anyone who works with his hands. She finds it quite exciting and looks at his hands now, seeing chipped, rather dirty nails. The thought of them touching her is vaguely titillating but distasteful too. But he is a good jiver, he has spun and twisted her round the floor in a way she hadn't thought possible. If he asks her to come again, she will.

The juke box is playing 'Rock Around the Clock'. It has a rhythm of its own, a new rhythm, demanding a response.

She taps her feet as she sips her coffee, her lips sinking through the vapid froth to the scalding liquid beneath.

'It's been a wonderful day,' she told Mark when they got home. 'I'll remember it for a long time.'

'Me too.'

They hugged each other sadly, with regret.

Tomorrow he would be leaving.

'You look absolutely ghastly, Phyl.'

'I feel it. It's been a ghastly three days. If anyone had told me . . . well I've never been a coper, not really.'

'Nonsense. You rally when necessary, like the rest of us.'

Phyllida looked strained and tearful. She put her hands over her face, smooth hands still, but fatter so that her rings cut into the flesh. She said painfully, 'It's so dreadful to see her suffer. If I could be sure it's doing any good.'

'You simply have to believe that it is.'

Phyllida began suddenly to cry. 'And what if it isn't, Ro? She'll die. Those poor children, what will happen to them? And Ben . . . I can't bear it.'

'Let's cross that bridge when we come to it.' Rowena heard the impatience in her voice and gentled it to say, 'Come on, dear, you're home now. Why didn't you bring Bob in with you?'

'Oh I don't know. I just wanted to be alone I suppose. There's been such a constant racket, Hannah pleaded a sore throat yesterday so I've had her moaning round me for two days, in addition to Kathryn. Not that she moans, I don't mean that, she's very brave. But I feel I have to try and make her eat and that makes her sick and the whole vicious circle begins again.'

'But she's better now?'

'Yes. Until the next time.'

'How long will this go on?'

Phyllida spread her hands helplessly. 'You tell me. She sees the specialist next week.'

'Spring's coming. Maybe everyone will feel better then.' Even as she spoke it sounded fatuous, the sort of palliative one offered to the stupid. Phyllida wasn't stupid but she seized on the words gratefully.

'Yes. I certainly shall. Rowena . . .' She hesitated.

'What's that?'

'Bob's asked me to go away with him for Easter. To the Cotswolds. Would you mind very much?'

Rowena was not entirely unprepared but she felt a brush of dread.

She said carefully, 'It will do you good. You go.'

'I wish you could come too,' said Phyllida, though she didn't.

Oh no, thought Rowena. Phyllida had always tried to include her against her will. She had only been married a month when Rowena was invited for the weekend.

'I'm never going to be rid of her,' she tells her mother, ungraciously, over the telephone.

'But you must go. Aren't you curious to see her house?'

'Not really. All that ghastly domesticity.'

'Well I expect she just wants to show it all off. It's understandable.'

This is precisely what Rowena fears. She doubts the enthusiasm of her response. 'By the way,' she says, 'I've been made Deputy Head of Department.'

'Darling! That's wonderful. Your father will be delighted.'

'I was going to come home and celebrate, but I suppose I've got to go to Guildford instead.'

'Well, give her our love.'

She cradles the telephone for a while before dialling Phyllida's number. It would be so easy to say no, but she can imagine Phyllida's hurt expression, and she can't put her off for ever. There seems no end to the ways she has to make Phyllida happy, it is unfair. But then life is unfair.

Henry meets her at the station. It is raining, the car roof is up, but she sees confetti still on the floor and protruding from the upholstery.

'We can't seem to get rid of it,' he laughs. 'To tell you the truth I don't think Phyl really wants to.' And he smiles indulgently.

She thinks, he sounds kind. Phyllida will respond to kindness, as if she were a household pet. Which, she soon realises, is almost what she is.

The kitchen smells of cooking and boasts an array of cakes and biscuits. Phyllida is pink and floury, wearing a long pinafore decorated with cherries, her hair a little mussed, her mouth bruised with kissing. Henry likes to make love in the mornings, indeed he had almost missed the train. She hugs Rowena with one arm, the other holding a wooden spoon.

'Welcome to The Maltings,' she says. Rowena thinks it sounds terribly pretentious.

She murmurs her delight at being there.

'I'll make some coffee,' says Henry, picking up the automatic percolator Rowena had given them. 'Phyl's still not too sure how this works,' he tells her, filling it with water and measuring the grounds.

Phyllida looks at him feigning crossness. 'Oh you!' She makes a moue and he blows her a kiss. Rowena says, 'May I go to my room? And where's the bathroom?'

'I'll show you.' Phyllida unties her pinafore, pushes at her hair, picks up Rowena's bag and hustles her eagerly through the hall, which Rowena sees with a sense of inevitability is square and panelled, and up a shallow staircase to a galleried landing. There are white doors, solid and shiny, with brass door furniture. One of these opens onto a pretty guest room with chintzy curtains and a matching bedspread on the double bed. There is a washbasin in the corner and a rail of pink towels. A small posy of flowers graces the dressing table.

'I want to do this room next,' Phyllida tells her. 'I thought a white candlewick bedspread, fitted, and Sanderson curtains. And a fitted carpet of course.'

Rowena rather likes the worn art deco square and the polished boards, but she says nothing.

'The view is nice.' Phyllida goes to the window, inviting her to look out over the late summer garden. 'Next year I'm really going to get to grips with the garden.'

'Oh Phyl. It looks as if someone has already got to grips with it!'

'What I mean is, I want to learn.' Phyllida has flushed. She is going on too much, showing off. Perhaps Rowena is jealous? 'Make yourself at home. I hope you'll be comfortable.'

Leaning from the window after she has gone, Rowena unkindly counts the hours until her train.

On Good Friday Rowena waved Bob and Phyllida off in the Jaguar, smiling brightly. Phyllida looked excited, girlish and almost coy as Bob handed her into the car. Rowena told herself to be happy for her. After all, she had as much right as anyone else.

As much right as Rowena herself.

She picked up the telephone and dialled Derek Stadden's number.

'It looks like a fine Easter, do you fancy a nice long walk tomorrow?'

When he accepted her spirits rose, she felt almost cheerful as she stripped the beds and generously made up Phyllida's for her. Phyllida still slept in a double bed, with sheets and blankets and an expensive padded coverlet that had come from The Maltings, that had taken over finally from the ubiquitous candlewick. As she smoothed tucked and patted she wondered about the bed that awaited them in Stow-on-the-Wold. For Phyllida was giving nothing away this time. Maybe, after all, she was past all that?

But, thought Rowena, gazing hungrily out of the window, I'm not.

I wish I was, but I'm not.

Next day Derek drove her to Box Hill, which was a mistake as everyone else seemed to have had the same idea.

'This was not very original I'm afraid,' she puffed as they struggled up the hill.

'Good ideas never are, everyone has thought of them before. Like clichés. Something only becomes a cliché because it's appropriate.'

'That's right of course. I never thought of it like that.' She looked at him with respect. 'I see there's a German film on at Studio Two. Should we go?'

'Why not. It would be a good test.' He smiled at her. 'It's a pity the classes have stopped for the summer. I shall be so rusty by October. At least you have your holiday to look forward to.'

She spoke without thinking. 'It's a pity you're not coming too.'

He laughed. 'I don't think a threesome is a good idea.'

But she had no idea what he meant, only that she agreed with him.

'Henry's giving me a birthday party,' Phyllida tells her on the telephone. 'Naturally, we want you to come, and stay the weekend.'

'Well . . .'

'Please come, Ro. Henry particularly wants you to.'

'Don't be silly, Phyl.'

'Well, *I* want you. Twenty-six – can you imagine it?'

Rowena can. She supposes that once more won't hurt. Besides, she is interested to see what Phyllida calls a party.

She buys a potted camellia and a card and loads them with her case into the boot of the second-hand Ford her father has helped her to buy. It has a radio which she keeps permanently set on Radio Luxembourg. Driving, she feels carefree, and excited by the mix of Bill Haley, Dean Martin and somebody new called Elvis Presley. There are advertisements for acne cream, but she no longer has acne.

She is singing along as she turns into the drive. A new song begins – 'Memories are Made of This'. And there is Henry, with a tennis racquet in his hand, smiling amiably and reaching to open the door.

'Good to see you', he says, as if he means it. Rowena is surprised to find that it is good to see him too.

'He's going to the club, he always plays on Saturday afternoons,' Phyllida tells her.

'Even when you have a party to prepare? I thought he would be in here making sandwiches.'

Phyllida blushes. 'Oh we're not having sandwiches. And we've got caterers coming in.'

Rowena raises an eyebrow. 'On a librarian's pay?'

Phyllida looks embarrassed. 'He has a little money of his own. From his parents. And he likes to spend it on me.'

'Of course.' Rowena is eager to apologise. 'It's absolutely none of my business, I'm sorry.'

Phyllida is pouring coffee. She seems to have got the hang of the percolator. 'It's marvellous that you've got a car. I haven't got the nerve to learn, I'm afraid.'

'Wouldn't Henry teach you?'

'He says he prefers to drive me himself.'

'Well, lucky you. I have to find my own way around.' Saying it, Rowena feels proud, strong, independent.

'I'll go on up if I may,' she says. 'I know the way.'

She sits on the bed to remove her shoes, but before doing so she folds back the new white bedspread, as she has been taught.

Phyllida is in her element, circulating amongst her new friends and neighbours offering canapés, directing the little waitress with her tray of drinks, reminding Henry, with a kiss, to change the records. The music is light orchestral, long-playing records played on a veneered radiogram which has pride of place beside the fireplace opposite the television.

Rowena finds herself searching curiously through the other records, finding Moura Lympany and Myra Hess, Rachmaninov, Donizetti, Wagner, Elisabeth Schwarzkopf singing lieder. She wonders when they play them.

If they play them.

When the caterers have departed, bearing off the left-overs and the dirty plates and glasses, and Henry has emptied the ashtrays and pushed the furniture back into place, they sit round the embers of the fire drinking hot chocolate and Henry says, 'I don't feel in the least bit sleepy, who's for a game of Scrabble?'

Phyllida makes a face. 'Not me. You always win.'

'Rowena?'

'Well. Why not?' She looks at Phyllida. 'Do you mind, Phyl?'

'Why should I? But I warn you, he cheats! Check everything with the dictionary.'

'You only say that because I win.'

'Oh you,' she says, kissing him fondly on the mouth. 'I'm off to bed.'

He fetches the game and tips the letters into the lid, turning them face downward.

'I shall expect some cracking words from you,' he tells her, turning up the Q and securing the first go.

They select their letters and he places xenium across the middle, scoring twenty-six. She raises an eyebrow. So that's how it's to be. She adds zeugma, scoring twenty-nine.

He laughs out loud, slapping his hand on his thigh.

They don't check with the dictionary. They are trusting each other not to cheat.

Derek and Rowena were playing Scrabble on Easter Sunday afternoon. She had just placed Basque across a triple-word square, but her heart was not in the game. It was raining outside and Derek's house felt chilly. The sitting room wasn't as snug as her own and she didn't care for the slippery leather furniture his wife had apparently picked up in a sale not long before she died.

'She was so delighted,' he'd told her when first he invited her to the house. 'I couldn't tell her I didn't like it. And now I can't bring myself to get rid of it.'

'I could!' said Rowena. Then, backtracking, 'But then I've never had to fit in with anyone else of course.'

But now she longed suddenly for her own gold Dralon and the comfort of a living fire. Also, she was beginning to feel foolish. Here she was, alone with Derek hoping for who knew what, when he was clearly only interested in playing Scrabble. She resolved to remedy the situation as soon as she decently could, if she was to have any dignity. When the game was over, with her the winner, she said, 'Would you mind if I go now? I've got a bit of a headache.'

He was sympathetic, making her ashamed of the lie. Driving home she felt depressed. Derek was a pleasant companion, why couldn't she be content with that? It was shameful to admit it, but it was partly because of Phyllida and Bob.

The telephone was ringing as she let herself into the house.

It was Stuart, Phyllida's son, ringing from Newcastle. She felt her throat go tight. She was never at ease, now, with Stuart.

'Your mother's gone away.'

'Is she at Kathryn's? I'm going to call her next.'

She had no idea if Stuart knew about Bob. Let Kathryn tell him. 'No. She's away with a friend.'

'Right. I was just ringing to say Happy Easter.'

He clearly wasn't going to say it to her.

'How is Jill?' She didn't care, but one went through the motions.

'She's in bed with flu.'

'Oh dear. Well – goodbye.'

She stared at the receiver thoughtfully.

Henry's voice is excited on the other end of the line.

'They've arrived! One of each, at half past three this morn-

104

ing. Phyl did splendidly. We're going to call them Kathryn and Stuart. Isn't it simply marvellous?'

'Yes, Henry, it's marvellous . . . congratulations.'

The front door burst open and Phyllida was there, Bob close behind her, their faces oozing a suppressed excitement.

Rowena narrowed her eyes, looking from one to the other.

'You've had a good time, I can see. Did it rain? It's been pouring here.'

Phyllida looked at Bob and they burst out laughing, gaily.

'I didn't really notice. Did you?' He looks at her mischievously.

Sexual jealousy took Rowena's breath away. She gripped the arm of her chair, hating them.

Phyllida came and sat on the sofa, drawing Bob beside her.

'We've something to tell you, Ro.'

Rowena thought, I don't want to know.

Phyllida's eyes were very soft and very bright. There was make-up in the creases of her lids.

'Bob has asked me to marry him. And I've accepted.'

The room spun, history turning like a merry-go-round, making her feel sick.

'Congratulations,' she said. The word was like a pebble on her tongue, to be spat out and got rid of.

Why was it always Phyllida?

'You'll have to come and stay when we're married,' Phyllida told her next day, 'like you always used to do. I'd never leave you out.'

'It hardly seems worth it in Croydon! It's just around the corner.'

'Oh, we're buying a house in Epsom. Bob's missing the racing scene. I shall use some of my money of course.'

'Of course.'

'It will be fun, Ro. Having you to stay. Just like the old times!'

And she smiled at Rowena, complacently.

*   *   *

The twins are in the back of the estate car, strapped into car seats, their feet encased in tiny sandals, red and blue. Stuart is sucking his thumb with drooping eyes. Kathryn glares crossly through the window. Rowena, seated between them, wonders why she has come. It is simply that it is easier to say yes than no in the face of Phyllida's blandishments. And there is something else, though she hasn't recognised it yet.

They are going for a picnic, out into the Surrey woods where bluebells are misty among the young bracken and the beech leaves are an acid green which almost hurts the eyes.

'There's absolutely nowhere suitable here,' Phyllida complains with a little whine which Rowena has noticed for the first time, this time, when the twins are sixteen months old. She looks tired, has even lost weight, but it doesn't become her. Phyllida needs to be well-covered.

'Can't we find a field? Somewhere in the sun?'

Henry says patiently, 'You want a field, we'll find a field.' He swings the car round a corner, lurching the babies in their seats.

'Careful,' warns Rowena, 'we're in the back here, remember.'

They travel the lanes until they find a field. It even has the remains of a haystack against which to lean their backs.

'It's probably damp,' says Phyllida. 'It's a bit early for a picnic.'

'Then why did we come?' asks Henry mildly. 'Anyway, I've got the groundsheet.'

Rowena meets his eye in complicity. Phyllida must be humoured. He spreads the groundsheet at the base of the stack and Rowena covers it with a rug. Their eyes meet again and suddenly she wants to laugh; she sees his lip twitch and looks away. That would never do.

Kathryn and Stuart stagger across the grass, alike as peas in a pod except for their pink and blue jumpers, Phyllida following behind with a loaded hamper and cushions.

'What on earth have you brought?' asks Rowena, taking the hamper from her.

Phyllida looks defiant. 'I like to do things properly. There's another basket in the car with all the twins' things.'

106

She looks pointedly at Henry but he is doing experimental golf swings with a stick he has found lying on the ground. Rowena goes to the car and gets the basket, helps Phyllida unpack the food and watches while she deftly changes Stuart's nappy.

It reminds her of seeing Mark as a toddler, fat and smooth with his little organ protruding like a finger, so useless yet so potent. She finds herself staring and looks away to see Henry watching her, and blushes.

He begins to toss a ball and the twins totter after it, giggling. It is the first time Rowena has heard them laughing like children and something melts inside her. It is the happiest sound she has ever heard.

Then Phyllida calls urgently, 'Come and eat, ants are getting into the food.'

She is brushing them away, frantically, distaste curling her pretty mouth.

There is salad, egg and bacon pie, mushroom vol-au-vents, cheese — far too much. The twins, unrestrained, poke and squeeze and smear and eat nothing. Exasperated, Phyllida is near to tears.

Henry drags Kathryn onto his lap. 'Here — eat!' he commands, thrusting a piece of pastry into her mouth.

'Henry! She'll choke.'

He looks long-suffering and, when she turns away, raises an eyebrow at Rowena. She dare not be drawn. She offers Stuart a chocolate biscuit and he presses it into his mouth, chocolate melting between his lips, onto his pretty blue jumper.

'Oh I've forgotten to put on his bib,' Phyllida exclaims in exasperation. 'Didn't anybody notice?'

Rowena chokes on her laughter. Why does everything seem so funny? She cannot explain the elation, the wild sense that this, after all, is how it should be, the cloak of perfection drawn aside, the honeymoon over.

She dare not look at Henry, who in any event is fumbling in the basket for the bibs.

After tea, things improve. She offers to guard the twins while Phyllida, and Henry after some persuasion, go off to pick bluebells. Idly, she watches them go, crossing the field in the low sunshine, the leaves bright about their heads, gathering the flowers. Stuart, thumb in mouth, lolls against her knee, his eyes drooping. Kathryn bangs a spoon on a plastic cup and shouts.

Rowena dozes. When she awakes it is to see Henry smiling down at her.

'A pretty sight. Phyllida has just remembered the camera. She took a picture of you all.'

Phyllida cries, 'How about another? Get up, Ro. Go and stand by the haystack with Henry. There's just enough light.'

And they stand side by side, her hand touching Henry's in the folds of her skirt, in his other a dangle of bluebells, limp and moist. The twins pull at Phyllida's skirt while she focuses and adjusts the lens. Then Rowena feels Henry's hand reach out and gently encircle her own. A white light of revelation takes her breath away, her knees want to buckle beneath her and then they are clinging on, desperately, as if their lives depend on it as they smile together at Phyllida who is laughingly calling, 'Say cheese!' Laughing even as they betray her.

And, so simply, it begins.

The Middle

SEVEN

Every year at the beginning of May Rowena met Barbara, a friend from university, for lunch at Barbara's club. It had gone on for decades, during which they had followed the gains and set-backs of their mutual lives, the menopause, the relentless passing of time.

Barbara had risen high in the civil service and now had an inflation-linked pension and a small flat in Highgate. Like Rowena, she had never married, though for many years, until he died, she had lived with a musician in the London Philharmonic. He had been married to a Catholic who had refused to give him a divorce.

And Rowena had envied her.

The weather was still wintry despite the bursting blossom on the trees. She dressed in her new cashmere and threw her wrap over her coat. Although Barbara herself was unglamorous and looked all of her sixty-three years, the club was smart, full of young business-women in masculine suits and large earrings who Rowena imagined were busy clinching details, disposing of funds, making contacts. In fact they were probably gossiping, like Barbara and herself.

Barbara ordered sherry and they looked at each other.

'You still haven't changed,' they told each other incredulously as they always did, laughing as they always did.

'I'm stiffer,' said Rowena. 'Arthritis setting in I suppose.'

'But you don't wear glasses,' observed Barbara, whose lenses were thick.

'Just for reading still. I used to dread the telephone directory!'

And they smiled at each other comfortably, in the way that women can.

There had never been any need to apologise to Barbara

about Henry. She had never passed judgement, never said, 'How could you, Ro?' or 'It will only lead to tears.'

Now she said, 'How's Phyllida? Still driving you mad?'

'Oh dear! Did I really tell you that! Well I shall soon be rid of her. She's getting married.'

'Married? Some people have all the luck!'

'Yes. Well, I suppose she's lucky. Bob wouldn't suit me but I have to admit they're well suited to each other.'

'More so than she and Henry?'

Rowena looked her straight in the eye. 'Yes. History won't be repeating itself.' She gave a smile but it was crooked with remembered pain.

'So she'll be leaving you. How do you really feel about that?'

Rowena sipped her sherry. When she looked up, her blue eyes were startled.

'Panic, I suppose. Sheer blind panic!'

'I've often wondered why you took her in. You've nothing in common.'

Rowena gave a short laugh. 'Except Henry. I expect you thought I felt guilty or something, and was trying to make amends. But far from it. My guilty days were long gone. No, when it came to it, my motive was one of self-interest. I thought it would be good to have some company. And Phyllida was so eager to come, I was able to disguise it as altruism. It serves me right that it didn't work out quite as I had hoped. I should have known.'

'That she'd irritate you to death?'

Rowena looked at her helplessly. 'That's right. But it's worse than that. In a funny way I've got used to it, and to contemplate life without her is equally unbearable. I can hardly admit it to myself, but part of me doesn't want her to go.'

'What do you think about me wearing white, dear? Would that seem ridiculous, at my age?'

'I don't know about ridiculous. But would you look your best? I mean, pink has always been your colour. Pink, or pale blue.'

'Bob has this thing about white. He thinks it's virginal!'

Rowena was amused. 'So it is. But are you?'

To her surprise Phyllida blushed. She had never liked to talk about such things. 'Well obviously not,' she said with difficulty. 'I have the twins!'

To change the subject, Rowena said, 'We'll go shopping tomorrow. There's not much time, if the wedding is to be in June.'

June. Next month, and she would be gone. Rowena sometimes woke up in the night, startled, imagining herself alone; then realisation would come, hitting her every time somewhere beneath the solar plexus, that soon she would be. That next time she woke, as once she had, raging with fever, feeling too ill to tell anyone how ill she felt, there would be no one there to call to, to ring the doctor, to spoon in chicken broth, plump the pillows and administer the antibiotics.

But, 'I'm beginning to wonder,' Phyllida was saying, 'whether it wouldn't be better if we waited until we've found a house. I mean that flat – well, it wouldn't make for a very good start, would it?'

Rowena was irritated. 'There's nothing wrong with it is there? I mean, it's quite respectable?'

'But you know how I've always felt about flats.'

'You can't always have everything as you want it! Either you want to be with Bob, or you don't.'

'I know, dear.' She paused then went on relentlessly, 'But at our age there are other considerations. Comfort. Privacy.'

'But you'll be married, Phyl. Marriage isn't private. At least, I've always presumed it isn't.'

It was only the unmarried who were private, isolated, separate.

And alone.

'Well if you want to put things off, you'd better tell him now. Before he makes any more arrangements.' For Bob was booking a cruise, making guest lists, bursting with excitement. Rowena doubted that he could cope with any delay. He was as passionate and doting as a teenage groom.

'I think I'd better. I'm not having second thoughts, don't think that . . .'

'I don't think that. But he might.'

She recognised a craven hope, irrational and pathetic, that he would be right.

She knew when she got back from shopping that Phyllida had told him. His face was dulled and despondent, and he looked bent and older as Phyllida handed him tea and cake at the kitchen table. She stood behind him, one plump hand fondling his neck, his cheek, as if she was fondling a dog. Like a dog, he looked up at her, wanting more.

'I do see Phyllida's point,' Rowena said, hoping to help. 'Once you get settled into the flat, you might give up any idea of moving. And that would be a shame. I'm sure you'd both enjoy starting somewhere new.'

'But at our time of life there's no time to waste.'

'What nonsense. You're sixty-four.'

'Sixty-five.'

'Well . . .' Rowena looked hopefully at Phyllida. It wasn't her argument after all.

'I've told him how disappointed I am,' Phyllida explained. 'And it won't take long I'm sure. It's a buyer's market.'

'But I have to sell the flat,' he reminded her.

Phyllida obviously hadn't taken account of that. 'Young people always want flats,' she said unrealistically, discounting the recession, the mortgage rate, the rapid rise in re-possessions.

Bob stood up. He was barely taller than Phyllida and almost as plump. Rowena thought cruelly that they looked like Tweedledum and Tweedledee. He put a short arm round Phyllida's shoulders, tweeking her chin with his other hand.

'Sorry to be so glum,' he told her. 'It's just that I want to be with you. You know that, don't you, precious?'

Despite herself, Rowena's heart melted. The poor man was so obviously in love. And he was suffering.

When Bob had gone Rowena said, 'Poor man. He really loves you. You're very lucky.'

Phyllida gave a little smirk. 'Yes. I never thought it would happen again. After Henry . . .'

Rowena said quickly, 'You're really very well suited. Do you love him too?'

Phyllida looked at her wide-eyed, surprised and thankful. 'Yes, Rowena, I do. He makes me laugh. He makes me feel safe. I can't ask for more than that, can I?'

'I'll call you. We must meet,' Henry mutters as he sees her to her car, hustling her ahead, away from Phyllida who follows behind with a bag of vol-au-vents from the picnic, and lettuce from the greenhouse.

She nods in a dumb and helpless joy, then turns and smiles brightly at Phyllida, accepting her gifts and the drooping bunch of bluebells that Henry thrusts into her hands. She drives away, too fast, her tyres spitting up the gravel, and in her rear view mirror she sees Phyllida take his arm possessively.

'Meet me,' he tells her on the telephone, 'next Saturday afternoon by the telephone box in Chawton. We can walk, and talk. And at the very least I can hold your hand.'

And she goes, on a dizzy dreamy afternoon of early summer, of foaming meadowsweet and tight-curled bracken, and they leave their cars face to face like friends – like lovers – on the daisied grass, and they walk from the village into the greening country where their hands touch and then their lips, then all the hungry length of their bodies there in the lane in the bursting heat of summer, and she knows that they have not come to walk and talk and that he must become her lover.

Afterwards, lying in the bracken looking up at the sky which is as bright and blue as the bluebells she asks him 'Why?', and he tells her, 'I think it should always have been you. And now I love you, it's too late.'

'And now, though it is too late, I love you too.'

And she knows it to be so.

*   *   *

Phyllida went with Rowena to see Helen, who was sitting in the garden of Adelaide House. Her knees were covered in a patchwork knitted blanket. Some of the stitching was coming undone and Phyllida said, 'It's disgraceful, letting them have such shabby things. I'll take it home and mend it.'

Rowena said, 'Phyllida has some good news for you, Mother. I'll let her tell you herself.'

Helen swivelled her eyes to Phyllida. Her hands perched like birds on the edge of the blanket, pale against the coloured wool.

'What is it, dear? Are you having another baby?'

Rowena and Phyllida looked at each other, their eyes meeting and dropping away. It was too horrible to be funny, too pathetic.

'No, dear, but I'm getting married. To somebody called Bob. I'll bring him in to meet you if you like.'

'Well then perhaps you'll have a baby. Rowena never did. It's such a pity.' She seemed to have forgotten that Rowena was there.

'Rowena never knew what it was like to be a mother,' she said. 'Not like you and me.'

And Rowena felt again the extent of her omission.

She has taken her mother to see the twins. It is their second birthday, Phyllida's mother is there too, exerting her grandmotherly rights. She has one child on each knee and is reading them a story, the book held between them while Kathryn joins in and Stuart sucks his thumb.

'Rabbit,' says Kathryn clearly. And 'Bang bang bang' when Rabbit bangs his drum.

Helen says to Phyllida, 'It's wonderful when the words begin to come. How are you getting on with potty training?'

'Kathryn's dry, though not at night. But Stuart has no idea.'

'Oh boys are harder. I remember . . .'

Rowena fidgets. It is one thing to be excluded, quite another to be invisible. But all her senses are concentrated elsewhere, in the kitchen where Henry is making tea. She wishes she had offered to help, in the past she would have but now, when every action is so laden, every action seems suspicious. It is an agony of excitement to contrive to be alone, when before they could have been alone without trying. Now she dare not go to him though every nerve is strained with the urgency of her desire. They have so little time, and she must be here, he there.

The door opens, he comes in carrying the tray and her eyes are already reaching for him, locking onto his own, careless of the others. He gives a tiny contradictory shake of the head. And Rowena thinks, how doesn't she guess? The very air is crackling with emotion. But Phyllida has other things on her mind.

'Put it here,' she says of the tray, 'I'll fetch the cake.' And she brings it in, iced half and half in blue and pink, each with its little candle, and Henry lights the candles and looks at Rowena, the flames flickering in his eyes, and the fire burns into her with the smell of wax and Kathryn's chuckles as she reaches towards the cake and presses into the icing the imprint of her tiny thumb.

Ben, Kathryn and the children were coming to Sunday tea, giving Phyllida the chance to bake while Rowena pushed the mower round the lawn and dusted down the garden chairs. They were kept in what had been the air-raid shelter, which was now converted to a store. Strings of onions hung from the hook that had carried her father's air-raid warden's helmet.

The mower was electric, the rotary kind which threw the cuttings in all directions, covering the newly turned beds with green. She found it exasperating but the mower was easy to use and all she could manage. She was clipping the edges and gathering the trimmings when Jake ran out of the back door and up the garden, gripping her round the waist.

Her heart lifted with pleasure at his cheeky face, the tufty rug of a new short haircut showing his ears which were clean and pink and rather large.

'Hi, Jake. That's a fine haircut.'

'Dad doesn't think so. And Grandma squeezed her mouth.'

Rowena laughed. That exactly summed up Phyllida's particular expression.

'Dad says I'm too young to be trendy, but I'm nine.'

'Quite old enough. Are you too trendy to help me clear up here?'

He seized the shears. 'I'll put these in the shed.' She followed more slowly, carrying the mower, and together they wound the flex and tipped the edgings onto the compost heap.

She put her hand on his shoulder as they walked back down the garden. 'How is your mother, Jake?'

He shrugged. 'Okay I suppose.'

'Good. And you're not worrying too much? She wouldn't want that.'

He looked at her wisely. 'Dad says there's no point worrying about something you can't do anything about.' Then uncertainty took over. 'But I think that's the best reason for worrying, don't you?'

She squeezed his shoulder. 'I expect he means that it doesn't really help. But I do know what you mean.'

Ben stepped into the garden. 'I'm to find the sun umbrella, Mother thinks Kathryn would be better in the shade.'

'And what does Kathryn think?'

'She doesn't seem to have much opinion about things these days.' He looked bleak.

'She's had a bad time. She'll soon be back to her old self.'

'At least you don't argue,' Jake interrupted. 'I like it.'

Ben met Rowena's eyes. 'Out of the mouths of babes and sucklings . . .' he murmured. 'Now, where's this umbrella?'

They settled Kathryn on a lounger in the shade.

'Are you still going to the caravan?' Rowena asked her. 'Your mother seems to think not.'

'She's right, I'm afraid. I don't really feel up to bunk beds and a chemical toilet. The children are disappointed of course. Maybe later in the year.'

'We could have them for you sometime, then Ben could

118

take you somewhere nice. That would be a better rest.'

She saw Phyllida looking at her with surprise. 'When Bob and I are married, of course, they can come to us.'

Pain coiled itself tightly round Rowena's heart, squeezing so she could hardly breathe. She closed her eyes. In all her imaginings she had overlooked the loss of Jake and Hannah. Suddenly it seemed the final straw. There was no end to it. She could not take any more.

'Are you all right, Rowena?' It was Ben, leaning towards her with a worried look.

'I've probably just overdone the gardening. A cup of tea's what's needed.'

'I'll put the kettle on.' Phyllida was looking at her curiously, with some alarm, yet unaware of the havoc she had wrought.

When she came back carrying the tray Rowena asked her, 'Will you stay here alone while I'm in Germany?'

'I hadn't really thought, dear.' She blushed. 'There's Bob of course. I mean we shall probably spend the time house-hunting. He's put his flat on the market.'

Rowena saw Kathryn reach for Ben's hand, and wondered. She had not seen them since Phyllida had announced her engagement. She wondered what they felt about the match, about her mother taking so bold a step. She knew a swift stab of jealousy. Whatever they felt, they would close ranks, support their mother, welcome Bob into the family. The children would learn a new allegiance.

She looked at Phyllida, remembering her own lack of charity when they were girls and feebly hoping to be dealt with better.

She and Betty were booked on the midday hovercraft from Dover. They arrived at half past ten and spent the time in the hoverport drinking coffee and browsing through the paperbacks. Rowena always found herself in a quandary about holiday reading. It was a time either for some serious reading or for a chance to try something light and undemanding – she never could quite decide. Accordingly, she always brought several library books of authors she admired, then at the last minute succumbed to thick and colourful blockbusters and family sagas which were discarded after the first few pages.

Now, tempted by the cover blurb and the Victorian costumes against a smoking mill, she bought a rags to riches novel which Betty professed to have been unable to put down.

'Then I won't be very good company,' Rowena laughed.

'Oh, I've brought the cards. We can practise our bidding.'

'And I've got travel Scrabble. I've always been fond of Scrabble.'

It was time to go. The hovercraft had crawled up out of the sea like some primeval monster, drenching the waiting cars with noise and spray then settling down onto its skirts like a snail. It was awesome, far more so than an aeroplane, which always arrived and departed in the distance. Betty started the car and they drove into its wet and oily bowels.

They spent the first night in a pension in northern France, then drove on through Luxembourg and Tricr, along the Moselle and down the Rhine, stopping twice along the way. Rowena would have liked to take a trip on the Rhine, but Betty had worked out an itinerary which didn't allow for that. She was proving to be a formidable travelling companion and their lines of responsibility were clearly marked. Rowena would talk them through, Betty would transport them; together, they would reach their destination near Freiburg on time and in one piece. Thus, at four o'clock on a rainy afternoon they drew up outside a balconied wooden guest house with a swinging sign showing a double bed, and claimed their room.

The beds were pushed together and hard, the mattresses set in wooden frames and supported on slats. Betty immediately pulled one away towards the window and dropped her bag of maps and guide books onto the crisp white duvet. 'That's better,' she stated. 'We asked for singles after all.'

'Only one pillow,' said Rowena, investigating. It was square and puffy. 'I suppose I could double it up.'

'Look in the wardrobe.' Betty's voice was brisk. And she was right. Gratefully Rowena took a second pillow and placed it on what was clearly to be her bed.

'We may as well unpack straight away.' Betty unzipped her bag. 'There's no chance of a walk in this rain.'

'I hope it doesn't go on like this.' Rowena pulled out shirts and light trousers and hung them tentatively in the wardrobe. She hoped she wouldn't take up too much space.

'Of course it won't. Think positive!' Betty set her walking boots on the floor of the wardrobe. 'This side is mine, is it? Not a lot of room – I hope you haven't brought too much.'

There were ten people in the small dining room, seated at polished wooden tables on carved wooden chairs with hearts cut out of the backs.

'A bit kitsch,' Betty remarked, unnecessarily loudly, Rowena thought. 'It looks like the gingerbread house.'

'I suppose it's what people expect.' Rowena rather liked it. It was what one came abroad for. Outside the rain had stopped and the doors to the balcony had been thrown open. The evening light was catching the tops of the hills and a profusion of geraniums tumbling off the balcony were a dazzling red in contrast to the green. She wanted to be content, was ready to be impressed, informed, persuaded by this new country. But Betty, looking at the menu, was saying, 'Well they certainly make no concessions on the menu. I hope your German is up to this.'

She glanced down. The writing was curly and continental, unlike the neat print of her text book and the phrase book in her handbag. But she had a sense of being on trial. How she deported herself now would set the tenor of the next ten days.

'I'm afraid,' she said at length, 'we'll just have to take pot luck and see what comes.'

Betty's look was one of disappointed accusation. 'Really! How long have you been doing your classes?'

Rowena found herself suppressing a sigh. After all, had this been such a good idea? She seemed to spend a lot of her time apologising, and at times even found herself wishing for

Phyllida's more compliant companionship. She thought wistfully of Joyce and Robert, attending on the birth of their grandchild, and wished with all her heart that they were here too.

Next morning the sun was sparkling on the geraniums as they left the hotel behind them and set out along the forest path outside the village. Betty carried a map in a plastic folder to which a compass was attached. Rowena found it hard to believe they would need the compass but had no doubt that should they do so, Betty would be able to cope. Indeed, Betty told her as they strode along that in her younger days she had been an orienteer, and went on to explain in detail the sport about which Rowena was ashamed to admit she knew nothing. It all sounded very admirable and character forming. Betty, her husband and children had all participated. Uncharitably, Rowena wondered whether the others would have been given much choice.

But she found her a surprisingly interesting companion, able to point out flora and fauna and fully appreciative of the scenery through which they passed. She was even generous about rests, and produced from her knapsack a bottle of fruit juice purchased at the bar and two bars of fruit and nut chocolate, just when Rowena thought she could go no further. They stopped frequently to take photographs of sun slanting through the pines, tiny wild strawberries ripening beside the path and a deer, standing in an open meadow against a backdrop of tree-clad hills.

Rowena was carrying the packed lunch – cold sausage, hard boiled eggs, rubbery cheese and fruit. 'Just like breakfast,' Betty remarked. 'What was it called? Froostick?'

'*Frühstück*. I rather like the meal. A change from our ubiquitous "full English breakfast".'

Betty said nothing, biting into an apple.

'We seem to be the only English at the hotel,' said Rowena. 'I'm glad about that.'

Betty turned to her. 'Why? Don't you like the Brits?'

'Not abroad, particularly. I don't think we show up especially

122

well. But apart from that, it rather destroys the atmosphere don't you think?'

'Possibly.' Betty thrust her apple core under a clump of heather and wiped her fingers on a paper napkin. 'Well, in that case you'll have to make do with me for company,' she said.

But in the event, she was wrong.

On their third day at the hotel they were approached by new arrivals, a couple from England who introduced themselves as Fay and Geoffrey. He was a solicitor from the Midlands, a keen birdwatcher. Rowena found their company a relief from undiluted doses of Betty. To her delight, Fay and Geoffrey turned out to be bridge players and after dinner, they took to playing a hand or two in the lounge. True, in the privacy of their room, Betty tended to be scathing about their play, but Rowena could cope with that. She was grateful that Betty had somebody else to criticise.

Then, the day before they were due to leave, there was a most distressing occurrence. On arriving back from their walk, they saw an ambulance drawing away from the hotel. Geoffrey, it seemed, had collapsed and died. This incredible fact was confirmed by Fay, distraught in the hotel lobby being comforted by the proprietor's wife, who gladly handed her over to Betty and Rowena. They took her to her room and brought her brandy. Betty, brusque and practical as ever, asked Fay what she was going to do.

'Really,' demurred Rowena. 'As if she knows that, yet. There'll be formalities, things to see to.' She turned to Fay who was sitting with her head bowed, staring dully at her brandy glass. 'Have you anyone who can fly out and help you? Children, perhaps?'

Fay shook her head dumbly. She hadn't begun to cry. Now she cleared her throat and said with difficulty, 'Actually, it's more complicated than you may suppose. Geoffrey isn't — wasn't — my husband. I'm married to someone else — and so is he. So you see, it's all a ghastly mess.'

Rowena had to agree that it was. There didn't seem a lot to say or do, yet she felt guilty that they were going. They left Fay telephoning England, and went away to pack.

They didn't see her again, but driving away from the hotel the next day Rowena said with feeling, 'I feel so sorry for Fay. Not only has she lost Geoffrey, but she also has to face all the exposure. I wonder if her husband will stand by her.'

'I feel sorrier for Geoffrey's wife,' said Betty brusquely. 'Fay's got what's coming to her. I've no time for such carrying on.'

'No,' agreed Rowena meekly. 'But it seems excessive, that Geoffrey had to die!'

They come down the steps of the hotel hand in hand, for no one can see them here, on the banks of the River Spey where Henry has hired a half rod for a week in March.

A steady drizzle is falling, the russet bracken sodden beneath their feet, yet spring is in the air somewhere, birds are singing and catkins hang on the trees. Rowena's heart is bursting with its own spring as she marches at Henry's side, matching her stride to his.

Suddenly he says, without warning, 'I have a dreadful secret, something I've never told you.'

She looks at him sharply, but he is smiling.

'The thing is, Phyllida has always been so scathing I've become rather ashamed.'

She waits for him to continue, but he doesn't. At last, laughing, she says, 'Well you've got to tell me now. I think I can take it.'

'The thing is,' he says slowly, 'I collect stamps.'

She stops in her tracks, laughter exploding. 'Really? That's unforgivable. I think you'll have to go!'

But he is looking shamefaced, like a little boy. She hugs him. 'Seriously, what is there to be ashamed of? What can Phyllida be thinking of?'

'She thinks it's childish. I think she would have thrown them all away if I hadn't convinced her how valuable some of them are. There are some from my father's collection, and he started me off when I was about twelve. I never thought I'd have to apologise for it, I'm sure he didn't.'

He looks genuinely upset. 'Oh darling,' she says, kissing him. 'You don't have to apologise to me. I want to know everything about you.'

'Well, since this is confession time, I can't play cricket. I have always been scared of the ball, since I was hit in the face at school!'

'Then I'm not surprised. Anyway, you play tennis. And squash. I think that's wonderful.'

'And I can't sing in tune.'

'Neither can I. We were obviously meant for each other!'

And they embrace, and kiss each other, lost in an ecstasy of happiness.

When finally they move on she asks him, 'Did you mind going to boarding school?'

'Oh yes, very much so at first. I was only eight. I can still remember watching my parents drive away. I didn't think I'd ever survive. But I did. One does, you know. It got better when I made a friend. Stephen. We're still friends now.' He pauses, then continues, 'Actually, I've told him about you. Do you mind?'

She feels a surge of pleasure. She — their love — had been acknowledged, made real. She denies fervently that she minds. In a wild, sudden excitement she says, 'Let's run. Catch me!' And she flies off across the sheep-cropped turf, away from him, knowing that he will follow, follow her to the ends of the earth, and they are laughing, and nowhere and nobody else exists.

Later, she sits alone on the river bank while Henry and the ghillie, up to their thighs in the rich brown water, discuss flies and casts and the whereabouts of the salmon, and she watches, revelling in him, content to wait. It is enough to be with him, pretending to be his wife. Waiting for them is the high-ceilinged room where thick curtains keep out the draught and heavy radiators creak and groan with heat. Soon, they will climb the stairs, holding hands, and he will open her waterproof and slip it off. She will step out of her boots, undo her heavy cardigan and place his cold hands against her breasts with a moan. They will not wait for night, will not even close the curtains, but fall together onto the accommodating bed.

She closes her eyes with a shudder of desire. Guilt stands not a chance.

EIGHT

When Rowena arrived back from Germany, Bob's Jaguar was parked on the drive and Phyllida was waiting for her at the door, her face a twist of worry.

'Thank goodness, Ro. There's been a call from Matron.'

'Let me get inside the door.'

Bob appeared and took her cases. Phyllida shut the door.

'It's your mother.'

'Obviously.' Rowena felt strangely philosophical. The worst could be that she was dead, and was that really so very bad? Her mother wouldn't be arguing, she was sure.

Bob took her arm gently. 'She's slipping away, my dear. They don't think it will be very long. We were hoping you'd make it in time.'

In time? In time for what? She felt a panicky obligation to be there at the end, to attend again at death's visitation, to experience that incomprehensible withdrawing of presence. To know again the absence that was in its way more deeply felt, ineluctable, impossible to ignore.

'Somebody died at our hotel,' she said, inconsequentially. But it wasn't of that death that she was thinking.

It is several years since her parents have had a Christmas tree but this year is special because both Mark and Rowena have come home. Her father has climbed into the loft and brought down the box of decorations and Mark has arrived with fairy lights from New York, and richly packaged chocolates and lavish parcels with gilded bows. He has come alone, to try and make amends.

Rowena kneels on the floor, passing the fragile baubles to Mark who hands them to their father who is on a chair, reaching for the top. It is a very tall tree, it touches the ceiling of the lounge, there is no room for the fairy. Rowena unwraps her nonetheless, smoothing the crumpled net of her dress, opening up her wings. The fairy stares at her over the years from painted celluloid eyes.

'Tinsel,' says Mark, stooping to gather the shiny strands. 'And that little clown, I remember him, I made him at school, and you made crackers, where are the crackers, we must have the crackers.' He is generating excitement to hide the fact that his parents seem to be nervous, treating him like a stranger, somebody with a sordid secret. He is missing Lawrence who will be clearing snow in Maine with his brother, who has accepted Mark as one of the family.

If it wasn't for Rowena, he would be wishing he hadn't come.

She gets a tactile pleasure from the tinsel's silky strands, running them between her fingers thoughtfully. She can hear her mother in the kitchen, smell the mince pies in the oven, the simmering spiciness of the wine they will drink with them.

She will never forget the smell of the wine, it goes into her memory bank along with corned beef pie and the wax of melted candles. For there is a brief cry from above and, glancing up, she sees her father's face contorted, surprised and pained and fearful, watches his hand go to his chest, sees his knees bend and Mark leap unsuccessfully to support him. Together, they crumple to the ground. She has to roll away to avoid being crushed, and they land on the cardboard box, on the remaining baubles which splinter into shining shards, with tiny glassy sounds. And the tinsel mingles with her father's hair.

His dead dead hair.

She is weeping and weeping, as her mother is, each of them supported by Mark in a dark suit of his father's, standing at the graveside at the church set in the fields, overlooking the house where he lived. Where they all lived, once upon a time.

Phyllida is there of course, in a black fur coat and a wide brimmed hat with a purple flower. She is wishing she had removed the flower. It looks too much like a wedding hat. She is holding Henry's arm, grieving both for the father she once lost and the only one she can really remember.

The wind blows icy round their legs though there is no warmth now to rob, they are all deathly cold, Mark, Helen and Rowena. They think they will never be warm again.

Rowena lifts her eyes and through her tears sees Henry, with Phyllida on his arm. His hand is on hers, but his eyes are on Rowena, full of a desperate pity. And she nearly chokes with anger, with the hopelessness of it all, for that is where she should be, and if it wasn't for Mark's supporting arm she would leap across the open grave, and into Henry's arms for ever.

'Do you think you should ring Mark? He'll want to come I'm sure.' It was Phyllida, plying her with coffee, being helpful, focusing her thoughts.

'I'll let him know. But he said his goodbye, last time.'

'You'd like him here, though.'

'Yes. But it must be up to him.'

But there was no answer from Mark's number in New York.

Rowena left her bags unopened and drove to Adelaide House where they gave her an unwanted cup of tea and sat her by her mother's bed. The other occupant of the room had mercifully been moved away.

'You can stay if you like,' said the nurse, indicating the empty bed. 'There's nothing we can do, and no point in moving her into hospital. If she woke, she would only be confused.'

'Do you think she's likely to wake?'

The nurse shook her head. 'I think she's too far gone. She's very peaceful. It's the best possible way to go.'

Better than the hand on the heart, the last desperate tumble from life. The ambulance in a foreign land . . .

'I'll stay,' said Rowena. 'But perhaps after all I could have more tea. And a sandwich? I've just driven back from Germany.'

Helen's breath was rattling in her throat. The death rattle, thought Rowena, how aptly named. And how tortured it sounded, how impossible to sustain. Yet it went on, hour after hour. Like a gyroscope turning of its own volition, so life continued from habit, to no purpose, bound by an agenda of its own.

She found herself kneeling by the bed. She had a sudden desperate longing to be a child again. This was her last chance, her absolutely last chance. After this she would be grown-up, finally, and it would be her turn next. She remembered her mother's hand on her head when she had measles, scarlet fever, earache; pouring warm oil, pressing hot towels, smoothing her forehead. She remembered the stories and the songs, but mainly the hand upon her head.

She reached beneath the blankets and pulled out her mother's hand, very gently for fear she would waken her for she did not, after all, want to look into those eyes again, it would be too fearful, too shocking after all this time. The hand was warm. She rested her head on the bed and laid the hand upon it, pressing it down with her own, feeling warm tears spill out between her closed lids.

'Mummy,' she heard herself, whimpering like a child. 'Oh Mummy . . .'

She began to sob uncontrollably, all the losses, all the pain, released in a tidal wave of childish grieving. After a while, across the sobs, she heard a voice.

Phyllida's voice. 'Oh Ro, don't upset yourself so. Get up, do. You'll disturb your mother.'

She looked up, spite and fury driving away the tears.

'Go away, Phyllida,' she hissed, with hatred in her voice. 'Go away at once. She's *my* mother, not yours. Why don't you ever leave me alone?'

* * *

Helen took two more days to die and each night Rowena prayed it would be the last, but still the rattling breaths went on.

'She's not ready to go,' said the doctor. 'She'll choose her own good time. Why don't you go home and get some rest?'

'I've waited this long, I don't want to miss it now,' she said, as if it were a celestial happening, a royal occasion, something she had queued for hours to see. She telephoned Mark again from the telephone in the hall, and this time he was home.

'It's not worth coming now, there can't be long to go.'

'Can I speak to her?'

'Mark, she's too far gone for that.'

'Let me speak to her anyway.' She heard panic rising in his voice, the panic of helplessness, of absence.

A divine spark of inspiration prompted her to lie. 'I'll put the receiver on the pillow,' she told him, holding the phone away from herself, against the wall of the cubicle. She didn't want to hear, the words were not meant for her. But as she stood she wept and a visitor passing by looked at her curiously and at the telephone talking, talking, to nobody.

It was like a powerhouse shutting down, Rowena thought, this slipping away of the accumulation of experience, of knowledge, of function and memory – the war, the sum of two and two, the recipe for pastry. The French for love. Love itself. Herself, Mark, her father. There was just one thing Helen had never known: Henry.

She stroked the dry hair, feeling the warmth beneath. Her mother was still there, somewhere. The doctor had told her to talk to her, in case she could hear. 'I'm here, don't be frightened. It's going to be all right.' She heard her voice; reasonable, kindly, loving, reassuring – but how could she know, how did any of them know?

When it came, it was quick and painless. The breathing paused, wavered, continued once or twice, paused again, then continued. Rowena was holding her hand. A nurse was

131

holding Rowena's other, squeezing it tight. Rowena was grateful for that. The next pause was the last. Rowena found she was holding her own breath, waiting, waiting, half willing, half dreading the dreadful rattle. When it didn't come she sat back, laughing and crying with relief.

'It's over. Oh God, it's over. I'm so pleased I was here. So pleased.' And she knew a wild and crazy joy that she had coped, that her mother had not died alone, that she had seen it through until the bitter end.

Her mother's will asked for a cremation, and for her ashes to be scattered in the churchyard near her husband's grave. Rowena went alone into the churchyard on a mild June evening. There were new rules now, the grass was closely mown and new graves could not have kerbs, which got in the way of the mower. Her father's had a kerb, and a fitted vase with holes in the top which she filled with water and into which she fitted roses from the garden, the garden he had created with her mother. She was soothed by the niceness of the continuity. She knelt there for a while, wishing she could pray, unaware that in her silent communion she was praying as fervently as any religious. Then she opened the casket and tilted it over the grave, scattering the ashes tenderly among the roses and into the gravel, whence it would wash down and down to mingle with the remains of her father. She rose, upended the vessel and patted it lightly, dusting the summer grass.

'Goodbye, darling,' she cried out loud in an ecstasy of sentiment. Her voice hung unanswered in the twittering evening dusk. Then she turned on her heel and walked back down through the fields.

Phyllida wept that night as she hadn't wept at the funeral.

'It didn't seem to be my place,' she explained quietly. She had been skirting round Rowena nervously since her outburst by the bedside.

'But I was very fond of Helen. She did a lot for me when I was young.'

Rowena nodded. 'She loved you too, Phyllida. She knew how you missed your father.'

'And if it hadn't been for Helen I wouldn't have married Henry.'

Rowena narrowed her eyes. 'How so?'

'I didn't think I was good enough for him. He was so much cleverer than me. But she persuaded me that he loved me, that brains weren't everything, that I could make him happy.'

Rowena said nothing but looked at her thoughtfully, re-assessing her mother's influence on her own life. If it hadn't been for Helen, perhaps . . . but then, she would never have met Henry. Impossible, now, to be sorry that she had.

They are sprawled on the sagging sofa in Rowena's flat, doing *The Times* crossword.

'Dictator chap, an admirer of Marianne. Beginning with F.'

Rowena chews the pen thoughtfully. 'Franco was a dictator.'

'Then there's a P. Francophil would fit.'

'Phil would be the chap. But what's it got to do with Marianne?'

'She's French, I suppose. An admirer of the French – Francophil.'

'So we settle for that?' He nods and she writes it in.

'Would you call yourself a Francophil?' Henry asks.

'Up to a point. France was the first foreign country I visited and I think that counts for a lot. I've only been a couple of times since but I like the food, and I like speaking French.'

He looks at her hungrily. 'I wish we could go together. I would like to walk with you on the banks of the Seine with the other lovers.'

'Oh Henry. And we have to be content with my flat in Andover!'

'Phyllida won't come to France. She says the food would upset the children, but really it's her. She's so unadventurous. I suggested camping, when we could do all our own food, but she says she couldn't sleep in a tent. Honestly, Ro, sometimes . . .'

He brushes his hands over his face in bewilderment, and when he removes them his expression is desolate. 'This is what I hate,' he bursts out angrily. 'This fault finding, this criticism, it's so disloyal. She does her best.' He leans towards her, his face desperate. 'I get so angry, and feel so guilty, and I know that ultimately I can't hurt her. Please try and understand.'

She says she does, but increasingly she doesn't. His guilt, and her dissatisfaction, are beginning to burrow like worms through the self-justification of their love. In panic she says, 'We ought to eat, you'll have to leave soon.'

He pulls her to him. 'Not yet, I need you again.' Afterwards he asks, hopelessly, 'Why did I ever marry her, Ro? But then, if I hadn't, I would never have met you.'

Bob and Phyllida had found a house.

'It's pretty, Ro. You'll love it. Quite small but it has a utility room, and a connecting door into the garage.' She was twittering with excitement, already arranging the rooms. 'Of course I got rid of so much stuff when I came here, we'll have to start again, Bob's isn't up to much. Well, you know, not my taste. It would be nice to start afresh. I do like nice things.'

'And what about the flat? Are you any nearer selling?'

Phyllida looked vague. 'I think a few people have looked round.'

'You can't do much until you do,' said Rowena sensibly. 'It would be best not to build up your hopes too much.'

'Oh Ro. Why are you always so . . . realistic?'

'I suppose,' said Rowena pointedly, 'because I've always had to be.'

She is driving towards Bournemouth, singing. The Beatles have taken over from Elvis, England is swinging, Carnaby Street, Union Jacks and thighs are coming into fashion.

They have three days, the first for months. Phyllida is taking the twins to see her mother, Henry has invented a conference, it is half-term and she is free. She swings into the hotel car park and looks for the Sunbeam, but it isn't there.

There is a message for her in reception; he cannot come, she mustn't ring, he will explain everything later.

She goes back to the car, dragging the leaden weight of her disappointment, her humiliation, her anger.

'This can't go on,' she tells herself. 'Yet how can it ever end?'

'It's the twins,' he tells her. 'They have chicken pox. Phyllida couldn't cope. I couldn't leave her.'

'Poor Phyllida.' Her voice is bitter. She begins to cry, great useless ugly gulps and gasps into the telephone. 'Poor you. Poor us! I cannot handle this.'

'Come and see us. I'll suggest to Phyllida that she asks you down. It will cheer her up.'

And she agrees, and waits for the invitation, waiting like a beggar for crumbs from the rich man's table.

The jigsaw pieces are spread out on the floor and Stuart is collecting the edges.

'You've missed a piece,' says Kathryn. At eight she is already a bossy little girl.

'Never mind, why don't you help him?' Rowena speaks soothingly, leaning down from the sofa to select some pieces of sky.

Henry is in the armchair, reading the Sunday paper. He looks depressed, has told her he is depressed, and she longs above everything to comfort him, but it is not her place, she has no right, no rights at all. From the kitchen comes the smell of beef, over-cooked cabbage and apple pie. Phyllida can be heard there, clattering at the sink. She should go and offer to help but she cannot move, cannot leave the room while he is there.

'Stop scratching, Stuart,' she says, seeing him reaching towards a scab. 'It will leave a scar.' He comes and leans against her knee but she does not embrace him, although he is Henry's flesh and blood.

Or perhaps because he is just that, and she fears she will crush him to her heart.

135

Henry is watching her over the paper. His eyes are a molten mix of love and pain.

'This just goes on and on,' he says, and his voice is full of wonder and a dreadful, hopeless acceptance.

They take the children out for a walk in the early winter dark. There are streetlamps in the lane; Guildford is encroaching despite Phyllida's objections. The children run ahead, enjoying the fresh cold air, and the three of them follow behind, their shadows stretching ahead of them as they pass the lights. And as their shadows fall behind he takes her hand and they watch, breathless, until their heads appear beneath their feet and then their hands part – together, apart, together, apart, a rhythmic conjunction that makes her want to laugh out loud at their audacity. And Phyllida is talking about a planning application in an adjoining field and how they must protest to the local council, it is the beginning of the end as far as The Maltings is concerned, the end of life as she knows it, with green fields lapping at her gate. She doesn't want to go back to suburbia, there is a snobbish exclusivity in having rubber boots by the back door and muddy lanes to walk them along.

She had always known he would never leave Phyllida. It had been agreed, right from the beginning.

'It's not her fault that she's the way she is. I never should have married her, given her the twins. I care for her, in a way. I cannot leave her just because I'm bored! Oh darling, I am bored, bored, bored! And I cannot live without you. But I cannot leave her either.'

She used to say, 'Of course you can't. And I couldn't do that to Phyllida. She's supposed to be my friend.'

But now she is beginning to hate her. She dreams of them all at night, she and Henry running, running, trying to be alone and always, always, there is Phyllida catching up, seeking them out, her innocent presence a silent castigation. How could you, Ro?

And she begins to think, very easily.

*   *   *

With a final twirl and twist, *Come Dancing* ended and Bob pressed the remote control to Off. Phyllida gave a sigh of satisfaction and settled closer into his arms.

'I'd love to be able to dance like that. Wouldn't you?'

'Believe me, precious, that's how it seems to me when I get you on the floor.'

She giggled coyly. 'Oh you! I bet you say that to all the girls.'

'Seriously though.' His voice was thick. 'I wish I could get you on the floor right now.'

'Bob!' She feigned disapproval though she was excited. She liked the way his hand was searching her body, it made her feel young and fierce. She had never expected to feel like that again.

His breath was hot on her face, his tongue insinuating between her lips. She parted them eagerly, at the same time listening to the sounds from the dining room where Rowena was playing bridge. When he began to unbutton her blouse she said, 'No, Bob. Not here.'

'Well where? How long is it going to be?'

'Not long. We'll be married soon.'

'But in the Cotswolds . . . you enjoyed it, didn't you? I mean I'm not past it, am I?'

She looked at him wickedly. 'No, Bob, far from it. Let's just say that in Stow-on-the-Wold you sort of sneaked up on me. Call me old-fashioned, but I believe there's a right way of doing these things. And the right way is to be your wife.'

She heard the dining room door open. Rowena was going into the kitchen for the trolley.

'I expect you'd like your hot drink now,' Phyllida said, firmly putting his hand aside. She patted her hair and buttoned her blouse. She really felt quite trembly and wondered if Rowena would notice.

She could hear the others in the dining room as she passed through the hall. There was the usual inquest. 'I thought you were bluffing with that call.' 'I felt certain that with the ace and the queen . . .' 'And then, when you trumped clubs on the first hand!'

Rowena was pouring water onto the coffee. 'All right, dear?' she asked for no particular reason, without looking up.

'I'm fine. I've just come to make our chocolate.'

'Well there's plenty of milk. I got extra.' She poured hot milk into a jug and swirled the saucepan under the tap. 'Would you like a piece of fruit cake?'

'No thank you, dear.'

'Betty's brought some holiday photos. I'll keep them to show you. There's one of Fay and Geoffrey, it's really rather upsetting.'

Phyllida was scouring the pan prior to filling it with milk. 'I don't approve, you know that, Ro. But I suppose it was rather a dreadful way to be found out.'

'It was a dreadful way to be parted! That poor woman.'

'His poor wife!'

And they glared at each other fiercely, miles apart as always, on opposite sides of the fence.

At the end of June, surprisingly, a buyer was found for Bob's flat.

'An insurance company. They want it for housing new staff while they find somewhere permanent. Isn't that a stroke of luck?'

'Absolutely, in today's market. So you'll be making plans.'

Rowena attempted to smother the panic, the resentment, the renewed sense of deprivation. Phyllida must not know how she felt. Not because it would spoil her happiness, but because Rowena had her pride.

'We must go out and choose your dress. When do you think the wedding will be?'

'Early August, we thought. And I want Hannah to be a bridesmaid. Do you think that's silly, in a registry office? It seems a charming idea, to have one's grandchild.'

'It's original, certainly. But I can't see her in pink frills.' She remembered vividly her own discomfiture. 'Hannah isn't a frilly child.'

'Isn't she?' Phyllida looked at her blankly. 'Will you help

138

me, Ro? Kathryn doesn't seem to be up to shopping trips.' She added, 'Though she did seem to rule out pink too.'

'Right, let's go on Saturday. We'll take Hannah with us.'

'Jake will want to come too.'

'Well he can't,' said Rowena firmly. 'Just tell him it's an all girls' day.'

But Jake was in the car when Kathryn delivered Hannah, looking sulkily out of the window. Kathryn looked pale and stark when she handed Hannah in at the door. 'I won't stop, Jake is being a pain. I promised to take him swimming.'

'Darling, you're not up to swimming. Couldn't Ben . . . ?'

'I won't go in the water. Ben's putting up the bean poles. A bit late, the beans are flopping over for lack of something to climb. But everything's disorganised this year.'

Hannah was tugging at Rowena's hand. 'Can I have ice cream for lunch?'

Rowena smiled. 'Who said anything about lunch?'

'Mummy. She said we'd be going out to lunch. Jake's cross about that.'

'Poor Jake.'

Phyllida said when they had gone, 'Bob and I will take Jake one day, you tell him that.'

Hannah tilted her head appraisingly. 'Can I come too? I've never had lunch with Bob.'

'We'll see. And you'll have to learn to call him Grandad, when we're married.'

They got into Rowena's car. Hannah leaned forward, holding onto the front seats. 'Where will you live, Rowena, when Grandma marries Bob?'

'I'll stay here of course. This is my house.'

'On your own?' Rowena could see her face in the mirror. The expression was wondering and pained. She turned round.

'Yes, but I'm used to it. Now sit back and do up the belt.'

Phyllida slid in beside her, pulling the seatbelt wide over her plump form.

Rowena thought suddenly, there won't be many more times

like this. I shall have to get used to driving alone again with only the radio for company.

It will be like it always was.

Her new car, a Hillman Imp, has a tape player and she is listening to Beethoven's violin concerto as she drives the Hampshire lanes. The plaintive lift and slide accompanies the rise and fall of her emotions; the meld of joy and dread, at seeing him again, at what they will say to each other. Over the years she has learned that the greater the highs, the lower the equivalent lows. The brighter the light, the deeper the shadow it casts. She senses that the shadows are growing, unbalancing the light.

There is a house, owned by the National Trust, where they sometimes meet, and walk in the grounds, and talk. Sometimes, riskily, they make love in the deepest part of the woods, where anyone could find them but no one ever has.

They sit, today, beside the lake. It is high summer. The trees are heavy with leaf, casting solid shadows on the sheep cropped turf. Across the lake the house, white and Palladian, stares back from blank windows. They have never been inside.

Henry says, 'Somehow it gets harder, not easier, to deceive. The more one gets away with it, the more trusting she is – the worse it is.'

'Yes,' she whispers, for after nearly six years, this is true.

After a while she says, 'It worries me that the guilt is outweighing the pleasure. After all, if this doesn't make us happy, whatever is the point?'

'The point is, my darling, that I can't do without you.'

'Nor I you. But you can't leave Phyllida. Or the twins. They need you.'

'More than we need each other?'

'No. But they have their rights. Though it kills me to have to say it.'

'And we don't?' he asks, and she thinks, I could persuade him, I could – but then, would I love him the less? Is it for his loyalty and his courage that I love him most?

140

Their eyes meet across the bleak vault of the future and they think, this will have to end — but not yet. Not yet . . .

She raises her hand and removes his glasses. His eyes are grave, urgent, questioning. She slides her hand behind his head and kisses him fiercely, desperately, on the lips.

The play is *The Cherry Orchard* and the curtain has just fallen on the sound of the axes destroying the trees.

Rowena sits back with a sigh of satisfaction. 'I love Chekhov. He really knows how to work on the emotions.'

Henry smiles. 'Well now we've seen them all. How long I must have known you.'

She narrows her eyes. No more Chekhov. No more . . . ?

They walk arm in arm down Villiers Street and onto the Embankment. Lights are strung along the river, reflected in the dark water. The bridges throw skeins of light from bank to bank, the traffic roars behind them as they lean over the wall and a train rumbles over Hungerford Bridge.

Henry says, 'I worry that Phyllida may be wondering. It makes me feel so fearful, it would finish her if she knew . . .'

Ice settles around her heart. She says nothing, and waits.

'Last night, I wanted to kiss her feet and tell her everything. It would be easier to expunge my guilt with her sorrow. To beg her forgiveness for what I had to do.'

She whispers. 'We had no choice. And now we have no choice. Do we?'

She withdraws her hand from his and looks at him, at his dear face, the fall of his hair, his glasses reflecting the lights and shielding the look in his eyes.

'What will we do?'

And he answers, 'What we have to do.'

They walk in silence, thinking of what they have to do.

He helps her into the train, solicitously, like an invalid. They are very gentle with each other. He waits on the platform, she leaning from the door, watching litter blowing round his feet like dead leaves, the leaves of autumn's dying fall.

The whistle blows and they kiss, without believing that it is for the last time, and the train moves away and they go their separate ways.

Rowena was wondering whether she would hear from Derek Stadden again when he rang and invited her to the theatre.

'You like Chekhov, don't you? There's a production of *Uncle Vanya* at the Fairfield Hall.'

It had been so long, yet still her heart could both lift and sink. She had never seen Chekhov since Henry.

'I'd like that, Derek. Will you have supper here first?'

'No. Let's eat there. I want it to be a treat.'

'Oh?' She was curious, but decided she could use a treat. She would buy a new dress, perhaps something that would do for Phyllida's wedding.

Phyllida herself had chosen powder blue, a swathed and pleated silk that treated her figure kindly. Rowena had to admit that it suited her. Bob would be delighted with his bride.

For Hannah they had found a navy dress she could wear afterwards. Phyllida had needed persuading over the colour and had only relented when a pinafore was found, embroidered with pale blue forget-me-nots, and a ring of forget-me-nots for her hair. Hannah herself was enchanted, swirling this way and that in front of the mirror in an excess of female vanity. Rowena decided to suggest to Kathryn that they put her hair up into a bun.

She went back into Croydon and found herself a silk two-piece in rusty gold and, for the wedding, a black hat which had a severity that pleased her. If it was funereal then so be it. She wasn't sure that she would be rejoicing.

'You're looking very nice,' Derek told her when she opened the door wearing the two-piece. 'I'm very flattered.'

'Well you said it would be a treat.' Briefly she wondered what he had in mind. She had been to the hairdresser, her hair had been trimmed and smoothed and as she picked up her handbag she caught sight of herself in the hall mirror. She was pleased with what she saw.

The play was well done, by a national touring company

which visited Croydon once a year. But Rowena found her attention straying, her mind casting wistfully back over the years, replacing Derek with Henry, the uncertain atmosphere of the evening with the piquancy of the past. The previously held wish that perhaps Derek would take her hand was replaced with a dread that he would. She was not sure whether she could cope; she would surely take his and press it to her lips and let hot tears fall through his fingers.

It was a relief to be out of the stuffy darkness and in the bustle of the restaurant serving late-night suppers. Now she was pleased to have him take her arm, to notice for the first time that he was wearing an unaccustomed dark suit and that his grey hair had been cut. A zest of anticipation replaced her melancholy and she allowed him to order her a gin and tonic, though she had always disliked gin.

'I've still to hear about your holiday,' he said, inviting elaboration, which she gave, describing eloquently the glories of the scenery, the charm of the carved and painted houses, the brilliance of the flowers.

'And your German stood up well?'

'Adequately. We always seemed to get what we wanted though Betty wasn't over-impressed.'

'And how did you find the food? If I remember it's fairly substantial and stolid.'

'That's right,' she laughed. 'Except the cream, which is watery and not a patch on ours.'

'And would you like to go again?'

She slid her eyes away, momentarily disconcerted. She wondered wildly if he was inviting her to go with him. Reason prevailed when he went on with, 'I think you're very adventurous. I seem to have lost the taste for foreign travel.'

'Oh?' She was surprised. 'Then why the German classes?'

'Just a mental exercise. I like the language, and the literature. It would be nice to read it in the original German. But I doubt I'll ever reach that standard now.'

'There's plenty of time,' she said encouragingly. 'You'll be coming back to the class in October?'

'That's just it.' And now he did reach out and take her hand, as if understanding the enormity of what he was saying. 'You see, I'm going away. To Wales. I've decided to go and live near my daughter.'

She was stunned. From a distance she felt the warmth of his hand, a warmth so fancifully imagined, granted now so late, too late ... She felt herself pulling away, lowering her hand to her lap where her napkin lay smooth and pristine like virgin sheets.

'I see.'

'Margaret's been asking me to go for quite a while. I suppose it was silly, but I was hanging on to my independence. Now that seems worth nothing compared with seeing more of my grandchildren. And if anything should happen, well, she'd be on hand.' He looked at her pleadingly, suddenly looking older, imperceptibly shifted a notch from potential lover to dependent grandfather. 'You don't think it silly of me do you? I mean I've lived here for over forty years. I have friends, interests. I don't want to feel I'm just throwing them all away.'

She wondered if he included her. 'I think,' she said carefully, holding her hands tightly together in her lap, 'that as we get older our priorities change. There's a lot to be said for security, for being with those we love.'

But who is there for me? From whence cometh my own help, the comfort of my own old age?

'I shall miss you at the classes,' she said inadequately. 'But I'm sure you've made the right decision.'

She rings him from the telephone box in the empty village street.

'I had to come. Will you meet me?'

He hesitates, confirming everything that had been understood between them, that last time was the last time.

'Why have you come?' he asks.

'Because I had to.'

And he tells her, 'I'll be there.'

She leaves her car on the daisy-strewn grass of the verge

144

and climbs a stile into a field overlooking the house. It is held in its warm hollow in a daze of afternoon, silent and apparently deserted. The summer seems only now to have matured, autumn held at bay. She sits on the grass, waiting with a futile hope.

She knows the sound of his car approaching along the lane, hears his step flattening the grass between them and looks round with a joy that hurts and a pain that is almost sweet.

She says, 'I'm sorry.'

'Don't be.' He lays a hand against her cheek and she jumps up, afraid that tears will spoil it.

'I thought we could go inside the house. We never have.'

He nods, and walks beside her across the field. She thrusts her hands deep into the pockets of her skirt to keep from holding him.

There is a man inside the hall. He sells them two tickets and a guide book. 'You'll have the place to yourselves. But we close in an hour.'

And as if in confirmation a clock at the foot of the wide curving staircase strikes four. The call is taken up by other clocks in other rooms – an echoing, meaningful chorus. When next they mark the hour, their time will be over.

Henry scans the guide book quickly. He says, 'We go this way,' and they enter the Tapestry Room, where the windows are shaded from the sun. In a voice not quite his own he reads, 'Flanking the fireplace, a pair of Charles II English stools of ebonised gilt decoration, covered in crimson goffering.'

'Well, they look dreadfully uncomfortable. There's a lot to be said for Parker-Knoll!'

And he smiles in gratitude that she can be trivial.

They find the sun again in the Drawing Room, flooding in across the lake and driving a thousand stars from the chandelier. Gilt-framed faces from the past stare down at them from damask walls.

'That one doesn't approve of us,' says Henry of a stern-faced puritan between gilded mirrors. 'He must know.'

'But what is there to know?' she asks. 'There's nothing now.'

And around the house in the empty rooms clocks call the quarter hour.

She asks, brightly, 'How is Phyllida? And the children?'

'She's well. And Stuart's learning the violin. You can imagine how awful that is! And you, Rowena?' He leans towards her anxiously. 'How are you?'

'I'm coping. I'm thinking of changing my job. It's time I moved on.'

'Yes. Of course. Well – good luck!'

They drift towards the door and a rose, heavy with blooming, trembles as they pass and drops its velvet petals.

Henry studies the guide book with careful concentration.

'Henry the Eighth and Anne Boleyn came here, as lovers. Do you suppose . . . ?'

The tester bed, dark and heavily carved, looks old enough. She smooths the fraying coverlet, ignoring the notice 'Do Not Touch', and he fingers the dusty hangings and they stare down at the bed, and up at each other, remembering.

They pass through the Library with its chained shelves and the Dining Room, set for a banquet with Minton and crystal glass. They walk the length of the Gallery, past the Chippendale console tables, the Indian lacquered cabinets and pair of K'ang Hsi plates.

The clock in the Nursery is of white porcelain and ormulu, smiling shepherdesses entwined in summer trees. They turn away and examine instead the furniture, the toys and the tiny embroidered garments.

And the white and gold clock strikes five.

'It's time,' Rowena whispers.

'Yes,' says Henry.

They descend the stairs into the hall and cross the unyielding tiles, black, white, black, white, leading their reluctant feet towards the driveway leading to the lane, and they reach the waiting cars.

'I'm glad I came,' she tells him.

'So am I. Somehow it seems more possible now.'

She shakes her head, tears trembling in her eyes. 'How can it be?'

'Please.' He touches her arm. 'Don't make it harder.'

He gets into his car, turns, and drives towards the village, past the empty telephone box and beyond. And Rowena goes the other way, up the lane to the main road. Behind them the distant clocks mark the quarter hour, and the grass verge is empty as it will always be, with only the broken daisies to mark their passing.

The End

NINE

Phyllida cracks the eggs into the bowl and beats them into the butter and sugar. It is an exercise she enjoys; the electric mixer Henry bought her sits unused on the formica surface. She is humming as she beats, something about flowers and peace and San Francisco. The low sun streams in through the wide window of the kitchen and lights on Kathryn, ten years old, pale and fierce, rolling and cutting gingerbread men and giving them sultana buttons, eyes and noses.

She is a daunting child. Phyllida glances at her, sees that she has dropped sultanas on the floor, wonders whether to mention it and decides against. But she stops humming, biting her lip as she folds in the flour.

'Daddy's in a mood,' Kathryn tells her suddenly, placing the last sultana and brushing flour from her fingers. 'He told me to stop watching television.'

'Yes, well it is rather a waste of time. When we were your age we had better things to do.'

'Like what?'

'Oh . . .' Phyllida looks up vaguely. 'Well, reading I suppose, riding our bikes. And sewing. I always liked sewing.'

'Well I'm cooking, aren't I?' Kathryn looks sulky, inferring a rebuke. Phyllida has been trying unsuccessfully to enthuse her with embroidery. 'I don't suppose Rowena will want gingerbread men, anyway.'

'Auntie Rowena, what have I told you?'

'But she's not an auntie, not really.'

'Well Rowena sounds cheeky, at your age.'

'She doesn't mind, she told me so.'

'Well I mind.' Phyllida sighs. She had expected confrontation when the twins reached adolescence, but not so soon.

151

'Put the baking tray on the middle shelf, the sponge can go on top.' She adds, 'Perhaps you'd sweep up the mess on the floor before you go. I washed it this morning.'

'Yes, Mum.' It sounds more insolent than amenable, but the job gets done.

'Where's Stuart?' Phyllida asks her as she leaves the kitchen.

'He went to Guildford with Daddy. Something about wine for tonight.'

'Right. Well – find something useful to do.'

It sounds lame, but she has tried. After a while she hears music emanating from the sitting room. Kathryn would be sprawled on the Sanderson print sofa, already acting like a teenager. But the song is catchy – something about a beautiful balloon. She finds herself humming again, and a smile of satisfaction widens her lips.

Sometimes, these days, she feels like a teenager herself. The past year or so with Henry has been something special, it is as though they had fallen in love all over again. He has become attentive, fervent, passionate. She especially welcomes the passion because for years sex had become a routine between them, and not a frequent one at that. In return, she has tried to lose weight, had her curly hair cut into a shorter, crisper style, shown more interest in his work. He is now Head Librarian of a specialist library of scientific works and has taken the trouble to talk to her about his plans for the re-organisation and cataloguing of the books. He has even asked her to go up and look around, and meet his assistants and the secretary who does his typing. She tried to show a proper understanding of the system. She was conscious of her position as the boss's wife, and sensed their awe of her. Driving home Henry said, 'You did very well, darling,' and he had taken her hand and squeezed it.

She plans to tell Rowena all about the new library, to show Henry how proud she is of him and how involved she is in his work. Rowena would be interested. She has always taken an interest in Henry's work, loving books as she does. Filling the sink, she wonders again about Rowena. It is nearly a year since she has visited. Phyllida finds her friend's life impossible to imagine and she shudders at the independence, the imagined loneliness. There seems to be no man in her life – if there is, she never mentions him. Phyllida can't understand it. Rowena is attractive enough. She herself cannot imagine anyone actually choosing life without a man. It doesn't occur to her that there may be different priorities. Rowena has changed her job and always pleads pressure and busyness when Phyllida asks her down. But this time she has agreed, though at the last minute her car has broken down, she is coming on the train and needs meeting at the station. Phyllida looks at her watch. She hopes Henry won't be late to meet her.

She wonders, idly, why he should have been in a mood with Kathryn. Usually, he is indulgent with the twins, as he is with her.

Drawing on her rubber gloves and plunging her hands into the bowl she reflects that she is a very lucky woman.

Rowena, leaning from the window as the train draws into Guildford, seeks out Henry, sees only the twins, feels a leaden weight of disappointment. It had been a device born of desperation to pretend her car was out of action. That way, there was a chance of fifteen minutes alone together in the car. Instead she hands Stuart her bag thinking, how he's changed, he must have grown six inches, how much time has passed. Henry comes up behind them. His eyes are veiled as he greets her with a light, brotherly kiss on the forehead. Her lips smart hungrily as she follows them from the platform and her eyes threaten tears. She is angry, frustrated, lonely, jealous; she should never have come but, finally, nothing could keep her away.

Phyllida hugs her. 'Oh Ro! You shouldn't have left it so long.'

Rowena shrugs. 'Oh, well, you know.'

Phyllida laughs. 'No, I don't! But then I'm not a busy career woman. Do you want to go to your room? Stuart, take Auntie Rowena's bag.'

'Oh please, they're a bit old for the auntie. Wouldn't Rowena do?'

Phyllida looks obstinate but she sees the triumph in Kathryn's eyes. 'I suppose in the end it's up to you,' she says reluctantly.

'I don't really see myself as auntie material,' says Rowena jokingly. She catches Henry's eye as she turns to mount the stairs but there is nothing there but evasion, a denial that is like a blow across the face. Once in her room, she shuts the door and huddles on the bed, regardless of the white coverlet, regardless of her shoes which might be dirty, regardless of anything but her misery. Perversely, she wants him to be miserable too. She wants them to be united in unhappiness. But he has shut her out, giving every appearance of contentment. It is as if six years had never been. She is bitterly hurt and seeing him with Phyllida is like a knife in the wound. And yet she cannot stay away. She cannot let him forget her. She cannot allow him to be free. She skulks in her room like a banished child, until Phyllida's bright voice calls her down for lunch.

Later, she dresses carefully for supper. There are people coming, a couple from Wisley, and a friend from Guildford whose wife has recently left him, taking the children with her.

'He needs cheering up. He needs to feel he still has something to offer,' Henry had said as they turned into The Maltings' drive. But she feels she is being palmed off, put in her place as a single woman, available, unattached. It is very evident that Henry regards her as unattached. So all right. Henry would see what he was missing.

She underlines her eyes with black eye-liner and clips on large black earrings. Unlike Phyllida she had never had her ears pierced, and wore very little jewellery. But Henry, on their first Christmas, had given her a gold chain necklace. She had always delighted in wearing it recklessly in Phyllida's presence. Now she fastens it in the open neck of her blouse, and this time the statement is meant for Henry.

*   *   *

The couple are called Judith and Michael, the deserted man is Nigel and he makes no pretence at putting on a brave face. He sits mournfully, staring into the fire cradling a glass of Henry's best malt whisky. Rowena finds herself hustled onto the sofa beside him, where they sit in silence while the others talk about the new estate which is springing up along the lane, and bemoaning the concrete jungle under which all of England is disappearing.

'I know people have to live somewhere,' Phyllida complains. 'But why does it have to be in my back garden?'

Rowena sees a nice irony. 'Once they did that, literally. What about Tudor Close?'

'Yes, well we weren't still living there. We've lost all our view.'

'Not quite, darling.' Henry takes her hand and in doing so drives a spike cruelly into Rowena's heart. 'And I suppose one can't blame the farmers, making a bit of money out of their land.'

'Have you ever seen a poor farmer?' It was Judith, waving a challenging hand loaded with glittering rings.

'And if it's not houses, it's caravans. The south coast is being ruined,' joins in Michael, a fat bank manager who always holidays in France.

Rowena asks irritatedly, 'Do you often go down to the coast?'

'Good heavens, no. Far too crowded. We've got a place in Brittany. Great beaches, no one else in sight. The children love it.'

'You should join us one year, Phyllida,' suggests Judith.

'Phyl isn't all that keen on abroad.' Henry looks at her tolerantly while Rowena remembers angrily how he used to complain at this lack of enthusiasm.

Phyllida looks at him crossly. 'It's only the food. Especially when the twins were little. But if we stayed with Judith and Michael . . .'

'Oh we like to eat out. It makes a change from the sort of rubbish you get round here.'

'Yes, well . . .' Phyllida laughs nervously. 'I hope everything will be all right tonight.'

'Darling, take no notice of him.' Judith puts a hand on her arm. 'Is there anything I can do to help?'

'No. Everything's under control.' Even so, Phyllida gets up from the arm of Henry's chair and bustles into the kitchen. Rowena watches her go then slides her eyes to Henry, daring him to meet her gaze. He does so and there is a brief frisson of melancholy, of remembered hunger, flickering between them, sending a shaft of excitement which makes her say almost gaily, turning to Nigel, 'Are you another Francophil? I'm taking a group of girls to Paris next Easter.'

He looks startled. She hears Henry clearing his throat behind her.

'Nigel's wife is French, she's taken the children back to Poitiers.'

'Oh. Oh, I'm sorry.' She empties the last of the sherry.

Oh well, she thinks, I tried.

She finds herself alone with Henry in the kitchen. The three of them have washed up together, then suddenly Phyllida is gone, carrying glasses back to the dining room.

Rowena panics. She is not prepared. But she has to say urgently, bitterly, 'You seem to be coping very well. How are you really?'

She wants him to break down, to reclaim their love. But he says, 'I think it's working. It just needs a hundred and fifty per cent application.'

'And no diversion?'

He turns away, closing his eyes. 'It's the only way I can play it.'

She nods, satisfied with his pain which begins to equate with her own. 'I still love you.' The words are low and strangled, torn out of her even as Phyllida returns to the kitchen.

She sees him incline his head. Accepting? Agreeing? He says to Phyllida, 'All done, darling? You did very well, you must be tired.'

Phyllida leans against him, pulling his arm round her waist. She smiles at Rowena complacently. 'I'm afraid Nigel wasn't much company for you. I'm not surprised Jacqueline left him.'

'Oh, he was quite interesting really, once he started to talk about his lectureship. I shouldn't be rude about your friends, but I preferred him to fat cat Michael.'

Phyllida looks puzzled. 'Michael? Oh he's a big name in Rotary. They do a lot of good work in the town.'

'I'm sure they do. Well, I'm off to bed. Thanks for the evening.'

She glances back as she leaves the room but Henry doesn't turn his head.

The following day, peeling potatoes while Rowena chops leeks, Phyllida is in a mood for confidences. She is so happy with her life that she wants to share it. Also, she is proud of herself. She feels she has done well by Henry.

'How do you think Henry looks?' she asks experimentally.

Rowena replies guardedly, 'He looks very well.'

Phyllida puts down the peeler and turns from the sink. 'We're very happy, Ro. More especially these days.'

Rowena doesn't want to hear this, it hurts too much. She applies herself to the leeks, cutting venomously. 'I'm glad. You're very lucky.'

Phyllida gives a complacent smile. 'Yes, I suppose I am.'

Then she asks the question that has so often been on her lips. 'How about you, Ro? Any man in your life? I can't understand . . .' She stops, thinking this is not kind.

'You can't understand what?' Rowena is irritated. There is a terrible compulsion to tell. Any guilt she felt has long disappeared. What had Phyllida lost after all? Rather, she had won all the prizes in their unfair competition. Now Rowena just wants to claim some part of Henry for herself.

'You can't understand why I'm not married. Well it just isn't that easy for all of us.'

Phyllida fills a saucepan with water, dropping in the

potatoes, counting as she goes. Better not allow any for herself. 'But has there never been anyone?' she persists.

'Yes of course. I'm quite normal, I have feelings just like you.'

Phyllida looks sympathetic. She comes to sit at the table, ready to be confided in. 'So – what happened?'

Rowena tries to keep her voice light. 'Let's say it wasn't meant to be.'

Maybe there is something in her eyes for Phyllida says, 'Do you mean that he was married? Oh – poor you.' She feels a frisson of excitement, sensing secrets. 'Do you want to tell me about it? You can, you know.'

Rowena looks at her consideringly. How would she handle the truth? Where would be friendship then? She shakes her head. 'No, I don't think I can. It's still too painful.'

'Oh poor you,' Phyllida says again. She feels peeved. Rowena has shut her out. What's more, she has experienced something Phyllida has never known – illicit love. Phyllida wants to know about it, she wants to share, maybe even offer advice. What she really wants is a warm, female confiding, but Rowena, tempted though she is, is not to be drawn.

Derek had put his house on the market but nobody had been to see it.

'So it looks as though I shall be around for a while. I hope you'll keep me company.'

'Of course.' Rowena didn't know whether to be pleased or sorry. Like Phyllida, he would go away and leave her, so why cling to the present any longer than necessary? But then, it gave him more time to get to know her better. Maybe time was all she needed.

'Come to supper on Saturday. Bob's coming . . . and Ben and Kathryn. There'll be wedding talk, I'm afraid. It's only a month away.'

'Right. If you're sure.'

She was perfectly sure. She had been feeling outnumbered and was considering asking Betty.

'I'll bring a bottle of wine,' said Derek. 'German I think, don't you?'

Rowena noticed at once that something was wrong with Kathryn. Her eyes had a haunted look and she hung onto Ben's arm uncharacteristically as they greeted Derek, who had arrived first with two brown bottles from the Rhine.

Phyllida however seemed unaware of the tension and greeted her gaily, drawing Bob up to kiss her also. 'After all, she'll soon be your daughter,' she pronounced with satisfaction. 'One big happy family.'

'Your plans are all finalised for the wedding?' Derek asked politely.

Bob rubbed his hands. 'We're all set. Four more weeks. It's going to be quite a day.' He leaned towards Phyllida, whispering so that they all could hear. 'And quite a night!'

She pushed him away, glancing nervously at her daughter, but Kathryn was staring out of the window, seemingly unaware.

'Sherry everyone?' Rowena passed round a tray of glasses and they all sat down.

'How's work, Ben?' she asked.

He shrugged. 'The usual. Not enough staff, underfunding . . .'

Phyllida was impatient. 'Never mind that now. We want to talk about the wedding. Make the final arrangements. Will Hannah come here to get dressed?'

There was silence. Phyllida glanced from Kathryn to Ben, for the first time sensing trouble. 'What is it?' Her voice was sharp.

Ben said oddly, 'I'm sorry, Derek, we didn't know you would be here.'

'Shall I leave?' He looked puzzled but rose from his chair. Rowena put out her hand.

'Please stay.' She looked at Kathryn in alarm. 'Do you have something to tell us, Kathryn?'

She saw the girl's face collapse momentarily as she glanced at Ben. 'Ben?' Kathryn took his hand and gripped it.

He spoke slowly. 'The fact is, Kathryn has to go back into hospital. To have a hysterectomy.'

'Why?' Panic straddled Phyllida's face.

'They think the cancer has spread.'

Bob put his arm round Phyllida's shoulders.

'I'm sorry,' said Kathryn in a helpless voice.

There was a long silence. Rowena watched as Phyllida's face crumpled and turned into Bob's shoulder. He patted her absently with his pudgy hand but Rowena could see his mind whirling. 'The wedding,' he burst out. Then added, looking confused, 'I'm sorry, my dear. So stupid of me.'

'The wedding must go ahead.' Kathryn looked at Ben. 'We've discussed it. I shall be home by then, even if I can't come.'

'But you must be there.' Phyllida looked at her accusingly. 'It wouldn't be the same.'

Rowena said warningly, 'Phyllida. It's up to Kathryn.'

Kathryn said crossly, 'I really can't be held responsible for your cancelling all your arrangements, and I can't be coerced into coming if I don't feel like it.'

'What Kathryn means,' added Ben soothingly, 'is that the most important thing is for you to go ahead as planned.'

Phyllida pursed her lips. 'I wish I could think so. It doesn't sound very good news to me. How can we all go ahead and celebrate?'

'Don't you see it's the best possible thing you can do, not to make too big an issue of it? It's just a routine operation, they're doing it every day.'

'But not for cancer. I thought at the time they should have removed your breast.'

'Mum . . .'

'You're not helping, Phyllida,' snapped Rowena. Out of the corner of her eye she saw Derek get up and make for the door.

'I can hear something boiling over,' he explained tactfully, and made his exit.

It was a miserable meal, with none of the festive spirit Phyllida had planned. She herself was overcome with fear and disappointment and a niggling sense of mortification that she had let her daughter down. Bob had sunk into himself in fear that once again his plans were to be thwarted and Rowena was seething with impatience at the pair of them. Derek did his best, carrying in vegetable dishes and pouring wine, and Rowena was touched and grateful. When he came to leave she apologised.

'I had no idea things would be so fraught. I would never knowingly have invited you into all that!'

He shrugged. 'I hope I wasn't too much of an intrusion. Sometimes an outsider is a catalyst and helps to diffuse a family drama.'

'Well I was glad you were there, anyway. I think I might really have lost my temper with Phyllida.'

'She's a very frightened woman.'

'So is Kathryn. Phyllida's useless. And selfish. She always has been.'

He raised an eyebrow.

Rowena was ashamed. 'You're right. I suppose I'm a bit upset myself. It doesn't sound too good, does it?'

'Well you know what I feel about cancer.'

Without thinking, Rowena leaned forward and kissed him on the cheek. 'I know. And thank you for your support this evening. Has anyone been to see the house?'

'One couple, this afternoon. But they didn't look as if they had two pennies to rub together.'

She tried not to be pleased. 'Never mind, someone will turn up one day. I suppose there's no rush.'

'No. But now I've made up my mind, I want to get on with things. There's a bungalow near Margaret which sounds ideal, if only I could get things moving. I really feel quite excited about starting again.'

Rowena nodded. 'I remember the feeling,' she said.

'I'm buying a house,' she tells them. 'You must come and see it.'

Phyllida looks impressed but surprised. 'On your own?'

Rowena laughs. 'How else?'

'It's just that it's unusual. I mean, without being married.'

Rowena feels a rush of irritation. 'Not everyone's married, Phyllida. But it doesn't mean they have to live in rented flats all their lives.'

'Well I think it's splendid,' says Henry heartily. 'Congratulations. Of course we'll come and see it.'

She wonders if he's patronising her but sees in his eyes a light of pride and something else that makes her wonder. Envy?

They come on a summer Saturday when the little garden is bright with the bedding plants she has been cramming in each evening after her return from school. She has mown the patch of lawn and sprayed the roses which fill the air with scent. Inside, her new furniture sparsely adorns the carpets her mother has passed on to her. It is Helen, too, she must thank for the curtains that flutter at the windows looking out onto a suburban street.

It is a far cry from The Maltings, but it is her own.

The twins, twelve-year-olds and tall, tumble out of the car carrying packages, and run excitedly up the concrete path between the pinks and petunias. Phyllida follows more slowly, carrying a cake tin. From habit, Rowena's eyes reach behind her for Henry locking the car, glancing up and down the street, finally turning towards her so that their eyes meet for an instant like warm hands touching across a space. Her heart contracts with love and hunger but his greeting is no more than brotherly – the usual kiss on the forehead and a nod of approval.

'Pleasant road. The gardens have come on well. How old is the house?'

'Just eighteen months. They're still building further down the estate.'

Phyllida is standing in the little hall peering into the kitchen. 'Awful, all these estates. They're simply creeping up on us at home.'

Henry rebukes, 'Phyl, that's hardly tactful.'

'People have to live somewhere,' adds Rowena tartly. 'Is that a cake you've brought me? You really needn't have troubled.'

'Well, I know how busy you are.' She hands her the tin with an awkward smile. 'No really, Ro, it's splendid. I really like it.'

'You haven't seen it yet. Not that there is a lot.' She pushes open the door of the living room, wondering anxiously how it will seem to them. It is a cosy room, its walls lined with bookshelves and pictures and a small television set beside the stone fireplace.

'I like the fireplace,' Henry tells her.

'And you've some lovely plants. They obviously like that window ledge.'

Stuart comes in through the open french windows. He hands her a flat parcel. 'Dad thought you'd find this useful. I bought it with my pocket money.'

'Oh Stuart, how kind.' She unwrapped the parcel and found a book on gardening for beginners. 'Well that's me all right! I'm going to find that very useful.'

'My present is stupid. We made them at school.' Kathryn hands her a pair of roughly made wooden salad servers wrapped in blue tissue paper.

'I don't think they're stupid.'

'Well Mum didn't want them.'

There is a painful silence into which Stuart neatly drops a question about lunch, and Rowena is able to escape into the kitchen to prod the potatoes.

'Will you carve?' she asks Henry, bringing in the joint. Defiantly she has left the beef rare, the cabbage crisp, but her Yorkshire pudding is not a patch on Phyllida's. She tells her so, apologetically, waiting for a comment on the oozing meat on her plate. But it is Kathryn who remarks, with a giggle, 'The meat's bloody. And you can't stop me saying that word because it's true.'

'Kathryn, calm down,' reproves her father, looking at the meat with appreciation. He gives himself a thick slice right from the middle, and ladles on the cabbage.

'Eat, everyone, don't let it go cold.' Rowena is anxious suddenly, watching Kathryn sliding the meat around her plate. Stuart seems to have no such difficulty and Phyllida makes a brave attempt. Serves her right, thinks Rowena ungraciously, thinking of the leathery helpings she has endured at The Maltings. When in Rome . . .

'Let's drive round to Tudor Close this afternoon,' suggests Phyllida. 'The twins have never seen where I grew up.'

'Does it seem strange, coming back to your old stamping ground?' asks Henry.

'A bit. But I like the school I'm at and I felt I should be nearer mother.'

'How is Helen?' Phyllida's face takes on a sympathetic shape.

'Lonely. I think she misses Mark as much as she misses Dad.'

'It puts a lot of responsibility on you,' says Henry.

'No more than on me,' protests Phyllida. 'Mother only has me, and has had for years.' She thinks for a while then adds clumsily, 'But of course she has grandchildren,' which earns her a stern look from Henry.

'Pudding?' asks Rowena brightly. 'I've made a cheesecake, a rhubarb crumble, or there's ice cream.'

'Can I have crumble *and* ice cream?'

'Of course you can, Stuart.'

She is disappointed when Phyllida says, 'I'll pass on the pudding, Ro. I try and watch my weight.'

'Surely just this once?' asks Henry.

'But darling, you're always saying you prefer me slimmer.' She makes a moue and Rowena looks away, gathering the plates.

'Kathryn, help Rowena clear away.'

The girl sighs. 'Why is it always me, just because I'm a girl?'

'Don't argue with your mother.'

'I'll do it,' offers Stuart, picking up the remains of the joint. Really, thinks Rowena, following him into the kitchen, he is the nicer of the two. He takes after his father. And something like a sob makes her run water fiercely into the roasting tin while Stuart reaches into the fridge for the ice cream.

Rowena sits in the back of the car between the twins, staring at the back of Henry's head and remembering another time, so long ago. Phyllida is once more niggling away.

'I said turn right at the pub. I do know my way around here, remember.'

'But the road was blocked with the brewer's lorry. We would have sat there for ages. Surely we can turn further down.'

She shrugs. 'I'm not sure I can find my way through further down.'

Rowena leans forward. 'It's okay, Phyl, I can.' Daringly she lets her hand rest on Henry's shoulder. 'Take the next right, then straight across at the lights.' She squeezes his shoulder lightly and he meets her eyes in the mirror and shakes his head. Rebuffed, she sits back thinking, He *will* remember, and says defiantly to the twins, 'The first time I sat in the back like this with you two you were toddlers. We were going on a picnic.' She stares into the mirror, daring him to look at her, but his eyes are on the road.

They get out in Tudor Gardens and walk into Tudor Close and Phyllida explains how it used to be, when she was the twins' age. A man mowing his lawn looks at them curiously and is even more mystified when Phyllida tells him gaily, 'It's all right, I used to live here.'

'Really,' says Stuart as they walk back to the car. 'I suppose Grandma was just as bad as Bert Riley, selling off her land to developers.'

Phyllida looks pink and annoyed. 'It was different. Our house had been bomb damaged. Bert Riley is just doing it for the money.'

'But as Rowena says, people have to live somewhere.'

Phyllida turns to Henry for help but he says nothing.

'Well I'm not going to argue about it,' she says, wrenching open the door of the car and getting in.

And suddenly Rowena feels Henry's eyes upon her and she looks at him across the car and he raises an eyebrow in exasperation and she knows that he is miserable.

TEN

As Jake and Hannah had broken up from school it was arranged that they should come and stay while Kathryn was in hospital. They brought with them a camp bed which Ben put up in the spare room, where a squabble ensued as to who should sleep on it.

'I'm too heavy and it wobbles,' stated Jake, bouncing on the divan possessively.

'But I'm a girl,' whined Hannah. She pressed the camp bed. 'This is hard.'

'Shut up you two.' Ben looked to be at the end of his tether, as indeed he was. 'We've more things to worry about than that.'

Jake immediately looked stricken.

Rowena said briskly, 'Give me a hand with these bedclothes, Jake. I think the best thing is that you take it in turns, don't you? You never know, you might find it fun. You could pretend you are camping.'

'Like in a tent? I wish we *could* sleep in a tent.'

Hannah looked anxious. 'I don't want to sleep in a tent.' She twisted her long hair nervously. 'We don't have to, do we, Rowena?'

'Of course not. Why don't you go down and help Grandma while Jake and I do this?' Hannah skipped off gratefully, holding onto her father's hand, and Rowena said to Jake, 'I don't have a real tent but we could make you a pretend one in here if you like.'

He looked excited. 'Dad could fix it for us.'

She shook her head. 'Don't let's bother your father. I should like to do it. With you of course. You're a cub, you're bound to have good ideas.'

167

'We're going camping next Easter.'

'Well, this will be a bit of practice for you.'

She fetched some sheets, drawing pins and a long piece of string which she fixed between the picture rails. Then they draped the sheets over the string, weighting down the bottoms with books. There was room beside the camp bed for a stool with a small table lamp, and Jake went inside and sat on the bed enthralled. 'It's like having my own room. I didn't want to share with a soppy girl. I'm going to show Grandma.'

He went to the banisters and called to Phyllida. Her expression when she saw the contraption was one of surprise and disappointment.

'What a mess you've made between you. I took such trouble to make the room nice.'

'But this is nice. I've got my own room.'

'At least it settled the argument,' said Rowena wearily. She had been looking forward to having the children but sensed it was going to be a source of further irritation.

'Well come down now and have some tea. Wash your hands first.' Phyllida's face was drawn and Rowena reminded herself that she was under a great deal of strain. Kathryn had cancer and to be realistic she might never recover. Ben seemed to have given in completely to his fears and between them she and Phyllida had to support him, and keep the children happy and confident. If this was what having families was all about, maybe it was safer after all to be alone in the world.

She followed Jake into the bathroom and helped him dry his hands. Then she pulled him to her roughly in a sudden excess of pity and affection.

'What's that for?' he asked in surprise.

'Because it's good to have you here,' she told him.

They quickly found that when it came to amusing the children, no one was better than Bob. For a man who had had no family of his own he had an amazing fund of games and tricks, and endless patience. Phyllida suggested they get used to calling him Grandpa. 'After all, it won't be long now, and I think he'd like it, don't you?'

'We've never had a Grandpa.'

'I know, Jake.'

He looked thoughtful. 'If Mummy dies, will Daddy be a widow?'

Phyllida flinched. 'Mummy won't die. It's just an operation.' She told herself desperately that this was true. Anything else was unthinkable.

'But would he?' Jake persisted.

'No. He would be a widower. But it's not going to happen.'

'Here's Bob,' cried Rowena gratefully, turning from the window. 'Isn't he taking you to Chessington Zoo this afternoon?'

'Are you coming too?' Hannah slid her hand into Rowena's.

'No, I shall be playing bridge.'

Hannah looked disappointed and Rowena was touched. But it was something they were all going to have to get used to. She forced a smile. 'Cheer up,' she urged. 'Maybe you'll get to ride on an elephant!'

They left after an early lunch and Rowena was waiting for Betty to pick her up when the telephone rang. It was Stuart, and she felt herself backing off.

'I'm afraid your mother's not here. They've taken the children to the zoo.'

'Right. How are things?'

'Going all right. Kathryn's feeling a bit stronger.'

'Well tell her I'm coming down. Will it be all right to stay with you?'

She was annoyed. 'We're a bit full up, with the children.'

'Ah. I never thought of that.'

You wouldn't, thought Rowena spitefully.

'I'm sure Ben would put you up.' She hesitated, thinking of Phyllida. 'Or there's always the sofa here, if you can bear it. How long would it be for?'

'A couple of nights. I'd like to see Kathryn for myself.'

'I'm glad to hear it. Well, come here. Phyllida would want you to.'

'Thanks. I thought I'd drive down after work tomorrow. I'll arrive latish, I'm afraid.'

'Someone will be up.' She paused. 'And Stuart, let's not have any hassle. We've got enough on our plates at the moment.'

'Rowena! Would I?'

'Yes,' she told him shortly. 'You would.'

The telephone wakes her early on a Sunday morning, a dark mid-winter morning with an iron-hard frost on the garden. It is Phyllida and her voice is strange.

'Ro? Are you awake?'

'I am now.' She shivers, drawing her dressing gown around her. 'What's wrong, Phyl? Something's happened.'

'You could say that.' She gives a funny, brittle little laugh. 'Henry's gone.'

'Gone.' Rowena has to fight down the sudden surge of triumph. She looks involuntarily at the front door. 'When? I mean, what's happened, Phyl?' A sudden doubt makes her pause. But if Phyllida had found out, she'd hardly be ringing her.

Or would she?

'Can you come down?' Phyllida's voice is a sob. 'I'm such a mess, I haven't slept a wink, and it's so cold.' There is a silence. 'I don't know what to do, Ro.'

'Are the twins there?'

'Stuart is. Kathryn's at college.'

'Does Stuart know?'

'Yes.'

'Is he any help?'

'He's fast asleep if that's what you mean. But he's as shocked as me. Please come, Rowena. I wouldn't ask, only . . .'

'I know. I'll come. Now, while you're waiting why not light a big fire, and make yourself some breakfast. You must eat. And get dressed in something warm.'

'I never got undressed. I'm in a cocktail dress. We'd been out . . .'

'Yes, well you can tell me about it later. Have a hot bath,

get into something sensible.' There is a sound of helpless crying. 'Can you hear me, Phyl? Will you do as I say?'

'Yes. I'll do it. But please be quick. I'm going out of my mind!'

Rowena replaces the phone, wondering how soon it will ring again, wondering where he has spent the night. Dressing quickly, she wonders should she leave a note on the door, the key hidden in the garden, decides it would be an invitation to burglars, then decides it doesn't matter, and writes a note while she drinks black coffee and the sky gradually lightens. *Henry*, she writes. *I have had to go to Phyllida but I will say nothing unless she does. The key is under the tub by the back door. Make yourself at home. PS. I love you but you know that don't you.* She puts it into an envelope, writes his name and attaches it to the front door with sticky tape. She puts the key under the pot then slips on a sheepskin coat, collects her car keys and goes out into the frozen dawn. She has to scrape the windscreen with the engine running, careless of her sleeping neighbours, careless of anything but the singing gratification.

'At last, at last, at last,' she mutters as she scrapes. 'Oh Henry, my darling, at last!'

She approaches Phyllida warily, but there is no reproach, no accusation, only a brimming grief and shock. She is huddled by a fierce fire, wearing furry slippers, a tweed skirt and a soft pink pullover. There is a coffee pot on the table and Rowena notes wryly that she seems to have done everything she was told. The tears which have been waiting in the wings spill over as Rowena comes into the room. Phyllida pats the cushions beside her but something makes Rowena sit down opposite, though she does reach out a hand.

'Tell me everything,' she says.

Phyllida gulps and scrubs her eyes with an inadequate embroidered hanky. She starts to speak with difficulty, but like her tears the words soon begin to flow.

'Well, we went to this party. A big house, just outside Woking. Someone from the tennis club. Henry didn't want to go, he said he was too tired and didn't care for the couple who were giving the party but I persuaded him, I said we hadn't been out for ages and I'd always wanted to see inside their house. So he agreed, but he was in a bad mood to start with. Then when we got there, having had no meal beforehand, we found there were only little nibbles, nothing proper to eat, and you know Henry when he's hungry — well maybe you don't, but he needs regular stoking, I always say he's like a log fire . . .' her voice falters.

'But surely he didn't blame you for that?'

'I suppose not. But he just sat himself in a corner with a drink and a bowl of nuts and let me go round on my own. It was so embarrassing. He said, "Just let me know when you've seen enough. Don't forget to inspect the bedrooms!" It wasn't like him, he sounded almost cruel. It made me angry so I didn't hurry, going the rounds and talking to everybody and making excuses for him, saying he wasn't well and we wouldn't be staying long. But on the way home, we left at about ten I suppose, I told him I had been embarrassed and then he just flared up and said I always worried too much about what people thought and what about thinking of him for a change. He said he seemed to have spent a lifetime trying to make me happy! Well I've never said he hasn't, have I, Ro? And I've tried, too.'

She looks bewildered. She kneels on the rug and arranges logs on the fire with excessive care, and remains there, staring into the flames. Her voice runs on, on oiled wheels. 'Then he sat in silence until we got home and when I got out of the car he just went on sitting there and I said, "Aren't you coming in, it's freezing?" And he said, "I don't think I want to come in, ever again."'

Rowena is watching and listening with a mixture of disbelief, excitement and a sort of hysterical joy. At the same time she feels a deep pity for Phyllida. She is so innocent, so unknowing, so confused. How will she, Rowena, be able to face her, when the truth is out? Realising that Phyllida has stopped she asks, curiously, for she has to know, 'And was that all? I mean, you didn't just let him go?'

'Of course not. I asked him what he meant, and offered to get him something to eat and opened the car door to let him out, but he snatched it from me and slammed it shut and said, "Leave me alone, can't you. Why don't you ever leave anyone alone?" And then I burst into tears and ran indoors and I stood in the hall waiting for him to drive away but after a moment he followed me in and Ro, he looked ghastly, old and ill and tired, I've never seen him like it, and I said, "You look awful, are you ill?" and he said he was just sick at heart, and he needed to get away, he would just take a few things and go, he didn't want to talk about anything, he'd be in touch. So you see . . .' And she shrugs, spreading her damp plump hands, 'I don't know anything. Except that he's gone. And I don't know why or where.'

Rowena stares, struggling for the right reaction. Then Phyllida throws herself down on the sofa, writhing and twitching and sobbing and, appalled at her own duplicity, Rowena nonetheless slips to the floor and puts an arm round her heaving shoulders and says, 'There now, let it all come out.' And she sits there for a long time until the sobbing stops and the convulsions cease, and incredibly, Phyllida is asleep.

She sits back in her chair and pours cold coffee from the pot into Phyllida's cup and drinks it down. The room is suddenly alive with Henry's absence and she wonders, is he there already, seated in my chair, drinking my coffee, waiting for me? Then the door opens and she starts violently, splashing coffee onto her trousers, and looks up to see Stuart coming into the room.

She puts her finger to her lips. 'She's asleep, don't wake her.'

He looks at her strangely. It is two years since they have met, he is a man now, with Henry's brown eyes and soft brown hair. During his teens she has begun to be fond of him, but now there is an evasion in his eyes. Uneasily, she says softly, 'I'll make some fresh coffee,' but he picks up the pot and leaves the room. After a moment she follows him, shutting the door gently. She finds him in the kitchen, making toast, staring out over the frosty garden. The kettle comes to the boil but he ignores it. She finds the coffee, refills the pot and puts two mugs on the table. She waits for him to speak but when he doesn't she says, 'I'm so sorry about this, Stuart. Did you see your father before he left?'

He shook his head, still staring at the garden. 'I was out. I found Mother at midnight in a state of collapse on the stairs. Just sitting there, tearing a handkerchief into shreds.'

She doesn't know what to say. It is too awful to contemplate. She should be feeling guilty, fearful of what is to come. Instead she feels disbelief and triumph, equally mixed. Belatedly she realises that Stuart is suffering too. She goes to him and puts a hand on his shoulder. For a brief moment it is as if she is touching Henry.

'I'm so sorry,' she says again, and is horrified at what she must apologise for.

He mumbles, 'I don't know what's got into him.' She thinks painfully that he is crying. But when he turns to her his eyes are hard and dry and appraising. 'Do you?' he asks.

And, looking into his face, she thinks, he knows.

By midday there is a threat of snow, the sky is a sullen yellow and the wind whistles in from the east. Rowena makes them all some lunch and persuades Phyllida to eat, then excuses herself.

'I don't like the look of this weather. I'd better get home.'

Phyllida clings to her but she doesn't argue when Rowena says, 'After all I'm not leaving you alone. You've got Stuart.' She is already straining to be gone and as the car leaves the drive she cries out loud, 'I'm coming, my darling,' and in the mirror she sees her eyes ablaze.

'There's something I want to ask you,' Phyllida says to Stuart when she has gone. 'That night, about a month ago, when you and your father went out for a drink. He was quite drunk when you got home. I've never known him to drink too much. Did he say anything to you? I mean, anything that might have indicated he was unhappy?'

He looks her straight in the eye. 'Nothing, Mum. He talked about work mostly. It was my fault he got drunk. But it was only wine.'

'I didn't mind. I hope he didn't think I minded. And I didn't think anything of it at the time, not really. It's only now that I'm looking for clues, anything to tell me what was wrong, or where he might have gone. I mean, I always tried to put him first. I thought we were happy. We were happy. Didn't we seem happy to you, Stuart?'

He is embarrassed by her pathos, her innocence. How can he tell her? He looks at his hands and murmurs, 'Yes, you seemed very happy.' And thinking of Rowena, there is hatred in his eyes.

The snow is settling on the suburban streets as Rowena approaches her house. Driving too fast in her excitement she goes into a heart-stopping skid on a bend and has to curb her onward flight. 'More haste, less speed,' she tells herself out loud. 'You've waited eighteen years, another few minutes won't hurt.' Even so she feels sick with impatience as she turns into her road and never for a moment does she allow herself to doubt.

For where else would he go? He loves her, he had always loved her, he had made a brave attempt all these years but finally had to admit defeat. Well she is here for him, as she had always been. No one else had ever measured up. She pulls onto the drive, scanning the house for signs. As she gets out into the damp cold she sees at once that there are footprints on the snowy path. He has come! But then why is her note still attached to the door, the white paper yellowed by the brightness of the snow? And why had the footprints turned, and gone back down the path? Her hand is trembling as she feels for her key, then she remembers she has left it under the pot.

She stares at the closed front door. Perhaps he is inside? It wouldn't hurt to knock. She raises the knocker, knowing even as she does so that it is a false hope. The sound echoes round the empty house, cold and hard as the stone in her heart.

She picks her way round to the back door and moves the pot. The key is still there, in a patch of dirty mud amid the snow. Picking it up she gives a bitter sob, feeling foolish, stunned with disappointment. But already she is making excuses. He would have wanted to speak to her before he came, he has probably been ringing all day. She hurries back to the front door and in her haste she drops the key onto the snowy step. She picks it up and inserts it in the lock, pushing open the door and calling 'Henry?' because this is what she had imagined doing, although at once she knows it is hopeless.

The house is silent, gloomy under the leaden sky. With a gesture of despair she pulls the note off the door and crumples it in her hand.

Stuart arrived from Newcastle at midnight and Phyllida embraced him tearfully in the hall, taking pride in his height as he towered over her just as Henry had done.

'It's been too long, Stuart.' She wiped her eyes. 'You should come down more often.'

'It's difficult since you won't accept Jill.'

She looked upset. 'It's not that I don't accept her. I just don't like your not being married. I can't help it, things were different in our day. And I miss Fiona. I always thought of her as a daughter, now I never hear from her.'

'No. Well I suppose that's a pity, but it's understandable now she's married again. But don't let's go over all that old ground again, Mother.'

She shook her head with a brave smile. 'It's still good to see you. Kathryn will be pleased. She seemed much better tonight, though she's a long way to go. That dreadful therapy. I dread it for her. And of course there's no guarantee . . .' She bit her lip. 'I get so frightened, Stuart. Nobody understands.'

'Of course they do. You've got Bob. I presume I shall meet him?'

'Of course. But you were always the one I could talk to. Not

Kathryn. She was unapproachable. But I could always rely on you. When your father left I don't know what I'd have done without you.'

He said impatiently, 'That was a long time ago.'

She turned away. 'Sixteen years. But it sometimes seems like yesterday.'

Stuart was playing in the garden with the children. Phyllida smiled at Rowena with pleasure. 'I've told him he must bring Jill down to the wedding, life's too short to make difficulties.'

'Perhaps seeing you and Bob tie the knot will encourage them.'

'Oh Ro, do you think so?'

'Not really. But you never know.'

'Anyway, I've decided it's time to accept her into the family. Family is precious, I realise that more than anything now. Do you think Kathryn will be able to come to the wedding?'

'Well it's only two weeks now, and she isn't even home yet. I shouldn't build up your hopes. Anyway, you know how ill she feels with the therapy.'

Phyllida shuddered. 'Who will look after her this time? I can hardly leave Bob, and then there's the cruise.'

'Ben said he'd ask his mother to come.'

'That won't be the same. A girl needs her own mother.'

Rowena sighed. 'Well then cancel the wedding, if you must. You really must sort out your priorities.'

To her horror, tears welled up in Phyllida's blue eyes. 'Don't be cross, Ro. This is a difficult time for me.' She blew her nose hard on a small handkerchief.

Rowena softened. 'I know. And I'm sorry things have been spoiled. Just try and relax, let Ben and Kathryn sort things out for themselves and you concentrate on Bob. You can't be all things to all people all of the time.'

Phyllida wiped her eyes gratefully. It was what she wanted to hear. 'I'll get the tea,' she said briskly. 'Perhaps you'd call the children in to wash.'

But before Rowena had a chance there was a shrill scream

from the garden, followed by another, and a shout and running footsteps and then Jake fell in through the back door.

'Hannah's fallen out of the tree. I think she's dead.'

'Nonsense. Dead people don't make all that noise.' Even so Rowena found herself running into the garden, followed by Phyllida who was crying, 'Tree. What tree? What on earth have you been up to?'

They found her at the foot of the apple tree, with Stuart kneeling over her. Her leg was twisted back beneath her and she had stopped screaming and was deathly white and whimpering.

'Stuart said we could climb it,' Jake stammered defensively. 'It wasn't my idea.'

'Never mind that now. Phyllida, you'd better call an ambulance. We shouldn't move her. Jake, get a blanket.'

'Tea, hot tea. The kettle's on.' Phyllida was wringing her hands helplessly, staring down at the child.

'Phyllida. Go and phone.'

When she had gone, stumbling up the path like a drunkard, Rowena turned on Stuart in fury. 'What on earth were you thinking of, letting her climb the tree? She's six years old, for heaven's sake!'

'But I was holding her. I wouldn't have let her go alone. She just sort of slipped.'

Hannah gave a little gasp and looked at them in terror. 'Hush now.' Rowena smoothed her forehead. Jake arrived with a blanket and a pillow and Hannah's bear which he held out to her tearfully. She shook her head but Rowena pulled him close and took the bear, tucking it in beside her. 'That was thoughtful, Jake. Now she looks quite comfy.' She tried not to think of the leg, wrenched so painfully behind her. She felt sure it must be broken.

'Will she be all right?' whispered Jake, seeing Hannah close her eyes.

'Well, she'll have to go to the hospital, just to let them have a look at her leg.'

'The same hospital as Mummy?'

It was a ghastly thought. 'Well, I suppose so.'

'So Mummy can see her.'

'I don't know.' She looked up gratefully as Phyllida arrived, carrying a tray of tea. 'I thought we could all do with some.' She looked pale and wild eyed. 'The ambulance is coming.'

Stuart hadn't moved, crouching uselessly beside Hannah's lifeless form plucking at the blanket. Phyllida looked at him reproachfully. 'I thought you were taking care of them.'

'I was.'

Rowena passed him a cup of tea, leaving the saucer on the tray. Trust Phyllida to bring out the bone china instead of practical mugs. She suppressed the desire to shout at Stuart to pull himself together. She took a cup herself, scalding her lips on the hot liquid. Phyllida was eyeing Hannah doubtfully. 'Do you think it's all right to leave her like that?'

Rowena was suddenly frightened. 'She didn't hit her head did she, Stuart? If so, she shouldn't be allowed to go to sleep.'

'No.' He looked at them wildly. 'No, I'm sure she didn't. She just fell straight down.'

Phyllida was still standing holding the tray. Her voice was trembly as she said, 'Of course you realise what this means. We shall have to cancel the wedding now.'

Rowena clenched her hands, stressed beyond belief with a mixture of emotions. Trust Phyllida to think of that, above all else.

And trust it all to be Stuart's fault.

'Take Jake and go and wait for the ambulance,' she ordered him peremptorily. 'You're not being much use here.'

He threw her an angry, shamefaced look, but he went, pulling Jake by the hand.

'Go easy on him, Ro, he's feeling bad enough.'

'But it's his fault. It's him you'll have to thank for ruining the wedding.'

Phyllida gave a little gasp. 'How am I going to tell Bob?'

'That's your problem, just as it's your decision,' Rowena told her unkindly.

Phyllida crouched beside Hannah, twisting her hands

frantically then reaching out and touching the child's hair. 'Is she all right?' She looked at Rowena, begging for reassurance.

'*I* don't know. I hope so.'

Then Phyllida leapt up. 'Where's the ambulance, for heaven's sake? People could *die* while they make up their minds to arrive.'

'Calm down. It has to take ten minutes to get here.'

Phyllida moaned. 'What on earth are Kathryn and Ben going to think? I was supposed to be looking after them.'

'It's certainly something they could do without.' She looked up, listening. 'There's the ambulance now. You go with her, I'll stay here with Jake. I'll send Stuart after you by car, he can stay with you and bring you home. And I'll ring Ben.'

Phyllida nodded passively. 'Thank you, Rowena. As usual you've got it all sorted out,' she acknowledged humbly.

It was ten o'clock that night. Phyllida poured hot milk onto the cocoa and brought it to the table. She sat down, looking exhausted. 'Oh, it's good to be home. What a day!'

'Poor little Hannah. Fancy being in traction at her age. I wonder how long it will be.'

'They said several weeks. Poor Stuart, he's very upset, especially about the wedding.'

'When will you tell Bob?'

'First thing tomorrow. I must get a night's sleep first. He's going to be devastated.'

'Then why do it? Why not just go ahead?'

'Because it doesn't seem right. Not with both of them in hospital.'

'Kathryn may be home by then.'

Phyllida looked obstinate. 'Well I wanted Hannah as a bridesmaid. And she's so looking forward to it.'

Rowena sipped her cocoa. 'I thought maybe, for Stuart's sake, let alone Bob's, you may have decided otherwise.'

'Bob will understand. It will only be a month or so.'

'And Stuart? You never like punishing him, and this will seem like a punishment.'

'Why do you say that, Ro? I was always very strict with him, I was with both of them.'

'When he was little, maybe. And he was a very nice lad, as a teenager. But you must admit he hasn't made much of his life.'

Phyllida looked distraught. 'It wasn't easy, after Henry left. I did my best.'

'Maybe. But it seems to me Stuart has wasted himself. He left school with no qualifications, drifted into the estate agents and didn't bother to take any exams, left that and fiddled about as a salesman, when that didn't work started all that silly nonsense selling cosmetics under franchise, got behind with the mortgage and was then surprised when Fiona left him for someone steady in the bank.'

Phyllida's voice was pained. 'That was a very unhappy time for him. He loved Fiona. I loved Fiona, I still miss her.'

'But he used you. You could never see it, but a grown man of nearly thirty moving back in with his mother! It isn't on, Phyl.'

'I was glad of his company.' She looked angry now. 'You'll never understand, Rowena, because you're not a mother. You don't stop being a mother just because your children are grown up. You're always there for them. Stuart knew that, I wanted him to know that.'

Rowena sighed and pushed aside her empty mug. 'Okay. Let's not argue. You should go to bed.' She crossed the kitchen and dropped a reluctant kiss onto Phyllida's fine curls. 'Don't worry,' she said, apropos of what she wasn't sure. But then Phyllida had never known just how much there was to worry about. Rowena had made sure of that.

It is a month since Henry left, and Rowena is at The Maltings. So far she has pleaded busyness but finally it has been impossible to resist Phyllida's pleas. Nursing a hurt of her own, she doesn't want to come, to go over it all again, to hear Phyllida expressing a loss she herself must bear in silence. Worst of all is his absence, from his favourite chair, from the wintry garden, from his place at the head of the table. It is like a bereavement, but one over which she has no rights.

And turning a knife in the wound is Stuart's likeness to his father. There has always been a resemblance but now it is startling, as if Stuart has grown to fill the place Henry has vacated. The same brown eyes, the silky hair which he brushes back constantly, the same smile. It is both a joy and a pain. She devours him hungrily with her eyes and when he meets her gaze she almost expects an answering flash of desire.

But at least Phyllida can give her some news. 'He's staying with a colleague in Highgate. Paul, his name is, I've met him. His wife's gone to America for a year, to university. Really, some people's idea of marriage.' For a moment she seems to have forgotten that her own has failed. Then she says almost complacently, 'Well, I suppose it's better than having him go to another woman. Hopefully, he'll sort himself out. He says he needs to think.'

Rowena feels her words like a deep hard punch and has to struggle for breath. She makes herself say, 'Perhaps he'll be back.'

They pick silently at their food and when Phyllida goes to make coffee Stuart tells her quietly, 'He won't be back. Don't build up her hopes.'

Rowena is startled. 'How can you say that? What do you know?'

'I saw Dad in London last week. Mother doesn't know.'

She feels a spurt of jealousy and a desperate hurt. Questions rush into her mind, questions she cannot ask. But surprisingly he goes on. 'Actually, I was amazed that he hadn't gone to you. I was bracing myself to cope with Mother.'

She is going to ask him why but realises that it is pointless. 'How did you know?' she asks instead.

'He told me, about a month before he left. He was terribly depressed. He needed to talk to someone, but it was only because he'd had too much to drink. I wasn't any too pleased, but I don't have to tell you that.'

'But it's all been over for years. We never wanted to hurt her.'

'Well now you have, indirectly.'

She hates herself for trying to engage his sympathy. 'I'm hurt too. Try and understand that.'

He looks at her consideringly. 'Did you expect him to come to you? After all this time?'

She cannot speak but her eyes give her away.

'I asked him why not,' Stuart says. 'He said your time had passed. Can you understand that?'

She nods, biting her lip.

'Actually, there's something I want to talk to you about. But not now. I'll ring you if I may.'

She is puzzled, but Phyllida is returning. It has been a relief to speak at last, but her relationship with Stuart has subtly changed and she suddenly feels very vulnerable.

He rings her two days later and his voice is different, cold and calculating. He speaks his lines as if from a script, carefully prepared: 'You've kept your secret all these years, and now it seems Mother need never know. I'm sure you'll agree that's best. After all she thinks of you as her friend.'

'I am her friend.' She waits uneasily.

'Of course, I could tell her, any time.'

'But why should you? Isn't she suffering enough?'

'I didn't say I would, it's up to you.'

'Why? What can I do?'

There is a pause. She hears her heart beating erratically.

'I need some money. Three hundred pounds. But I need it urgently and I haven't got it. I wondered if you could help.'

She cannot believe it. She sinks down onto a chair, weak-kneed and sweating. 'That's blackmail, Stuart. I've known you all your life. I can't believe it.'

'Maybe I've put it too strongly. I'm simply asking for your help. There's this girl, see. And as I said, it's urgent. I told her I'd help.'

'An abortion?' She hugs herself, feeling sick.

He doesn't answer.

'Why didn't you just ask for help?' Her voice is weak but his is strong and ironic.

'Oh come now, would it really have been on?'

'I'm an old friend, or I liked to think I was. I really don't deserve threats.'

'Well, anyway, can you help?'

'It won't be that easy. And it would have to be a loan. I'm not well off.'

'I need it this week.'

She is thinking, trying to control her spinning thoughts. 'I can't believe you'd tell your mother. How could you be so cruel?'

'Let's just say I'm desperate.'

'Well, if I lend you the money it won't be because of the threat. I can't believe you'd stoop so low. I can let you have a cheque in the post. But it's just this once. It can't go on . . .'

'It won't have to.' Relief lightens his voice. 'Thank you, Rowena, I knew I could rely on you.'

She cannot bring herself to say goodbye but replaces the receiver abruptly. She is shaking all over, feeling sullied and used. 'Oh Henry,' she moans, rocking on the chair. 'Was this all it was worth? Didn't I deserve better than this?'

ELEVEN

Kathryn came home from hospital and Jake and Phyllida were there to meet her. Phyllida was shocked at how frail her daughter looked. Propped in a chair in the hospital ward she had looked pink and encouraging; now it seemed she could not walk from the car without Ben's help.

Jake ran to her but Ben fended him off. 'Wait till we're inside, old chap. You don't want to knock her over.'

The boy bit his lip. 'I wanted to help.'

Kathryn put her free hand on his shoulder. 'Then so you shall. Let me lean on you.' Her face was grey. Phyllida stood back to let the three of them pass into the house, then went to get Kathryn's bag from the car. Quite suddenly she didn't want to follow them indoors, she wanted to run away.

When she reached the kitchen Ben was already making tea and Jake was setting mugs and milk on the kitchen table. They had thrown the back door open and the cat sat in a patch of August sunlight. There was a vase of daisies on the table which Phyllida had picked, and upstairs there were roses beside the bed. A casserole simmered in the Aga, filling the room with the rich scent of pork and onions. She hoped Kathryn was glad to be home, but all Kathryn said, tearfully, was, 'Oh dear, it's dreadful without Hannah. She looked bereft when I went to say goodbye.'

'Of course, poor lamb. But you can still visit.'

Kathryn looked doubtful. 'It's going to be difficult. But you'll go with Ben?'

'Rowena and Derek are going tonight.'

'That's good of them.' Kathryn put her head back weakly. 'I really think I'd like to get to bed soon,' she murmured.

'Of course, love.' Ben went and stood behind her, kneading

her shoulder with his hand. Her own hand went up to his. His eyes met Phyllida's, dark with dread. She poured the tea busily and gave a mug to Kathryn. 'Drink this first, dear, then we'll help you upstairs.'

Jake sat at her feet, drinking orange squash. 'I made some cakes at cubs but they weren't very good. I don't expect you want one?'

Kathryn smiled down. 'Not now, do you mind? But I'm sure they're great.'

He shook his head, then jumped up. 'I want one. Do you, Grandma?'

'Well . . .' They were rock cakes, dry and knobbly. 'Well, all right, since you made them.'

Jake offered the tin to his father who took one absently, bit into it then set it on the table. Jake said, 'Next week we're going to make stew in a syrup tin. Bob's been telling me what to do.'

'How is Bob?' asked Kathryn. 'He must be so disappointed about the wedding.'

Bob had been devastated, but Phyllida wasn't going to say so. Instead she said with rare restraint, 'He understands. We've fixed a date at the beginning of October. And we were able to get our money back on the cruise, so that's been re-booked as well. So you see, nothing's lost. And this way, you'll be feeling much better too.'

'What about the house? Hasn't Bob sold his flat?'

'Yes. He's moving to Epsom next week. It will give us a chance to get everything as we want it before I join him.'

Kathryn looked at her mother with some surprise. 'You sound very philosophical.'

Actually, that was far from what Phyllida was feeling, but she said uncharacteristically, 'No good getting in a state about things which can't be helped. The great thing is to have you and Hannah with us, even if she is in plaster.'

'Which she will be. I've been talking to the consultant,' said Ben. He picked up his cake then put it down again, watched anxiously by Jake.

Phyllida took one and bit into it enthusiastically. 'Lovely, Jake,' she told him. 'But next time, use sultanas, they're not so dry as currants.'

'Rowena gave me the currants.'

'Yes, well Rowena's not used to making cakes.'

'But she makes great spaghetti bolognese.'

'I expect so.' Phyllida didn't care for pasta, finding it too difficult to eat. 'I'm not an expert on spaghetti.'

Ben said, 'Hannah's getting fed up with hospital food, perhaps you could make some cakes for her, Jake? With sultanas?'

'Could I, Mum?' He looked at Kathryn eagerly.

'If Grandma will come and help you.'

'But I can remember. I wrote it down.'

'We'll see.' She sighed and held out her mug. She looked up at Ben who was still standing behind her. 'Bed?' she said, and he smoothed her hair gently before helping her from the chair.

Rowena and Derek sat either side of the bed while Hannah held court between them. She wore a skimpy pink nightdress and white knickers and her leg, grotesquely enlarged by the plaster, was strung at an angle by a contraption of wires and pulleys. It didn't seem to trouble her at all though Rowena ached in sympathy.

'Nurse Rachel says I'm a star,' Hannah told them. 'She says I don't complain. But I did cry when Mummy went, she used to sit with me a lot.'

Derek spoke in a jolly voice. 'I see people have been signing your plaster. Can I add my name?'

'You need one of my felt tip pens. They're in the locker.'

Rowena smiled as he wrote his name and drew a beaming face at about the level of Hannah's knee. He really was a very nice man. 'There, that will keep your chin up,' he told her, capping the pen.

Rowena took her hand. 'I think we'll have to go now. They'll want to settle you for the night.'

Hannah's face seemed to shrink. 'Must you?'

187

'Daddy will come in the morning. Be a brave girl.'

Tears began to run down into her hair. 'I want to be home with Mummy. I want to look after her.'

'Mummy has lots of people to look after her, she just needs you to get well and strong.'

'I want to walk at Grandma's wedding.'

'Well you will. Just be patient a little while longer.'

She bent to kiss her. 'Don't forget, you're a star,' she whispered, wiping the tears away with her finger.

Then Derek reached onto the floor and brought up a paper parcel. 'Here's something to amuse you when we've gone. It's a favourite book with my grandchildren. You should be able to read some of it yourself. It's called *The Giants Who Squabbled*.'

Hannah tore off the paper and grinned. 'They've both got one red sock and one blue one,' she said, looking at the cover.

'That's because they squabbled.'

'I squabble with Jake, sometimes.'

'Everyone squabbles, sometimes. Goodbye, darling.'

They turned at the entrance to the ward to wave, but she was already immersed in the book.

'Dinner?' suggested Derek as they got into his car.

'Lovely. There'll be nobody at home.' She shuddered, for that was how it would always be. The postponement of Phyllida's departure brought her little comfort, for it only put off the inevitable. On the other hand her patience was nearly exhausted. Jake on his own since Hannah's accident had proved an endless bone of contention about what he ate and what he did. He had wanted to stay in his tent but Phyllida had swept the sheets away in a cavalier fashion, declaring that at least now they could get the room straight again.

Rowena had protested. 'It's hard enough for him having Hannah whisked away to hospital. Why make it worse? He was having fun in there.'

Phyllida chose to infer renewed criticism of Stuart for his part in the accident. 'Leave it alone, Ro, Stuart said he was sorry.'

'That's not my point. I just don't see why Jake has to lose his tent.'

Phyllida pursed her lips. 'He's my grandson, please let me decide. Surely he'd prefer a proper bed.'

Rowena wasn't so sure, and neither was Jake, who gave a howl of disappointment when he found the tent had gone.

'I was being an explorer,' he complained.

Rowena looked at him sympathetically. 'Well perhaps you can pretend your journey's over and you've got safely back to a hotel somewhere.'

'Or maybe I can pretend to be in hospital, like Hannah. Can I have my leg tied up?'

'No you can't,' Phyllida told him brusquely. 'Whatever next.'

Remembering this, Rowena gave a little sigh. Derek said, 'You're not looking forward to her going, are you?'

She looked surprised, for that wasn't what she had been thinking. However, she had to be honest.

'Well I suppose, despite everything, no, I'm not. It will be hard to be alone again.'

He nodded. 'Loneliness is the single biggest problem of modern man. Worse than ill health, poverty or unemployment. And it's not only the old, either.'

'But when you're young, you have hope and optimism. What is there to look forward to when you're old?'

'At least when you're old you don't have expectations, which so often are unfulfilled.'

She laughed. 'Oh dear, how depressed we sound. Where shall we go to eat?'

'There's a new Italian place in Coulsdon. Or would you prefer a quiet pub somewhere?'

'Let's drive out into the country and find a pub. I fancy trout with almonds or a nice steak.'

They found a redbrick Kentish roadhouse with a beer garden full of over-blown roses and nodding cosmea in pink and purple and a mock wishing well surrounded with gnomes.

'I can't abide gnomes,' said Derek, 'but then again there's something very appealing about some of their faces. Shall we have a drink outside?'

'I don't think it's really warm enough now the sun's gone down.'

They sat on an oak settle beside a fireplace filled with pine cones and hung with brasses, drinking beer while they waited for their food. Rowena wondered whether Derek had found a buyer for his house, but could not bring herself to ask. There was something very pleasant about the evening, and she needed no reminder that this, too, was a pleasure she would soon have to forgo.

'I had a letter from Mark today, he suggests I make a trip when the wedding's over.'

'And will you? That sounds like a good idea.'

'I think I will. I've never been. Well, that's not strictly true, but it was a long time ago.'

'Does he have a family? I mean do you have nieces and nephews with lots of children to visit too?'

She spun her glass thoughtfully. 'No. Mark never married.'

Some peculiar compulsion made her go on. 'Actually, Mark's a homosexual. He used to live with someone, Lawrence, but he died. They had been together all their lives. Like a marriage. It's hard to imagine that, isn't it?'

'It is. I can't understand them, but I don't disapprove. I dislike the terms "queer" and "gay". And I simply can't stand jokes about homosexuals. I find them quite unfunny, and it must be very hurtful. After all they didn't ask to be different, and for them it's normal.'

She looked at him in relief. 'I'm afraid my parents found it very hard to feel like that. I think they thought him something of a freak.'

'Are you sure it wasn't just that they were concerned for him? After all, life is hard enough without swimming against the tide.'

'Actually, they never talked about it with me. Maybe I should have tried to discuss it. But I shall never forget the day

I found out. Mother was making cornbeef pie, meat was still rationed, I remember the smell to this day, and father was hammering away in the garage. I knew even before Mark told me that it was a crucial day in our lives.'

She wondered why she was confiding in him like this, but it was a curious relief. 'So, now he's all alone, as I shall be. Yes, I think I will go, there's nothing to keep me here.'

Their food arrived together with cutlery wrapped in red paper serviettes.

'The size of this steak is ridiculous! It's obscene, with half the world starving.' Derek smeared the meat liberally with mustard.

'Well you don't have to eat it all. But what good would that do?'

'Would we ever have believed it during the dark days of rationing? Not that we did too badly, my grandmother lived in Devon on a farm and I seem to remember various secret little packages arriving and being opened with great excitement by my mother. We always had a turkey at Christmas and it would be stuffed round with eggs and butter. I'm not sure that it was allowed.'

They began to reminisce about the war. Derek had lived in Harrow and his parents had sunk an Anderson shelter in the garden in which he spent many nights. 'My father was wounded at Dunkirk so he was in a desk job in London, something very secret but at least we had him home most nights. I suppose we were lucky.'

Rowena told him about Keswick, and how she had met Phyllida. 'So we go back a long way. Yet curiously that's all we have in common, our memories.'

Well not quite all, she thought. 'I can't think why I'm telling you all this now,' she said with some surprise. 'I mean, you'll be leaving soon.' Maybe, she reflected, that had made it easier to talk.

He put down his knife and fork. 'Ah yes. I've been meaning to tell you. I have a buyer for my house, and they want to complete in a hurry.'

'Good.' She smiled bravely. 'And how about the house in Wales?'

'It's still on the market so I've made an offer. I could be gone within a month.'

'Oh dear.' She stared down at her plate, at the neatly stripped fish bones and the slice of lemon. Then she looked up, smiling again. 'I'm sorry. I'm very pleased for you. It's just that life seems to be full of goodbyes.'

He smiled back. A kind smile, reaching his eyes. And she thought wildly for a moment how nice it would have been if he had asked her to go with him.

Phyllida was very depressed when she got home from Kathryn's. She found the house dark and empty and was disappointed. She had counted on Rowena being there for her.

She had found the last three weeks terribly trying, looking after Jake in addition to visiting Kathryn and Hannah in hospital, coping with Bob's disappointment and her own feelings of guilt over the wedding. She had sensed, too, Rowena's growing impatience with her and realised sadly that Rowena would be glad when she had gone. It never for one moment occurred to her that part of Rowena's irritability stemmed from fear and envy. She resolved to try very hard for the few remaining weeks. She wanted Rowena to miss her when she'd gone, not to slam the door behind her in relief.

Meanwhile, Ben had reminded her that it was his and Kathryn's wedding anniversary in a few days' time. He had asked Phyllida to come and baby-sit if he could persuade Kathryn to go out somewhere for a quiet meal, and Phyllida had agreed while privately feeling that it would be impossible. Kathryn had looked so frail and ill. Now, sitting alone at the kitchen table, Phyllida dropped her head into her hands and allowed herself the luxury of tears.

Rowena found her there when Derek dropped her off after their meal.

'Phyllida? What's wrong? Kathryn got back all right?'

Phyllida wiped her eyes. 'Oh yes, if you can call it all right. She's so weak, Rowena, I can't believe she'll ever get better.'

'Well, it's a big operation. And the chemotherapy always takes it out of her.'

'She's not having it this time. Just radiotherapy. They think that will be better.'

'Well, there you are then. I'll make some Horlicks, you just sit there. I won't have any, Derek took me out to dinner.'

'That's nice. Where did you go?'

'The Boar's Head, near Westerham – it made a nice change. But he'll be moving soon.'

She waited for a sympathetic response but none came. Instead Phyllida said, 'It's Ben and Kathryn's wedding anniversary on Thursday. He wants to take her out somewhere but I don't think she's up to it.'

'How many years have they been married?'

'Twelve years.'

Rowena stirred the milk into the mug. She hadn't blended the powder carefully enough and big yellow globules floated to the top. Phyllida would hate that but for once she didn't care.

She was thinking, twelve years . . .

Phyllida is on the other end of the phone. For once she sounds happy and excited. 'Kathryn's getting married.'

Rowena too is suddenly unbearably excited. 'When?'

'Soon. A month or so. Ben's got a job down here and they've found a house.'

Soon! She would see him soon. Rowena sees her face in the hall mirror and is thankful there is a telephone line between them. She says evenly, 'That's very good news. You must be pleased.'

'Henry will give her away, of course. We've talked it all over.' Phyllida sounds self-important, smug, momentarily reinstated.

'Of course, I wouldn't have expected anything else.'

'You won't be away I hope. it will be late August.'

'Don't worry, Phyl, nothing would keep me away.'

Nothing. She hugs herself to contain her joy.

Consumed as she was with anxiety over Kathryn, Phyllida found herself, curiously, wishing for her mother. She had been dead for years and in her lifetime had offered Phyllida precious little support, but Phyllida longed for someone of her own in whom to confide. Of course there was Bob, but Bob was preoccupied with arrangements for his move, and secretly she thought that he resented her family for coming in the way of his plans. He never said so, was unfailingly tolerant and generous, but she couldn't help realising how she would have felt if the position were reversed.

'You worry too much, precious,' he told her.

'That's what being a mother means. Take Kathryn herself, her own child is in hospital and there's nothing she can do for her.'

They were sitting at his kitchen table wrapping china in newspaper and packing it in tea-chests. 'Do you really want all these jugs?' she asked. 'I mean, I have plenty of pretty ones, and how many jugs can we possibly want?'

'Leave them then, if you don't like them. Though,' he added after a pause, 'I should like to have some of my own things about me.'

'Of course!' She laid a soft hand on his, seeing them both grimy from the newsprint. 'You must have what you like,' she said generously, while privately relegating the jugs to the back of a cupboard.

'You are what I like,' he said, shaming her with the adoration in his eyes. He squeezed her hand. 'As long as I have you, I'll be happy.'

'Oh you.' She was embarrassed suddenly at the strength of his love, wondering if she deserved it.

'Five weeks, then you'll be all mine.' He looked at her roguishly and she felt a frisson of excitement, like a young girl approaching her wedding night. She was pleased they had waited, except for that one time, and she was glad of that too because now she knew it would all be all right.

She said suddenly, 'I think Rowena will be happy to be rid of me. I wonder whether it wasn't a mistake after all, moving in with her.'

'Surely not.'

Phyllida thought that it was not something she would have admitted, had escape not been so imminent. If it wasn't for Bob, she would have been glad enough to have a safe refuge with Rowena, and done everything possible to make it work. She remembered how it had been when Kathryn, then Stuart, left home to get married.

'I hated living alone,' she admitted. 'I never told anyone of course, but when Fiona left Stuart and he asked to move back home I was delighted. Isn't that dreadful?'

He smiled tolerantly. 'I can understand it. You're the sort of woman who needs looking after.'

'And then, when he got his job in Newcastle I was desperate. It was my idea that I move in with Rowena. I thought she seemed pleased. After all, she'd lived alone all her life.

'She didn't want me to put any money into the house, and it's just as well as it's turned out. She always said, what would happen to her if anything happened to me – she'd stand to lose her home. So I've paid her rent all this time. It helped her with the extra mortgage she'd taken out to buy the house from her mother. And we share the bills of course.'

'Precious, I don't really need to know all this. It's your business, yours and Rowena's.'

But she went on relentlessly. 'Of course, it wasn't like The Maltings, but I hated that little box I had to move into when Henry sold. Modern houses have no character.' She modified the comment hastily. 'Well, I don't mean ours of course, I think it's charming.'

'I should hope so. And you're going to make it even more so.'

They had come to the end of the pile of china. He stood up, brushing his sticky hands together. 'And I shouldn't be surprised,' he said, crossing to the sink, 'if Rowena is expecting to miss you very much indeed.'

She looked hopeful. 'I should like to think so.'

He soaped his hands, then turned to her playfully. 'Come over here.' When she joined him he dabbed her nose lightly, crowning it with bubbles. 'You worry too much about things, precious. Now, let me wash those little hands.' Obediently she slid her grubby hands into his slippery grasp, feeling him caress each finger in turn, watching the suds grow grimy. He twisted her engagement ring so that the stones gleamed up through the bubbles. 'Not long now and there'll be another one. I can't wait.'

She leaned against him, languishing against his solid warmth. 'Nor me.' Then, excitedly, 'Oh, I just love weddings.'

She helps Kathryn to dress, buttoning the tiny buttons up her back and smoothing the satin skirt. She wishes her daughter had a floral headband and a long veil, but Kathryn has chosen a hat with a wide white brim supporting satin roses. It shows off the severe lines of her face which a veil would have softened, but it is too late now. Standing behind her Phyllida sees her own face in the mirror, prettily flushed, her fair curls carefully arranged around a pale blue pill-box hat with a tiny veil, and thinks that in a way she looks like a bride herself. She hopes that Henry, when he sees her, will feel a pang of regret, but she knows it is a foolish hope.

There is one bridesmaid, Olivia, a college friend of Kathryn's, and she hands Kathryn her bouquet of roses and stands back, with Phyllida, to admire. Then Phyllida's mother calls up from the hall, 'The photographer's here, and Henry,' and together they go downstairs and out into the garden of The Maltings and Phyllida sees Henry crossing the lawn towards them, tall and slim as ever in new, metal-rimmed glasses, and suddenly she wants to cry.

He takes her hand formally, like a guest.

'You're looking well. How are you feeling?'

'Weepy. It's a big day.'

'Yes.' She thinks, it wasn't supposed to be like this, you just popping in to give our daughter away, then going back to your bachelor flat and leaving me alone.

He turns to Kathryn. 'Wonderful. You look wonderful. You always had such style.'

She takes his arm possessively. 'Hello, Dad. I want a photograph just with you, down by the shrubbery.' She leads him away and the photographer follows, leaving Phyllida alone with Olivia, who smiles sympathetically.

'She always adored her father,' she says unnecessarily.

But later in the church, when he has given Kathryn away, Henry slides into the pew beside Phyllida as he was meant to do. She longs to take his arm as the responses are given but instead sits apart and stiff, dabbing at her eyes and trying not to sniff while he looks straight ahead, staring at Kathryn's back with its tiny buttons disappearing into the folds of her skirt. When Ben takes her in his arms and kisses her, Henry looks down at Phyllida and says, 'So, that's that. A job well done,' and she thinks bitterly, by whom?

Outside the church, with the bells ringing and clouds pulling back from a bright and timely sun, Rowena comes to her side. 'Hello, Phyl. It's all quite gorgeous. I love Kathryn's hat.'

'Do you? It seemed a bit unconventional to me.'

'It's very fashionable. And it suits her style.'

Rowena herself is wearing navy and emerald green and looks striking. She asks, 'How's Henry?' watching casually as he lines up for the photographer. He beckons to Phyllida, who almost runs to his side, leaving Rowena to stand and stare.

It has been five years. She had expected to find him changed, aged, careworn and sad. But if anything he looks younger, and happy. She has seen him look like that before. She notices how he towers over Phyllida whereas Kathryn comes to his shoulder. They made a handsome pair, he and Kathryn. He had used to say that she and he made a handsome pair. They still could do. Her eyes slide along the line to Stuart, as tall as Henry and the image of his father. It isn't fair that he should be so blessed, when underneath he is so different. A wash of remembered shame and resentment makes her mouth taste sour and she turns away.

Phyllida's mother greets her. She is tiny, frail, leaning on a stick. She will be dead within a year. All she says as Rowena joins her is, 'Phyllida's never got over Henry going. Poor Phyllida.'

Rowena nods. Poor, poor Phyllida.

She finds herself next to Stuart at the buffet.

He is cool as a cucumber. 'Hello, Rowena. Can I introduce you to Fiona? We're getting married in the spring.'

She shakes hands with a pretty girl in a lemon dress whom she barely sees, for anger is coiling up thickly in her throat, spilling out in words.

'You still owe me three hundred pounds.' She doesn't care if Fiona hears or not. 'I really ought to charge you interest.'

He looks at her blandly. 'Didn't I do that ages ago? But of course, we seldom see you now.'

She wants to shake him, to blurt out the reason for the loan in front of his pretty little fiancée, but some residual control takes over.

'Please see to it,' she manages crisply, turning away to help herself to salmon mousse. She is trembling and the salads blur before her eyes. 'Let me help you,' says a waiter solicitously, and she wonders if he thinks she is drunk.

She finds a seat by the window at a table where she knows no one and doesn't have to talk. Her eyes scan the room, which is panelled and dimly lit with wall lights despite the sunshine outside. She sees Henry, with Phyllida at his side. Phyllida is not going to let him out of her sight today. It is how it always was. She forces down the food, washing it down with wine. Whatever she had thought would happen is obviously impossible. It is unlikely that they will even speak.

After the speeches and the cake, she wanders into the garden, carrying the remains of her champagne. Desolation sweeps over her, dark as the evening shadows which are lengthening on the lawn. She had devoured the sight of him as a starving man devours food, yet he had barely met her eyes. Useless to pretend it was emotion that held him back.

Rather it was shame. Yet she wants no apology, no explanation, just some acknowledgement of the past. She takes a path that leads to tennis courts and a swimming pool, deserted now but with yellow sunbeds and umbrellas and dirty glasses bearing witness to the summer afternoon. She lowers herself onto one of the beds and leans back, cradling her glass and closing her eyes, letting everything – hope, desire, disappointment – drift away.

'Rowena?'

She starts awake, knowing his voice at once. He is leaning over her as he has done so often before. She thinks, wildly, that he is going to kiss her.

'Henry.' She sits up, spilling champagne down her emerald blouse. He takes the glass, gently, and dabs her with his handkerchief. Tears fill her eyes. 'Oh Henry, I didn't think you'd speak to me.'

'And I didn't think you'd speak to me. And then you disappeared. It was Kathryn who saw where you went.'

He sits on a wrought iron chair. 'It's good to see you again. There are things I need to say.'

Suddenly it's too much. She shakes her head. 'There's no need. I understand. But are you happy? I need to know you're happy.'

He looks at her consideringly as if assessing her strength. 'I am now. But I'm going away.'

'Away?' As if it made a difference.

'To America. With Hope.'

'Hope? You mean hopefully?'

He hesitated. 'That too. No, Hope's a colleague of mine, an American who's been over here on a year's sabbatical. She's returning to the States next month and I'm going with her. We want to get married.'

Hope. For whom? The blue pool and the yellow umbrellas spin round and round and she closes her eyes. 'That's nice. But will Phyllida give you a divorce?'

'I haven't asked her yet. I wanted to get Kathryn's wedding over with.'

'She's always said she won't.'

'Then I'll divorce her. It's five years, I can do that.'

'I see.' Poor Phyllida.

'I'm sorry, Rowena.' He takes her hand. 'I know it should have been us.'

'Nonsense. We always said . . .'

'I know what we said. But for years and years you were the one. Don't ever forget that.'

She clings to his hand and her voice chokes. 'I'll always love you. I shouldn't say it but it's true.'

He looks infinitely sad. 'Don't cry. I can't bear to see you cry.'

But she doesn't care and lets the tears slide. 'It will break Phyllida's heart,' she tells him, and is viciously pleased. Then she hears someone calling, coming along the path towards the pool. It is Stuart, looking at them accusingly, with Henry's eyes.

'Mother sent me to tell you they are off.'

Henry releases her hand and stands. 'There's a poem,' he says. 'By Frances Cornford.'

'Tell me . . .'

'I'll send it.' And he smiles, and touches her shoulder lightly, and passes from her sight.

She dries her eyes, and follows slowly, feeling in her bag for the brightly coloured confetti.

A week later a small package arrives. Inside it is a slim blue book, and inside that a note in Henry's hand: *Page 58. Goodbye.*

She turns to the page and reads.

> My love came back to me
> Under the November tree
> Shelterless and dim.
> He put his hand upon my shoulder,
> He did not think me strange or older,
> Nor I, him.

She screws his note so tightly that her nails cut into her palm, and lets it fall. She puts her hand to her face, but her tears, as hot as blood, slip through her fingers onto the page.

TWELVE

Derek came to say goodbye.

Rowena was picking runner beans with bees buzzing lazily round the last of the red blossoms in the late September sunshine. There were courgettes, already grown too big beneath their bright yellow trumpets. The smell of cider rose from apples rotting in the grass. She felt a sense of everything drawing to a close and it was difficult to smile as he came down the garden towards her, carrying a chrysanthemum in a pot.

'Not exactly a farewell gift,' he said, holding out the plant. 'It seemed silly to take it all the way to Wales, I wondered if you would give it a home.'

'Of course.'

They walked back down the garden, he still carrying the plant, she with the trug of vegetables.

'Will you have much of a garden in Wales?'

'Enough. Mine had got too large really.'

'As this will soon,' she said, looking round. The grass needed cutting and the edges were shaggy, spoiling the beds. 'I shall have to find someone else to do the lawns soon.'

'You'll miss Phyllida's help.'

'Oh, she just potters and fusses. Most of it's up to me, though she likes to think of herself as a gardener. You'll have a cup of tea?'

He looked apologetic. 'I can't stay long, I'm still packing. The van arrives at eight-thirty tomorrow.'

'Well, just a cup of tea. Phyllida's been baking.'

There was a chocolate cake and a tray of scones on the kitchen table. Phyllida had disappeared. Rowena put the kettle on and went to call her. Suddenly she didn't want to be alone with Derek, she wanted his leaving to be a casual thing, impersonal, not poignant and meaningful when really it meant nothing.

But when he left he said, 'I'll write of course, let you know how I'm getting on. And I shall expect to hear from you.' She smiled gratefully, feeling as if she had been thrown a lifebelt.

She watered the chrysanthemum carefully, resolving to keep it alive.

Phyllida was unusually solicitous. 'He's a nice man. I'm sorry he's left you.'

'He hasn't left me, he's gone away to join his family.'

'Well, you know what I mean. You could have done with him when, you know, after I've gone too.'

Rowena said defensively, 'That really doesn't come into it. Derek was just an acquaintance.'

Phyllida cleared the table. 'You're very touchy. I didn't mean to upset you.'

'I'm not upset.' Yet she knew she was, and Phyllida knowing she was made it worse. She picked up the milk and opened the fridge. 'Oh Phyl! You've been at it again.' She eyed the greasy butter papers with distaste. Phyllida pushed passed her and snatched them from the shelf. 'Never mind,' she snapped. 'You'll soon see the back of me.' She dropped them into the bin with a little sob and turned towards the sink.

'Phyl?' Rowena looked at her uncertainly as she ran water into the bowl.

Phyllida said nothing.

Rowena offered, 'I'm sorry. Maybe I am upset at Derek leaving after all. I shouldn't have snapped.'

'I do try. You always said I must think of it as my home too.'

'I know.'

Phyllida rinsed a cup. She always rinsed things, squandering hot water recklessly, but Rowena told herself it didn't matter now. She stared at her rigid back, not knowing what to say.

At last Phyllida turned round and there was something pleading about her expression. 'I have been grateful, you know. And now you'll have your house back, and be able to do things your own way.'

'I suppose so.' Rowena struggled with her pride. 'But it won't seem the same,' was all she managed.

Phyllida looked at her hopefully for a moment, then said, 'I'll fetch the washing in.'

She went into the garden. Rowena went to the pedal bin and found herself staring ludicrously down at the discarded butter papers, panic beating like wings about her head.

It is five years since Henry went to America. Rowena has made the best of those years, and is now headmistress of St Margaret's, as independent girls' school housed in solid grey stone with redbrick extensions and not a portacabin in sight. Her own office has floor-length curtains and a sofa on which to seat visiting parents. She spends her day dealing with the problems of staff and pupils, in balancing the precarious books and, very occasionally, taking a lesson with the sixth form.

She misses teaching, but she enjoys being in charge. For the first time in her life she feels fulfilled.

Nonetheless she has things on her mind. There is the problem of her mother Helen, who can no longer carry on living alone. There is a personality clash in the A-level biology group which looks like jeopardising one girl's chances of getting in to Cambridge. And there is a pregnancy in the fifth year. The aggrieved prospective grandparents are due to see her this afternoon, and she must decide whether their daughter can come back after the baby is born.

And Phyllida has left a message with her secretary. She is coming up to see her this evening. Throughout the day, annoyingly, Rowena finds herself wondering why.

She eats a sketchy supper, sitting at the kitchen table leafing through the paper which she never has time to read until the evening. She is tired, as she always is at the end of term, and the summer term is the worst, with exams and sports days, lists of entrants for September, new timetables. The following day she has to interview applicants for the job of her secretary as the indomitable woman who has held the post for twenty years is leaving. She doesn't know how she will manage without Mary, who knows the school better than she does. She puts the paper aside and rubs wearily at her eyes.

She does not want to see Phyllida.

But at half past eight she arrives, paying off a taxi at the gate. She is wearing a black suit with a too-tight skirt. She has put on weight since Rowena saw her last and there is a suggestion of grey in her blonde curls. Rowena opens the door before she rings and knows at once that the news is bad. Phyllida's face has the look of one who has been slapped down and rolled in the dirt, without knowing why. Rowena's heart sinks. She hasn't the energy to offer comfort. Instead she pours sherry and seats them on the sofa beside the open french windows. The garden is gilded with evening sunshine and she says lightly, 'My garden's looking a picture, don't you think?'

Phyllida nods. She is gripping her glass tightly, her knuckles shine white and her rings glint. She says in a voice which wobbles tremulously, 'There's no easy way of saying this, Ro. Henry's dead.'

Rowena's glass is cold in her hand, cold and hard and brittle. She clings onto the sensation as everything else gives way to the flood of shock and grief. At the same time there is the need for composure which causes her to ask stiffly, irrelevantly, 'How do you know? How did it happen?'

'I had a letter from Hope. He went in for a straightforward operation for gallstones, and died under the anaesthetic. You'd have expected better than that, in America.' Her voice is bitter.

Rowena gathers her self-control about her and touches Phyllida's arm. 'What a shock. I'm so sorry. But it was good of Hope to tell you. She must be pretty shattered herself.'

Phyllida begins to cry. 'At least she was his wife. She has a right to grieve. What rights do I have?'

'You have every right. Remember, you had him longer than Hope did. Henry would want you to grieve.' Tears are rising to Rowena's eyes too. 'Good heavens, *I* am grieving. Henry was an old friend.' Deliciously, she realises she can give in,

Phyllida will be comforted by her tears. Together, they sit and weep, and sip their sherry, and wipe their eyes, and smile at each other, then Phyllida says, 'It's good of you to share it with me. I'm grateful. But you don't know how I feel, not deep down inside. How could you, after all?'

And she gives her a look of patient, possessive sorrow.

Suddenly Rowena wants to tell her exactly how she knows. She wants to snatch away some of the rights of mourning, she wants to howl and rage and beat the air and destroy for ever Phyllida's patronising sense of superiority. Instead she says, 'I'll make some coffee. I think we could do with it.'

Phyllida follows her into the kitchen. 'Do you think he ever thought about me?' she asks pathetically. 'I mean, you can't just forget someone, after all those years. Can you?'

Rowena has wondered the same, many times. 'I'm sure he thought of you,' she says reassuringly. 'After all, he kept in touch with Kathryn and Stuart. Have you told them yet?'

'Stuart read the letter. He's gone to tell Kathryn. She'll be devastated. It's not a good time, with Hannah less than a month old.'

'I guess it's never a good time.'

Rowena pours the coffee. 'Is the taxi coming back for you?'

'Yes, at ten o'clock.'

Rowena glances at the clock. Half an hour. She begins to count the minutes, as Phyllida drones on relentlessly about the new baby, about Jake and his two-year-old achievements. With relief she hears the ring at the bell and sees Phyllida out into the last of the light. In her black suit she disappears quickly into the dusk. How like her, thinks Rowena, to wear black, as if it was a funeral.

But, she supposes as she shuts the door, perhaps it was. It was the nearest either of them could get to burying their dead.

She stands quite still in the dark hall, letting her feelings flow. She is deranged with grief, her thoughts scud around her brain, colliding with each other, screaming in pain. But her tears have quite dried up.

She cannot cry and she can say nothing.

It is only when Mary, her secretary, a week later asks, 'What's up? You look bloody awful,' that she tells her, 'Someone I loved has died. I can't say more than that.'

Hannah came out of hospital a week before the wedding on crutches, her leg still encased in plaster. Kathryn, who was having a good spell, invited Phyllida and Rowena to supper to celebrate. It occurred to Rowena that it would be the last time she went to Kathryn and Ben's. Over the years she had come to think of them as family, but it would be deluding herself to think that they felt the same. She was Kathryn's mother's friend, who might reasonably be supposed to have a life of her own. There was no way that they could tell that Rowena was staring into an abyss out of which there seemed no way to climb.

She was getting old. There could be no other explanation for this clinging dependence on someone with whom she had nothing in common and had always resented. Rowena sat silent while the family chattered on, and it was Ben who finally noticed and said, 'And what are your plans for after the wedding, Rowena? Perhaps you'll just be glad when life returns to normal.'

'Not at all.'

'Rowena's off to New York to see her brother,' Phyllida told them. She had Hannah on her lap, her leg supported awkwardly on a chair. She looked happy and self-satisfied. 'Bob says we can go to the States next year. Not New York, too dangerous, but I'd love to see San Francisco.'

'I'm sure Rowena will be quite safe with her brother,' remonstrated Ben. 'After all, he lives there.'

'He's going to move up to New England. I shall go up with him, househunting. He wants something by a lake.'

'New England in the fall,' said Kathryn wistfully. 'That's something I've always wanted to see.'

'One day you shall,' Ben told her almost fiercely.

I wonder, thought Rowena, looking at Kathryn's thin face. So far the treatment seemed to be working, but with cancer one never knew. It lurked insidiously beneath the surface like evil, waiting to strike. When Kathryn got up, gingerly for she was still sore, Rowena leapt up too, offering to carry in the plates for supper. Ben took the casserole and Jake the potatoes. When they were all served Phyllida said complacently, 'So, we're all set for the thirtieth?'

'I am going to be bridesmaid, aren't I?'

'Of course.'

Hannah looked doubtful. 'Won't my dress be spoiled, with the crutches and things?'

'Not at all. You'll look very pretty.'

'And at least it will be original,' Ben told her teasingly. 'Not every bridesmaid has her leg in plaster!'

'We could put flowers round it,' giggled Jake, mashing his potatoes into the gravy.

'Don't mess your food,' Kathryn said automatically. She had taken very little herself and, noticing this, Phyllida said, 'That's not enough to keep a fly alive. You need to build up your strength.'

'Don't fuss, Mother. I've no appetite.'

'I'll get you a glass of milk.' Ben left the room and Kathryn looked at her mother warningly. 'You only worry him,' she said irritably.

Rowena intervened quickly. 'We've made an appointment at the hairdresser for Hannah. They're going to put her hair up into a bun. If you agree of course.'

Kathryn shrugged. 'Why not?'

'We'll go together,' said Phyllida, reaching over to cut Hannah's meat.

'Leave her, Mother, she can manage.'

'And they'll fit her head-dress at the same time,' went on Rowena. 'She can come back with us to change. Is that all right?'

'It would seem sensible. We'll see you at the register office.'

Ben returned with the milk. 'Drink up, there's a good girl,' he said, looking at Kathryn tenderly. Rowena was moved. His devotion was touching. Any tensions between them seemed to have disappeared. She watched as Kathryn obediently emptied the glass like a little girl, then smiled at him, her top lip white with milk, her usually stern expression soft and vulnerable.

The last week wore inexorably away and the house gradually emptied as Phyllida's possessions disappeared into boxes. Little lamps with pleated shades, which Rowena had thought fussy, left strange, painful spaces. The silver removed from the sideboard left the drawer light and hollow. Phyllida wrapped her fish slice in green baize, saying, 'I can't think I'll ever use this again. I might as well sell it. Bob doesn't care for fish.'

Memory tore painfully at Rowena's dwindling reserves. Salmon, Scotland. Henry. And now it was Bob, and he was taking Phyllida away, taking away all the lamps and cushions and magazines and embroidery and homemade cakes. The curious comfort of having another person in the house. She found herself saying impulsively, 'I'm sorry, Phyllida.'

Phyllida looked up, startled. 'For what?'

'Oh, I don't know. Everything I've ever done to you I suppose.'

'What have you ever done to me?'

Rowena hesitated. 'I can be pretty impatient at times.'

Phyllida looked maddeningly self-righteous. 'That's true.' She started to pack the silver in a box. 'But then again, I expect I can be irritating. We all have our little ways. And of course you've never lived with anyone before. You don't know what it's like to give and take.'

Rowena was astonished and felt irritation flare. 'Believe me, I've become a past-master at give and take. Have you any idea how difficult it's been, after years of suiting myself?'

Phyllida nodded with a self-satisfied air. 'That's just what I mean. You'd got very selfish.'

'Well it wasn't through any choice of my own. Don't you think I'd have liked to marry and have a family? You were always so smug it never seemed to occur to you how lucky you were. You had everything. *Everything.*' Rowena found she was trembling and clenched her hands. Control. She must get herself under control.

Phyllida was trying to fit the fish slice into the box. Finally she gave up and put on the lid. The slice, loosed from its baize wrapping, gleamed on the table. She said quietly, 'Well I ended up with nothing, just like you.'

Nothing? Was that how Rowena's life seemed to Phyllida?

'You have your children. And Jake and Hannah. And now you've got Bob. A new house. A Mediterranean cruise. In fact, Phyllida, you don't know you're born. You even had me to take you in when you were desperate and alone.'

Phyllida's hand went to her mouth. 'I thought you wanted me, Ro. I thought I'd be company for you.'

'Yes, well I didn't ask you to come.'

'But you agreed.' Phyllida's voice was whining, like a child wanting a favour. She didn't believe what she was hearing. Rowena was looking at her as if she hated her. Her eyes had gone bright and hard and she seemed to have lost control of her mouth, which was pulled this way and that as if she was fighting with her words.

After a long silence Rowena said in a strange, harsh voice, 'All my life you've been there, wheedling your way in when you weren't wanted, hounding me, pursuing me, showing off . . .'

'No, no . . .'

'Worming your way into my family, making me be your bridesmaid when we were hardly even friends, dragging me down to your house so that I could see how well set up you were . . .'

Phyllida sank down onto a chair. 'Stop, Rowena. Please stop.'

But Rowena couldn't stop. Everything was coming apart, bursting out in an ugly rush of pent-up envy and resentment. 'I never wanted to be your friend,' she shouted, gripping the table and leaning towards her. 'Why didn't you just leave me alone?'

'Rowena, please. It wasn't like that. I always admired you,

you were clever and confident. And I envied you too. I always felt left out when we were children. I was proud to have you as my bridesmaid. Why didn't you say you didn't want to be?'

She was beginning to cry. Rowena snapped, 'Oh for God's sake don't cry. I've never known anyone turn on the tears like you do,'

'That's because you're hard, Rowena. You don't cry because you're hard. Henry said you were hard.'

'What? Henry said *what*?'

'Well, not hard, exactly. He said you were self-contained. When I said to him once that it was a pity you weren't married, he said you didn't need to be married, that you were self-contained. Your own person. I knew what he meant.' She scrubbed her eyes with a handkerchief. Her heart was thudding painfully and she was shocked and frightened. Rowena seemed to have turned into a stranger, and just when she had wanted everything to be right between them. Now Rowena was looking at her incredulously.

'I don't believe Henry said that about me.'

'Why not? I wouldn't make it up.'

'Because . . .' The words were there, trembling on her tongue. But at the last moment something intervened. The habit of deception was not easily cast away. In a fury of frustration instead she seized the fish slice and brandished it in the air. 'Because,' she said through gritted teeth, 'I'm not like that. Which only goes to prove you don't know me at all.'

'Rowena.' Phyllida stretched out a desperate hand. She was terrified. The slice flashed from side to side, brilliantly, showing her blurred and cringing figure in its shiny surface.

She stood up and grabbed Rowena's wrist. With a strength born of fury Rowena wrenched away.

'Don't touch me!' she cried. She pulled back with the slice poised like a dagger, then of its own volition her hand shot out and she felt the metal engage with the soft skin of Phyllida's cheek.

Phyllida's hand flew to her face. She was so shocked she didn't make a sound, and simply stood and stared with huge eyes as Rowena put the slice slowly down on the table. Rowena looked confused and rubbed at her eyes. Then she sat down at the table and put her head in her hands.

'Oh God,' she murmured. 'What on earth has happened?'

'It's all right.' Phyllida was so relieved it was over she was prepared to be generous. 'It's only a scratch, it's hardly even bleeding.' She looked at her fingers curiously, seeing the red smear in amazement. She wondered what to do. Always it had been Rowena who had taken control in a crisis, but Rowena was bent over with her arms wrapped tightly round her chest, rocking backwards and forwards, looking bemused.

'I'll make some tea. Or do you think a glass of brandy?'

Rowena said nothing.

'Brandy, I think.' There was a bottle in the sideboard. Phyllida poured two glasses and slid one across the table. She didn't care for brandy but she took a few desperate sips to steady herself.

'Drink it, Ro,' she urged. Rowena picked up the glass. Her hand was shaking and the liquid slopped onto the polished surface of the table. She wiped at it absently with her finger.

Phyllida sat down opposite her. She didn't know what to do. Her cheek was stinging and she wanted desperately to go and look at herself in the mirror, but something told her she shouldn't leave Rowena, who was now slowly drinking the brandy.

Hesitantly, Phyllida began to speak. 'I'm sorry, Ro. I didn't realise it had been like that. I thought we were friends.'

Rowena said nothing. She looked across the table and her eyes were haunted.

Phyllida persisted. 'We still are friends as far as I'm concerned. But of course you need never see me again after Saturday. I'll be out of your life for good.'

Rowena's mouth was working. Her voice when it came was strangely faint and distant. 'I don't know what to say. You'll never forgive me.'

Phyllida's face broke into a smile. She was being asked to be magnanimous. 'Of course I forgive you. I didn't know how it had been for you. You never said. But I'll be gone soon, you can get back to normal. Do things your own way. I never wanted to be a burden.'

Rowena's voice was flat. 'You weren't a burden. You're right, I was glad of your company. I'm going to miss you.'

'Really?' Phyllida was beaming now with pleasure. She was hearing what she wanted to hear. It was worth a small scratch. But was it a small scratch? It was two days to her wedding. She got up and went into the hall, leaning towards the mirror to inspect her cheek.

'I'll have to say I got tangled up in a rose bush. Or something.' She stood in the doorway looking at Rowena earnestly. 'I shan't tell, Rowena. I would never, ever, tell.'

Rowena lay in the dark, staring up, sleepless, towards the ceiling. Her heart was pounding noisily and erratically and she twisted restlessly. She felt both curiously purged and wound up like a spring. The look of hurt in Phyllida's eyes as Rowena had bathed her cheek and smoothed on antiseptic had burned into her as inexorably as the patient forgiveness of her smile as they drank tea together, quietly, at the kitchen table, trying to be normal.

Phyllida, too, was lying awake. For her, it was the words which had wounded more than the wound. The implications were so awful that she could only reject them. She had said to Rowena, 'Let's forget all about it. Pretend it never happened. And when you get back from America you must come and stay and everything will be just the same. You'll see.'

But that's exactly it, Rowena had thought. Everything will be exactly the same, exactly as it always was. But she had said nothing. She was frightened, and deeply ashamed. Let Phyllida believe what made her happy. The fact remained that she had struck her. Lying awake, she wondered if she would ever be the same again.

It was a relief when morning came. Rowena got up and made tea. She knocked tentatively on Phyllida's door, carrying a tray. There was no reply. She opened the door quietly and saw that Phyllida was asleep, her head thrown back, breathing loudly through her mouth. The scratch stood out pink and ragged on her pale cheek, and there was a hint of bruising. Rowena stared, appalled all over again. Had she really done that? And suppose it had been worse?

She put the tea on the bedside table and Phyllida opened her eyes. For a brief moment Rowena saw a flash of fear and compunction seized her. She explained quickly, 'I've brought you tea. It's a bit early, but I couldn't sleep.'

Phyllida pulled herself up. Her pink nightgown slipped down, revealing soft full breasts. Rowena looked away. The profligacy of Phyllida's body had always made her uneasy. Phyllida said, 'I took ages to get off too. It must have been the brandy.'

'Of course it wasn't the brandy. You were upset, as I was. And on the eve of your wedding . . .'

'There's still today. Let me take you out to lunch, once the removal men have been. I'd like that.'

Rowena looked at her in disbelief. It was as if Phyllida was apologising to her. As if somewhere in the dark watches of the night she had decided on unconditional forgiveness, chosen to take the responsibility on herself. To disabuse her would be to add to her unhappiness.

'All right,' she said at last. 'If you have the time.'

'There's nothing to do, once my things have gone. I'm not seeing Bob today, it's bad luck. You and I will have a nice day together, like we used to do.'

'All right,' said Rowena again. Let Phyllida have things her own way. It was the very least she could do. The very least.

The day turned out wet with a dismal rain polishing the changing leaves and soggying the geraniums in the front garden. Summer was over; soon there would be frosts and fog. Watching as the men carried cases and boxes and small pieces of furniture down the shining path Rowena reflected that she must lift the geraniums before she went to America. She would have a week, just a week to get through before she could escape the empty house and the dying garden.

Phyllida was bustling and happy, giving instructions to the men and making them coffee before they left. Then she rang Bob. 'They're on their way. But remember, don't unpack anything. I want to do it all when we get back.'

Rowena saw her smirk, then say, 'Oh you!', looking pleased. Then she added, 'Me too. Take care, and don't be late tomorrow. We have a date!' She blew a kiss down the phone and hung up. 'He's such a love,' she told Rowena. 'Don't you think so?'

'Well . . .'

'I can't think what I've done to deserve him,' Phyllida said with unexpected humility. 'I wish you could find someone too, Ro. I do really. Only I never thought you minded.'

'I didn't. Not really.'

Phyllida came across and hugged her. 'You will be all right, won't you?'

Rowena said stiffly, 'Of course. I've my trip to look forward to, and my bridge and plenty of friends.'

'And your German classes. You mustn't give up your German.'

'Well, maybe.'

Phyllida nodded with satisfaction. 'Everything will be fine, I know it will. And remember, you've still got me.'

'Yes.' Rowena turned away. 'Well, I suppose we'd better get ready for our lunch.'

She went into the kitchen to clear the cups. Phyllida followed her. 'It's going to be a wrench, leaving here,' she said unexpectedly. 'I've been happy.'

'Good.' She heard the scrape of a chair as Phyllida sat down, but didn't turn till she had washed the cups and wrung out the dishcloth. When she turned Phyllida was leaning her head on her hands. Her face was deathly white.

'What's up, Phyl?'

'I'm sorry, I suddenly feel dreadfully sick.'

'It's excitement. I'll help you to the bathroom.'

Phyllida's forehead was shining with sweat as she helped her up. She seemed a dead weight on the stairs. 'Will you be all right?' Rowena asked when they reached the bathroom.

Phyllida said nothing. She was breathing heavily and sat down on the side of the bath. Rowena pulled the door to and went into her bedroom. She sat on the bed listening for sounds of vomiting. There was silence. She didn't know whether or not to change for lunch and thought on balance it was better not. Phyllida would not feel like going out. She felt obscurely disappointed. It had been a good idea to mark the occasion and she blamed herself for not thinking of it. After a while she went onto the landing. Maybe Phyllida had left the bathroom without her hearing. The door was still closed. She went to it and knocked. There was no reply. She pushed, but the door didn't give. Possessed with a sense of urgency she pushed harder and saw through the gap Phyllida's white woolly arm lying across the carpet. She pushed again and forced herself through the gap, staring down at the floor with a hideous foreknowledge of disaster.

Phyllida had slipped from the bath and fallen across the floor. Her cheek was bleeding where it had struck the lavatory seat, the modest scratch of yesterday quite obliterated by an ugly gash. Her skirt was pulled above her knees, her plump hands loose. Her eyes and mouth were open and Rowena knew at once that she was dead.

They make a miserable procession, those who should have been a wedding party, standing in the rain about the grave. Kathryn is pale and frail, supported by Ben and Stuart, who look stern in dark suits. Rowena grasps Jake's hand encouragingly in hers, but Hannah needs her hands for her crutches and stands alone, tears running down her cheeks and mud splashing up onto the plaster cast.

Bob is tiny and annihilated by grief. His camel coat is saturated, his suede shoes sodden, his eyes dissolved. He has as his support a small plump sister who Rowena sees with surprise is not unlike Phyllida. She is glad he has someone.

216

As the first clods fall on the polished wood she waits to feel something. Loss, sorrow, guilt. The death certificate said it had been a stroke, a cerebral haemorrhage, caused by stress and excitement. The doctor had been reassuring. Marriage and moving house were two of the most stressful occupations there were. He had said nothing about being attacked with a fish slice by a trusted friend. Rowena knows that she will have to deal with this sometime in the future, but for the moment she has Jake to see to and he has knelt on the wet earth staring desperately into the grave. She bends down to him tenderly, pulling him up. 'Come away, Jake.'

His face is distraught. 'Is Grandma really in there?'

She nods.

'But she'll get wet!' And then he begins to sob.

She supposes she should cry. It must seem strange that she alone is dry-eyed. Hard, Phyllida had called her. Maybe she was right. Or maybe it is just that there is such a conflict of emotions raging inside her that they can't find their way out of her eyes.

Bob comes up beside her and says in a waterlogged, helpless voice, 'We should have been in Venice today,' and his sister pats his arm and leads him off like a child.

The last of the cars pulls off, taking away Phyllida's family which has promised to be her own. 'We'll visit,' they say. 'We'll keep in touch. Mother would have wanted it.'

But Rowena doubts it. She will soon be getting old. She will become a nuisance, but not their nuisance. She must make arrangements, soon, about her future, because there is no one else to do it.

But meanwhile Mark is waiting for her in New York. Her case is packed, her tickets and passport ready on the dressing table. There are cards there too, of condolence in her terrible loss, from Betty, from Joyce and Robert, from Barbara in High-gate. The message they contain is unreal. What loss? The emptiness of the house is something she had come to expect. She has yet to understand the difference, that Phyllida is dead.

That at last she, Rowena, is free.

She opens the drawer of her bedside table. Under her handkerchiefs there is a slim blue volume of verse and, marking page fifty-eight, there is a photograph. She and Henry are standing beside a haystack. Their hands are hidden but she can still feel his flesh burning into hers. Bluebells dangle from his other hand and they are smiling at Phyllida, even as they betray her.

She wipes her finger once across the picture then stands it up, defiantly, against the wall.